Murder at the Summer Theater

A "Double V Mystery"
Number 5

Jacqueline T. Lynch

Published by Jacqueline T. Lynch
P.O. Box 1394, Chicopee, Massachusetts 01021

ISBN: 9781791318796

Acknowledgements

Cover art by Casey Koester. Author photo by Gretje Ferguson. My special thanks to proofreader John Hayes.

Rear cover photo of the salt marsh along the Hammonasset River by the author.

To join my mailing list for updates and special offers, please see my website at www.JacquelineTLynch.com.

Rehearsals grow tense at a summer theater on the Connecticut shore. The lead actress goes missing – or was she murdered?

Juliet Van Allen and Elmer Vartanian, the "Double V" duo, are called in on the case, but even with Juliet pretending to be an actress and newcomer to the cast, the players are guarding their secrets closely. There are spurned lovers, jealous wives, scene-stealers and heartbreakers, with enough spirit of vengeance to fill up the loge. Will the show go on? Even when a body is found?

Murder at the Summer Theater is the fifth book in the Double V Mysteries series set in New England in the late 1940s and early 1950s.

If you like the charm of a classic film, this "cozy noir" will return you to an era of soft ocean breezes and a glamorous game of suspicion played between acts. The painted backdrop is the heyday of summer theatre, when greats from the New York stage and Hollywood performed in barns and tents on New England's famed "straw hat circuit." Passionate accusations and grim consequences lurk in the dressing room. Join the nervous producers on the veranda for a champagne cocktail.

It's a seaside caper where murder is in the spotlight in the summer of 1951, and Juliet and Elmer are on the verge of a new professional – and personal – partnership.

Chapter One

Elmer Vartanian walked the several blocks from Colt's Manufacturing Company to his tenement apartment in the south end of Hartford, Connecticut, ostensibly to give expression to his Puritan sense of guilt for quitting a good job that he needed. Mostly, he walked to save the bus fare that he was probably going to need for food if he didn't get another job soon. He knew without too much weighing of his conscience that it was really more in celebration, not guilt. He was glad to be walking out of that dark, noisy gun factory, to be breathing the fresh air again and enjoying the summer sunshine. He felt like a free man again.

Freer even than his first walk outside of prison gates two years earlier.

The Colt factory, one of Hartford's, and Connecticut's, most historic industries, was no prison like the state penitentiary, not to the thousands who happily worked there. He just wasn't one of them. Was he lazy? He asked himself this as he observed cracks in the sidewalk and gave sidelong glances to busy Saturday traffic passing by on Main Street.

No, he felt he was not lazy. He was hardworking and disciplined; he had trained himself to be in repentance for his teen goof-off years and the stupid stunts, and the crime that had sent him to prison. No, he had learned better, learned the hard way.

But he was not a 9-to-5 man, he told himself, at least not indoors. He had enjoyed driving a truck, and working on a tobacco farm, jobs that kept him outdoors. Maybe it was his seven years at the Wethersfield State Prison that made him claustrophobic at the thought of spending the rest of his days inside the walls of a factory.

Maybe it would be different if he worked in a store? A drugstore, or a department store. A place with windows where a guy could look out and see the daylight, with customers he could talk with and not just keep his nose glued to a noisy machine, risking the wrath of the foreman if he dared look up from the monotony of his drill press. Would one of those grand old stores downtown hire him, like G. Fox, or Sage-Allen, or even just a five-and-ten, like Kresge's? Would they hire an ex-con?

He had liked working at the Wadsworth Atheneum art museum as a janitor. It was quiet, and it was a place of beauty. But he had quit there, too, to avoid too much contact with Juliet.

It was all different now. He looked forward to seeing her this afternoon, had thought about it all day. He was to meet her for a late lunch at the Connecticut Room at G. Fox and take her shopping. Or wander behind her while she shopped, which was what all men did when they shopped with a woman, which was okay with him.

He arrived at his building, sidling through the kids in the neighborhood as they chased around each other, making their roughneck, happy noise. He threw a smile to a little boy on a tricycle who lazily rode in circles in the middle of the sidewalk.

The building was old, shabby, soot-stained brick, but it was home. He trotted up the stairs to his second floor one-room apartment, the sounds of radios and loud conversations from other apartments echoing in the hall.

He took his key from his pants pocket and opened the door to his room. A telegram lay on the floor. He immediately drew back and looked up and down the hall, foolishly, as if to see if he were being observed opening his own mail, as if there was something wrong with that.

He entered his one-room furnished inner sanctum, closed the door and sat down at his old wooden kitchen table on one of the two chairs.

The telegram was from Danny Martin.

He knew nobody named Danny Martin.

"CALL CIRCLE-923 SOONEST STOP JOB STOP."

Elmer felt tingling in his body, almost a chill despite the warm day. *JOB.*

Something akin to a premonition, a good feeling, made Elmer decide to call this Danny Martin now, but not on the payphone on the first floor. There was never enough privacy in this building where neighborly curiosity ran high. He left the building again and walked down a block to a mom-and-pop variety store where there was a phone booth.

The door to the store was propped open by a wooden case of Cokes; unlike the bigger stores calling themselves *supermarkets*, this little hole in the wall wasn't about to get air-conditioning anytime soon. Elmer went to the trademark red cooler inside, fished out a cold Coke, flipped off the bottle cap on the built-in bottle opener on the side and put a nickel on the counter. Eddie, the owner, hunched over the far end of the counter, listening to a ballgame on the radio. He chewed on a toothpick and waved Elmer off as if to say, *yeah, I see you—don't bother me.*

Elmer hiked back to the phone booth in the back of the store and closed the squeaky cantilevered door. He took out the telegram and dropped a handful of change in the box when the operator connected him. After five rings, Elmer was about to hang up, but then a male voice answered, "Yes, who is it?"

Elmer was halfway into a slug on his Coke bottle. He swallowed and belatedly answered, "Is Danny Martin there?"

There was a pause, and the speaker drew a breath. "Is this Elmer Vartanian?"

The question startled Elmer. He had also downed the Coke too fast, being thirsty from his walk home, and released a deep carbonation-infused belch. He swallowed hard and recovered, "Who wants to know?" And felt suddenly foolish because it sounded like something a gangster would say in the movies.

"Look, is this Elmer or isn't it?"

Something about the voice seemed familiar. Elmer took a chance. "Yes. I got a note to call Danny Martin at this number. Are you Danny Martin?"

"Are you alone? Can we talk?"

"Yes." Elmer frowned at the telephone and glanced out the booth window to where Eddie was concentrating on the radio. Kids came to buy candy and Eddie was clearly annoyed at them for bothering him.

"Where you calling from?"

Elmer answered, "A phone booth. I'm not going to play twenty questions with you. *I'm* asking the questions now. Who are you and why am I supposed to be calling you?"

The voice on the other end let out a ragged sigh, then Elmer could hear the strike of a match and what sounded like the man drawing in on a cigarette he had just lit. The voice answered, "It's Leon Welch."

Now Elmer remembered the voice. Leon Welch, the husband of Juliet's friend Betty Ann, one of the many houseguests that New Year's Eve over a year ago at the mansion of Juliet's wealthy father. There'd been a murder, and Juliet had called Elmer to help. Together he and Juliet got to the bottom of it, just as they had the year before when they had first met, when Juliet's husband was murdered. He ruefully mused their relationship was a based on a string of corpses.

"Elmer? Are you still there?"

Elmer had liked Betty Ann but he thought Leon was a weasel. "Yeah, Leon, I'm still here. Who's Danny Martin?"

"I'm Danny Martin. I mean, I just wanted to leave a fake name. I wanted you to call me but I didn't want to just leave a message with my name on it. I have a job for you, Elmer, if you're interested, but it requires discretion."

Discretion was a word Elmer had heard before in these matters. It seemed these rich people were more interested in discretion than they were in ethics. Still, it always meant a pretty good pay envelope at the end of the shenanigans for him.

"What's it all about, Leon? Or should I say, Mr. Martin?"

"You know that I run the Hammonasset Playhouse down here on the shore? Well, an actress in the cast has gone missing."

"Why don't you call the cops?"

"Here's how it is: The girl's been missing since last night. The cops won't even consider her missing for three days. Meantime, I have this show to get up. We open on Monday night. It's not like this girl to just walk out. And there's something else... The thing is, she and I... Well, I hope you're a man of the world enough to understand how it is."

Elmer took another, much slower sip from the soda bottle. "No, Leon, why don't you tell me how it is?"

"You know what I'm saying, I've been seeing the girl."

"What exactly am I supposed to be discreet about, Leon? The fact that you've been cheating on your wife, or the possibility that you have something to do with this girl being missing?"

Leon answered, "I'm not paying you to be my conscience, Elmer."

"What are you paying me for?"

8

"Find the girl, or find out what happened to her, and keep my name out of it. I will call the cops when it's time to call, but if she's still missing by then, they're going to start looking for suspects and if it ever gets out that I've been seeing her, I'm going to be the chief suspect. I want to save my wife that trauma." His voice sounded a little too self-righteous at the end of that sentence.

"You want to save *yourself* that trauma. Incidentally, how much would you be paying me?"

"I read in the papers how you solved the murder mystery over at that art bunker in the Berkshires this past winter. They make it sound like you've gone into business for yourself as a private detective. I suppose you're charging standard rates? I thought fifty dollars a day."

"I'm not a licensed detective."

"But you solved four murder mysteries so far, pretty well-publicized ones."

"With Juliet's help."

Leon paused and took another drag from his cigarette. "The papers are full of her being blacklisted, you know, the feds catching up with her commie past."

Elmer answered angrily, "Knock it off. Juliet's no commie. It was a frame-up."

Leon replied, "Take it easy. I'd rather you handle this case by yourself, Elmer. Juliet attracts the wrong kind of attention these days. I have a very conservative clientele at my playhouse. I don't want the FBI coming down on me, thinking I'm guilty of being a commie by association with Juliet. These are dangerous days. Anybody in business has to watch out for that sort of thing. If your name gets tainted, you're done."

"Yeah, Juliet's finding that out. It's nice she has such supportive friends."

"Does that mean you're not going to help me?"

Elmer answered, "One hundred dollars a day, plus expenses."

Leon cursed. His voice rose to nearly a little girl's shriek. "You're crazy! You're not even a professional!"

"But I'm discreet." Elmer sneered as he said it and drained the eight-ounce bottle of Coke.

"Okay. But no Juliet. Don't tell Juliet about this."

***

G. Fox department store owner Mrs. Beatrice Fox Auerbach would build a five-level parking garage for her customers this year of 1951. Hartford began to grow vertically. Public parking here cost forty-five cents per day but was free to customers of G. Fox with their receipt.

Inside the store on Main Street, Juliet Van Allen glanced morosely at the "career dresses" department on the second floor before proceeding with Elmer to the Connecticut Room restaurant, still mourning for her career as an administrator at the Wadsworth Atheneum that had been derailed when she had been blacklisted.

Juliet mumbled over the menu, "We have to stop at the bakery here and get some cupcakes for my father."

Elmer smiled the at thought of the patrician Jonas Van Allen succumbing to so human an affliction as a cupcake vice. Elmer was pleased that Juliet thought of her father; their relationship had never been very good, though in their last caper, the old gentleman's help in assisting Elmer to free Juliet from her kidnapper was nothing short of heroic. Poor old Mr. Van Allen had been recuperating ever since, and cupcakes were surely part of his recovery as much as his reward.

Elmer asked, "You shopping for anything in particular today, or is this just an outing?"

"An outing, I suppose. I'm bored and restless, and the job hunt is not going very well. Being blacklisted as an accused communist has further reaching consequences that I imagined. Sometimes it doesn't even come up; it's just implied. How can you defend yourself against someone's suspicions, especially when their suspicions are not even articulated? I had no idea when I was eighteen years old that a six-month membership in a college club for global politics would make me a social pariah and an enemy of the state a decade later."

Elmer did not bother to read his menu. He watched her. She was tastefully, immaculately dressed as always, in a form-fitting light blue suit, her white gloves and her purse casually tossed to the side. She had shorn her former hairdo, which was usually combed back off her face and tucked into a neat chignon or a bouquet of cluster curls at the back of her neck. This summer she adopted a short, curly "bubble" cut; her tight blonde curls escaped in wisps under her "half Breton" straw cap. In a moment, she would fumble for cigarettes but for now she gripped the menu and tapped it on the tablecloth a couple of times to punctuate her sentences. He knew she was not really reading it.

He replied, "Maybe you are shooting for a field that has too-high visibility. Is there some other administrative job in your line of work where you won't be so public? Or maybe a place where they won't take this kind of scrutiny so seriously?"

"Is there such a place? I don't know. I don't know." Her light green eyes lost their brilliance and she could focus on nothing, not the present and certainly not the future. She saw only bleakness there.

Elmer cleared his throat. "Leon Welch contacted me. He's got a job for us."

Juliet looked up, her brow furrowed, and she looked almost comically dumbfounded. She sipped from her water glass, as if needing to ponder this for a moment. She answered, "The only kind of job 'us' had has been solving murders, and that was entirely incidental, and if I may say, accidental. Don't tell me he's got a body in the library?"

Elmer smiled, ruefully. "A body, yes, but not dead—missing. She's an actress in his latest production at the Hammonasset Playhouse. She went missing, he thinks, yesterday. Officially, she's not a missing person yet, at least according to police, but he us wants to get a jump on finding her. He thinks if we can find her that will save the show, and possibly avoid bad publicity."

Now she fumbled for cigarettes, in agitation and excitement. While she opened a fresh pack, Elmer reached over for her purse, retrieved her lighter from it, ignited the flame and held it up for her cigarette. A slight smile played on her lips, and he knew she was pleased with the gentlemanly gesture and also amused, because Elmer did not smoke. He thought the practice ridiculous and he wished that she would stop.

Immediately upon drawing in and releasing a stream of smoke through the side of her mouth, she began, "What on earth are we supposed to do? Does he really think we're private investigators? It must be Rat Fink's columns in *The Hartford Times*."

"Rattinger."

"*Double V Investigators*, that fool said, Vartanian and Van Allen. Who would have thought Rattinger would end up being our publicity agent?" Juliet rubbed her forehead and giggled.

Elmer was glad to see her finally smile over something. He chose his words carefully, partly to entice her to come along and partly to avoid

---

mentioning that the missing person was also Leon's mistress. He intended to withhold that information from her.

"I told him we'd help. I'll go alone, if you'd rather. But we make such a good team that it seemed only natural to work together."

"Elmer, are you serious? You really want to go down to Hammonasset to look for this person? Where do we begin?"

"The same way we always do: By observing, asking questions, and perhaps even pretending."

"Pretending what? Oh, you mean using fake names again? Who are we supposed to be?"

He answered, "Well, I'm going to be me. He wants his other actors to know that someone is on the case looking for this girl. He wants to calm his backers and assure the police if there is an eventual investigation with them that he did everything he could to find this girl on his own so he's not legally negligent. You, however, are not going to be you. Here's what I think: You will be an actress."

"Oh, my lord."

There's a woman who was supposed to be playing one of the minor roles that's now stepping into the role of the actress who went missing. So, you are going to be taking over her original part. It's a smaller role. I just need you to spend time with the cast, get to know them, listen to whatever dirt you can find. There should be a lot of chatter backstage that the boss never hears. That will help a lot. I'll question them, of course, but they're going to be on their guard with me."

"I can't believe this. What am I saying, I could hardly believe any of the other capers we were involved in, either. Well, at least there's no dead bodies in this one."

"I hope not."

She asked, "Do you suspect murder?"

"I don't know what to expect. Exciting, isn't it?"

"I think you've found your niche, Elmer."

He grinned. "Right in this room, two years ago, did I not watch you trap a killer over lunch, with the Hartford Police watching you from the sidelines? I think we both found our niche, Juliet."

Juliet was loath to recall the traumatic experience of her husband's murder in the late spring of 1949 and the equally traumatic discovery of his infidelity, and that he had married her only because of her family's wealth. As humiliating and horrific as the experience was, it did bring

Elmer into her life. She was still sorting out what that meant. They were friends. They helped each other to survive a very bleak time for both of them. They continued to call upon one another in need.

Would it ever be more? After two years she still didn't know what he wanted and did not know what she herself wanted. She looked into his dark eyes and his rugged face with a crooked nose like a boxer's that she would not call handsome, except that it appealed very much to her. He was looking at her. She blushed and looked down at the cigarette nestled in her slender fingertips. It burned slowly and the smoke rose in wispy ringlets to the ceiling.

Elmer asked, "You've been to Leon's playhouse before, haven't you?"

"Yes. Many times. It had once been a barn, as is the case with many New England summer theaters. It's right on Route 1, on the shore. It's quite pretty. He's put a lot of money into it, or his family did, I should say. There's a big veranda that he built around it, which is kind of nice in the summer evenings when they have intermissions and one can step out for a breath of sea air and get a drink at the little bar they set up there under a string of lights. I think he sometimes holds fundraising parties there as well. It's a spectacular view of the ocean from the veranda of the playhouse. They've had some terrific productions with the best actors from theatre, both stock and Broadway. I understand a lot of Hollywood actors are touring now, what with the breakup of the studios. It's a great little place to see some top-notch theatre."

Elmer said, "It sounds nice. I remember when I was a kid, one summer in one of the parks they had some WPA actors put on a play. It was some old-time hokey melodrama, you know, the villain holding a mortgage over the homestead kind of thing, with corny jokes, but we ate it up. Kids, parents, everybody went. I think it was a nickel. That was the only play I've ever been to."

Juliet looked into his eyes again but said nothing. She had made too many observations of surprise on his childhood poverty; they were no longer appropriate or polite.

"It will be my first time seeing the ocean, too," he added.

This, Juliet could not pass by. "Oh, Elmer, how could a Connecticut boy grow to manhood without ever seeing the ocean?"

He smiled that sardonic world-weary tight-lipped smirk. "I can tell you plenty about the Naugatuck River, but that's the extent of my geography. Actually, I almost did go to the ocean once when I was a boy. Our church was having an annual picnic and that year took a couple of school buses down to Ocean Beach in New London. But as usual, I did something dumb, got caught, and my father wouldn't let me go." Elmer's voice trailed off and there was a softness mingled with pain in the expression of his dark eyes that she imagined might have been there when he was eleven years old.

"I'm sorry you didn't get to go to the beach." Juliet said, "but we can certainly make up for that now. Madison, the town where the playhouse is located, has a very nice state beach right next to the playhouse property, with an enormous boardwalk and pavilion. You'll love it. We'll bring our swimsuits."

"I don't have one. Not since that ugly, striped woolen one-piece I had when I was ten. I'll spare us both the embarrassment of that."

She giggled. "Well, here we are in a department store; you can buy one here. Not a striped woolen one-piece."

"Then you'll go?"

She answered, "Yes, of course, if it means I get to ogle you in swim trunks. Can you swim?"

"Yep, Naugatuck River-trained."

"That's fine. Actually, I really would love a chance to see Betty Ann again. She's halfway through her fifth month of pregnancy and I haven't had a chance to see her since she told me she was expecting."

Elmer looked suddenly serious. "Betty Ann's expecting a baby? Leon didn't mention that."

She said, "You know, I'm suddenly starting to look forward to this. Shall we take the Cosmo down, or would you rather take the train?"

"I think the car would be best. Juliet, one more thing—I want to take Robert with us."

"Are you sure? It could explode into one sweet mess," she answered.

"I know. But he's too much for his grandmother to take right now. She's old. He's an angry ex-con. I don't want to babysit the guy, but I don't want to leave him on his own right now. He's messing up."

"He's lucky to have you. Did someone pick you up from prison? How did you get home?"

"I didn't have a home. I was expecting to go to my wife's cousin to see my daughter Linda again. You know how that turned out."

"Yes," she said softly, wincing at the memory of how they learned about his daughter's death.

He continued, busily perusing his menu now, "I tried to see my parents in Waterbury but they didn't want to have anything to do with me. No, when I left prison, I took the old prison bus out of the gates. They would have taken me to Hartford but I asked to be dropped off in town, right there in Wethersfield. I wanted to get to Hartford on my own. I hitched rides. When I got to Hartford, I checked in with my parole officer. He got me a room in a boarding house that accepted ex-cons, and a job for me on the tobacco farm that accepted ex-cons, and I was pretty much on my own until I met you."

She reached her left hand across the tablecloth and placed it on his hand that had rested beside his plate, his fingers drumming intently as he spoke. His strong fingers became still and relaxed at her touch.

Chapter Two

A couple days earlier, Elmer drove with one hand on the steering wheel and the other casually resting out the open window, buffeted by the warm summer breeze. The breeze was stirred by the car's forty-mile-an-hour cruise down the country road, making his left hand cooler than the rest of his body, which was sweating in his light summer suit. He occasionally brought the hand back to the steering wheel to navigate turns. Juliet's big 1949 Lincoln Cosmopolitan was fun to drive, and she had teased him more than once about being in love with it. A demanding mistress that required his attention on turns, and he gladly gave it.

He borrowed it for this trip and hoped that Robert would not think he was putting on airs. Elmer had no car of his own, and the light summer suit he wore was only slightly better than the one he'd been given on his release from prison two years ago.

He was going back there now for the first time since his release. He had hoped never to see the place again, but for Robert's sake, he could take it.

Elmer slowed the car, traveling now through the historic town of Wethersfield, a charming, stately, quintessential New England town. Finding his own way home from prison seemed to him to both test and prove his independence, his worthiness of his new freedom. When he had arrived at the company rowhouse in Waterbury where his parents lived by the factory, he discovered they had not wanted him there.

He took a bus to Hartford and began his new life under bitter and tragic circumstances. The best thing that had happened to him was meeting Juliet, on what turned out to be the worst day of her life. The murder mystery in which they were both involved was a bizarre welcome for him back into society but it began a new friendship and an odd new partnership, and a string of other mysteries fell upon them to gradually change their lives.

He had written Robert about this, but when he arranged to pick him up on his release, he had not articulated that he hoped to ease Robert's way back into society, starting by giving him a ride in a car back to Hartford, taking him to lunch, bringing him back to stay with his grandmother, who wanted desperately to see him.

The car rolled with quiet ease to a stop in front of the prison gate. In the distance, the red brick Federalist-style buildings, which could resemble a college or a private academy except for the bars on the windows, was Elmer's first look back at the place where he had spent seven years. Even on the day he was released, walking towards these main gates from the other side, in the ill-fitting suit they gave him and the ten-dollar bill in his pocket, he had never looked back.

As eager as he was to see Robert, Elmer had quashed a nagging, uneasy feeling on the ride down, and could only admit to anxiety at coming back to this much-hated place. Now that he was on the outside of the gates looking in, he could regard the buildings in the prison yard as something from another time that would not reach through the fence and snatch him back. He had safely made it to the other side. He was determined never to risk anything to put himself in there again.

A figure in the distance walked away from the brick buildings and toward the gate. He wore a dark suit and a wide-brimmed Fedora. Elmer looked at him, fancifully, as if looking at himself two years ago in the same clothes. But this man was a black man, who took his time walking and did not briskly march away from the buildings with his head down as Elmer had. Robert had been imprisoned three years longer than Elmer. Robert looked back at the buildings once, and then twice, and even nodded in a friendly manner to the guards at the gate. When Elmer had left, he had not even looked them in the eye, too afraid to pause even for a moment, as if the slightest hesitation might result in his being kept there.

Robert appeared to see him now, but he did not smile or gesture, he only looked back at the prison walls a third time, as if regretting to leave.

The strange, surreal irony of the image gave Elmer a sense of dread.

Robert carried a brown paper shopping bag with handles. It held a few possessions he had accumulated after ten years in prison. Elmer had not chosen to take anything with him when he was released. Not even the Bible that had been given to him, which he never read. He wanted nothing from that world to infect his new life, though after two years, he still did not feel as if he completely belonged. He wondered now how to make welcome another ex-con when he still had such doubts about himself.

Robert grinned at the guard at the gate and doffed his wide-brimmed gray hat at him. Elmer smiled ruefully at Robert's bravado. Here was a man who perhaps would be all right no matter what. Robert carried a kind of armor plating on himself. It had sustained him in prison where he was the most vocal, yet likable and frequently outrageous man in the pen, especially when it came to his recitation of Shakespearean plays. He always liked to take books, especially that single book of Shakespeare's plays, from the prison library and read the parts out loud, sometimes enlisting Elmer to read with him. Robert was the only friend Elmer had made in prison; Elmer preferred to keep to himself but Robert was not the kind of guy one could dismiss or avoid. If he wanted you in his life, there you were.

At last the gate was opened, and Robert strolled through, swinging his shopping bag with a happy-go-lucky Easter morning attitude. Elmer got out of the car and walked to the middle of the road, not venturing to go any closer to the gate, as if it might snatch him up. He took off his own hat and squinted in the hot July afternoon sun. Robert tipped his own hat back away from his forehead, glanced at the car and jauntily considered Elmer with a smirk.

The two men approached each other and clasped hands in the middle of the hot, empty road, pumping each other's arm with a firm handshake and a feeling, at least on Elmer's part, of victory. It suddenly occurred to him that he had left a big part of himself in prison and maybe that part was Robert, and maybe now that he was out, Elmer could finally really be free as well.

"So that's the Lincoln Cosmo," Robert said glancing over Elmer's shoulder. Robert was a head taller than Elmer, so seeing over him was no great feat, but he made an exaggerated lean as if demonstrating the fact that he was giving the car the once over.

Elmer, almost overcome by the moment, was suddenly speechless. He continued to pump Robert's hand, losing any words of welcome thought of on the way here.

Robert said, "Well, you're just gonna have to introduce me to this Juliet of yours. She must be all right if she's gonna let you drive around in a car like that. I wouldn't trust you if that was my car."

Elmer finally caught his breath and released Robert's hand. "I can't tell you how glad I am to see you."

"Yeah," Robert said. "What do you say we go get a beer or something a little stronger? It's been a long time since I had a drink in my hand."

"There's a bottle of beer in the fridge at your grandma's house. That's where we're going, chum. I promised her."

"Fridge?" Robert scoffed, "She had an icebox when I went in the pen. Everybody did."

"Well, now you don't have to empty the drip pan anymore, because she's got a second-hand fridge with a loud motor and more ice than you can hold in any drink."

Robert said, "Oh, come on Elmer. It's my first day out. Let's go to a bar, for crying out loud. Let's have some fun."

"I know it's been ten years for you, pal," Elmer said, "but it's also been ten years for her. I promised your grandmother that I'd bring you straight home. I promised her. That's where we're going. You can have your beer there in her kitchen. If I know her, she's probably already got the gingerbread made."

Robert shook his head, "My grandma was a gingerbread junkie. I forgot about that. It got so I was sick of it. Come on, Elmer, we'll go to her place after we have a drink, huh?"

"Can't do it. I'm sorry. I made a promise. She's a sweet old lady and she just wants to see you again. How about later on tonight? I'll bring you to her place, you can have a little reunion with her and then I'll come back for you say around nine tonight and we'll go out for that drink, and the drinks are on me. What do you say?"

They walked to the car, Robert still making exaggerated examinations of the car. "If the drinks are on you, I guess that seals the deal. But I think you're a cold man to make me wait for that drink, Elmer. Yes indeed, a cold man."

They got in the car, both men tossed their hats in the back seat and loosened their ties. Robert settled into his seat, stretched his legs and rested his arm on the open window. He looked out the window at the prison again and kept his eyes on it, Elmer noticed, as he put the car into gear and turned it around in the road and they slowly headed back to Hartford.

Robert was quiet for the first couple of miles, then he looked over at Elmer. "So, what you doing now? I know you said you left the truck driving job. But then this whole thing came up with my parole and you never got back to talking about you."

"I was working at Colt, but I quit that, too. I've got a temporary job of sorts coming up. I've got to go down to the Madison area, down on the Sound. You remember I wrote you about that house party New Year's Eve last year where Juliet's friend was murdered?"

"Yeah, you and your girlfriend playing Sherlock Holmes and Doctor Watson. I still can't get over that. None of the boys in the pen would believe me. You wouldn't have anything to do with anybody when you were there, and we couldn't imagine you solving a crime, getting involved with people, let alone getting involved with your rich lady friend. How's that shaping up?"

Elmer ignored the question.

Robert grinned, as he played with the radio, and let loose a loud burst of Les Paul and Mary Ford performing "How High the Moon." He looked out the window.

Elmer recalled that in his first days, even weeks, after his release from prison he could not look at the world hard enough. The trees, the grass, every pebble in the street was a miracle to him, because he could see it and that made him part owner of it, just because he was free. He respectfully allowed Robert's moment of gazing out the window, like a mother who enjoys watching her child eat, but when Robert turned and rested back in his seat, he seemed to stare out the windshield not with wonder, but with empty eyes. His expression was a hardened blank.

"I'll help you, Robert," Elmer said quietly. "I'll help you get settled, get a job, ease your way into this. You're not alone."

Robert shot him a dark look. He had a thin, lean face but with the deep lines around his mouth of a person who laughs easily. He left a short burst of unmistakably derisive laughter.

Elmer said nothing, felt a little hurt, but at the same time he remembered the mistrust he had of people when he had left prison. It was a valuable thing to be reminded of, he thought. He could trust Robert implicitly in prison.

Could he trust him here, on the outside?

***

The look on Mrs. Kincaid's face when she opened her apartment door and saw her grandson Robert standing in front of her was something Elmer thought he would remember all his life. It was a picture of rapture and gratitude, and the thought that he had made that happen— for surely, he did make it happen by dragging Robert here against his will—would be one of the greatest achievements of his life. It gave him such a rush that it occurred to him in an instant epiphany why he was so drawn to private detective work—because it gave him the means to help people. It gave him the perhaps self-centered bliss of being in a position to help people. It gave him the momentary, fleeting authority, to be the one to bestow favor. It was perhaps inherently arrogant, he mused, but to be on the giving end of aid instead of the receiving end was so sweet a feeling that it was almost akin to a powerful drug.

Was his relationship with Juliet also based only on the fact that he had been able to help her and continued to help her when she needed it? Was there any love, in fact, or only the thrill of being a hero?

Love was not something he and Juliet spoke about; they circled around the idea, but they were both careful not to face it head-on.

"Oh, Robert, Robert, Robert!" Mrs. Kincaid put her hands on her grandson's face and drew him down to her and covered him with kisses and tears, snaked her arms around his tall, thin frame and like a wrestler would not let him go. Robert smiled weakly and shook his head to shrug off his embarrassment. For all his proclaimed discomfort, Elmer sensed that Robert was as glad as he was to have given this sweet old woman the opportunity to be happy at last.

But the expectations of being able to continue to make her happy were beyond his ability, and not his responsibility. Elmer hesitated at the door and was about to leave, which Robert evidently sensed because he reached back and grasped Elmer's shoulder.

"No, you don't," he said, "you're not leaving me with this crazy woman. Grandma, I hear you and my boy Elmer are old friends."

"Oh Elmer, Elmer, thank you so much! Thank you so much!" Mrs. Kincaid sobbed, laughing at the same time and snaking an arm away from Robert to throw it around Elmer's shoulders and pulled both men into her embrace.

Much later, after gingerbread and a lot of talk, Mrs. Kincaid went regretfully to bed, first kneeling beside it to say her prayers of thanksgiving, and then to try to sleep although she was too excited.

Elmer took Robert out afterwards, as he promised, though a little later in the evening than they had planned because they did not want to interrupt Mrs. Kincaid's joy. It was ten o'clock when they left, though Elmer felt the excitement of the day taxing on him and feeling almost jealous of Mrs. Kincaid that she could go to her bed; nevertheless, he would not break his promise to take his friend out for a drink.

They took a booth at a bar downtown and Elmer joined Robert in a Scotch, but soon Robert left him behind when he requested a bottle be left in front of them and he spent the next few hours sleepy-eyed and silent, drinking morosely, glass after glass. Elmer realized that Robert was in a different place than Elmer had been when released from prison. He did not know how to counsel Robert or help him make the transition. He now knew the humiliation of not being able to help at all.

"Robert, what do I do? You know I will help you."

Robert sat back in the booth, regarded Elmer with a slight smile and a snort. "I got all the help I need right here, chum." He poured himself another glass.

"You're not going to be in any shape to check in with your parole officer tomorrow."

"I'll be in the shape I want to be."

***

Robert was hung over and silent the next day, but Elmer made sure that he went to the parole officer's to check in. Robert would live with his grandmother, not that he really wanted to, but it would save him rent money. He had no interest in the job that had been set up for him in a machine shop and was less amused and more annoyed the next two days when Elmer started bringing him to work to make sure he got there. In part restlessness and part rebellion, Robert spent the second day getting drunk. He was fired. His grandmother was distressed. Elmer was by turns furious and heartbroken. Since all Robert had requested of him was to meet Juliet, he decided to bring her over to Mrs. Kincaid's and accept an invitation to dinner.

They drove there after their afternoon shopping at G. Fox. Mrs. Kincaid greeted Juliet with a warm hug. "It's so nice to see you again, honey. You and Elmer have gotten so famous. I read about you in the newspaper finding the bad guys." She had also read about Juliet's being suspected of being a communist in the caper last March, but with discretion kept that part to herself.

Robert chugged his fourth bottle of beer when they sat down to dinner. It was roast beef with baked potatoes; though the weather was growing increasingly warm for a meal that required the oven to be on all afternoon, Mrs. Kincaid could not resist showing off one of her best dishes.

Robert greeted Juliet warmly and glanced every now and again to Elmer. There was less sarcasm in his tone of voice and his expression, even though he was now on his sixth beer and Elmer had discovered what he had not known prison—that Robert was an ugly drunk. However, he seemed genuinely impressed with Juliet.

"So, you're Elmer's—*partner* in crime." Robert dropped his admiring gaze from Juliet's green eyes and snickered into his beer. "You could say I used to be his partner in crime."

Elmer noticed that Mrs. Kincaid's worried eyes darted frequently to her grandson. He had come home a stranger to her. It did not take much imagination to know that her heart was breaking. Elmer could feel a rise of anger at Robert for being insensitive to it, despite his sympathy for his friend, knowing what it was like to be just released from prison and to be more scared about freedom than exhilarated.

Juliet's answer was calm and warm and utterly unconcerned. "We're more like a pair of stumblebums who rely heavily on luck." She bestowed a wry, humble smile on Robert, but Robert's dim eyes had risen to meet hers only for the briefest of moments, and he looked away again, throwing his head back and gazing at nothing. There was a wall still around him.

Elmer sat back in his chair and spoke more directly towards Mrs. Kincaid. "Juliet and I are driving down to the Sound tomorrow. We actually have a new case to work on."

Mrs. Kincaid hastily removed her apron and joined them at the table, her eyes darting back and forth between Elmer and Robert. "Another murder mystery? How exciting! Do you think you'll be gone long?"

Juliet answered, "No, not a murder, thank goodness, but a missing person. I don't know if we should say much about it yet," she looked at Elmer for his opinion, "but hopefully, we'll get lucky again and find some answers. It certainly is a strange avocation we've gotten ourselves."

Robert swore, which made his grandmother gasp in consternation, and he sputtered sarcastically to himself, "Sherlock Holmes meets the Keystone Kops."

Elmer said, "Robert, why don't you come with us?"

Both Mrs. Kincaid and Juliet looked at him as if he had two heads. Juliet frowned and tilted her head, questioning him with a warning glance. Robert mumbled halfhearted vulgarities and drained his beer. He lifted the empty bottle by the neck and swung it back and forth, the way a magician would try to hypnotize someone with a watch, as a signal for Elmer to get him another beer. Elmer took the bottle from his hand and put it gently down on the table.

"Why don't you come with us?" he repeated.

Robert slurred his words, "I'm not going anywhere. Where you talking? I'm not going no place."

"Why don't you come with us down to the Sound, to the Hammonasset Playhouse. It's a summer theater. Remember all the Shakespeare we read in prison? '*To thine own self be true, and it must follow, as the night the day, thou canst not then be false to any man.*'"

Robert retorted, resting his face on his folded arms, "*A plague o' both your houses.*"

Elmer couldn't help but smile. He glanced over at Mrs. Kincaid, who seemed near tears with the sudden hopelessness of not knowing what to do. Elmer reached across the table and put his hand on hers.

"We're going to leave first thing tomorrow. Why don't I take Robert home with me tonight? He can stay with me in my apartment. That way I won't have to come back here and pick him up. We'll contact his parole officer. Robert can stay with us for a few days down there while we're doing what we have to do. We have a connection with the owner of the playhouse and maybe we'll find something for Robert to do, something to keep him occupied and keep his interest. Maybe when he's had a few days of this adventure, he'll see things a little more clearly. Would that be all right?"

She sighed. "Thank you, Elmer." Then she added in a soft whisper so that Robert would not hear, "I don't know what to do."

He nodded and patted her hand.

Robert, by this time, was in a half-sleepy stupor and did not put up much resistance. Elmer pulled him away from the table and half dragged, half carried him down the stairs when the evening was over and Juliet followed behind with a few roast beef sandwiches for the road that Mrs. Kincaid had put into a paper bag.

***

The next morning, Elmer shaved with less concentration and more cuts as he kept craning his neck out the bathroom door to look in on Robert, who was still sprawled across the Murphy bed they had slept in, though he had grunted and mumbled a few times that he was up and awake. Robert was about Elmer's age, a tall black man, taller than Elmer, making it impossible for Elmer to lend Robert his clothes. All Robert had was the suit given him when he left the Connecticut State Prison in Wethersfield. Elmer reckoned he could buy him another pair of pants and a couple of shirts, some underwear and socks. Mrs. Kincaid would likely not be able to afford too much in the way of providing for Robert, and Robert didn't look yet as if he had any intentions of providing for himself.

Elmer had not dressed yet. He had one more big job to do and decided it would be better to wait after it was done to put clothes on. He removed his pajama top, and only in the bottoms, he went over to the Murphy bed and pulled Robert out, muscling him into the shower. He turned on the cold water and Robert struggled, sputtered, swore, and complained he was about to have a heart attack.

Robert fumbled for the faucets and turned the shower off.

"I'll lay you out on the floor, idiot," he growled.

Elmer wiped his face with a towel and handed one to Robert. "You've got ten minutes to put your suit on. We're going down to the diner to get some breakfast and a pot of hot coffee in you and then we're going to check in at your parole officer. Then we're going downtown to get you a few more things to wear. Then we have to pick up Juliet. So look sharp."

"Why the hell don't you just go without me, fool."

"Because you won't let me."

Robert scoffed. "*I* won't let you?"

"If you had behaved yourself at your grandmother's and made plans to go to see your parole officer by yourself and sound like you're actually looking forward to new job referral that you're going to be getting, then I could go off my merry way with a light heart. But you didn't, so I can't."

Robert stepped out of the shower and dried himself off. "Sorry I'm not letting you enjoy your murder."

"It's not a murder. It's a missing person. I hope."

Robert was still hung over, but cooperative, and when they both were dressed, they went down to Juliet's maroon Lincoln Cosmopolitan that she had let Elmer drive home. They ate at the counter of the Aetna Diner, a stainless-steel shell streetcar dinner manufactured by the Paramount company, on the corner of Laurel and Farmington Avenue, but Robert just picked at his toast and concentrated on his black coffee.

Later that morning, they finally drove to the Van Allen mansion on Farmington Avenue and Robert was aghast at the old-money pedigree of both the home and the woman he assumed to be Elmer's girlfriend, although Elmer had never referred to her as such in his letters.

Juliet came out quickly; she had been waiting for them. Elmer put her suitcase in the trunk and she scooted across the bench seat and sat next to him, and Robert was about to move to the back seat, but Juliet said there was room in front, so he slipped in on the other side of her. They pulled out of the long drive and Robert craned his neck to look at the mansion.

"That some shack you've got there, Juliet," he said.

"It's my father's shack."

Downtown, past the businesses and the department stores and theaters, Elmer conducted a tour of Hartford for Robert. He wanted him to see the magnificent city, to remember what it was when he'd gone to prison and see how it was changing. The giant multilevel parking garage for G. Fox—who would have ever thought there would be so many people going shopping in their *cars* that they would need something like that.

Juliet replied laconically, "Elmer, I see your girlfriend is playing at the Strand."

Robert perked up and looked at the marquee. Someone named Ann Blyth was appearing in some movie named *Katie Did It*. He looked quizzically at Juliet; she smiled superiorly.

"Robert, don't bother forming an attachment for Ann Blyth, Jo Stafford, or Dorothy Collins, because Elmer has culled them out of the herd for himself. Madly in love with them."

"Never heard of them," Robert answered, and then to tease them, he added, "I thought *you* was his girlfriend."

Juliet huffed but smiled and said nothing. Elmer looked out the driver's side window and said nothing.

***

They followed Main Street along the river. Once out of the city, rural areas showed drastic change—new worlds being carved out—the suburbs. Elmer pulled up at a filling station to add water to the battery. Across the street had once been a family farm, a fallow field that had been turned over and steamrolled and paved with driveways on staked-out quarter acre lots, connected by a web of new subdivision streets. Construction workers and contractors perched on the wooden skeletons of several would-be houses down one new street, hammering and sawing. Other houses had only the cellar holes finished as yet. There was no grass, no landscaping, there was not a tree in sight. It was all open, baked in the sun like a desert.

Juliet remarked airily, "Welcome to the continuing phenomenon of what is known as post-war housing, Robert. What you will see before you is a housing development devoid of any originality or beauty. Each tacky three-room bungalow with a kitchen and bath has got to be exactly identical to its neighbor, so that no one fool enough to buy one of these homes will have to face their foolishness alone, but bask in the holy grail of conformity."

Elmer turned on his heel and looked back at her sharply and then looked out over the vast field of individual construction sites.

"People need a place to live," he said firmly, in a hard voice and not looking at her. "Maybe they lived in tenements before this, or maybe army barracks, or maybe in Hoovervilles in some town dump or under a bridge. Now they can have a place of their own, a big neighborhood so new they'll all experience it together as equals. Maybe it's the new start a guy needs."

Robert noted Juliet's rebuff. She lit her cigarette and blew a stream of smoke across the car roof. Robert asked her for one; she held up the pack so that he could draw one and put it to his lips. She flicked her cigarette lighter for him, and he put his hand on hers to help cover the flame from the breeze.

"Thanks."

Juliet resentfully looked across the former field dotted with new cement foundations and framework in various stages. The sound of hammering, drills, and electric saws filled the air as did the occasional shouts of the construction workers. It was like an assembly line but instead of the house moving along a conveyor belt, the construction workers moved from house to house. The framers, and the masons, the cabinetmakers, and the finish work, the plumbers, and the electricians, and the painters would all eventually have a turn. A slab of tar would be rolled up to the back door and that would be the driveway. Finally, landscaping would complete the project, which consisted only of rolling flat the dirt in the front yard and the backyard and then a sprinkling of grass seed. What was not eaten by birds—though, indeed, without a tree in sight, without a shrub, without any vegetation at all the place was not an inviting habitat for birds—but what was not eaten or washed away in violent summer thunderstorms, just might germinate. Then blades of grass, not so close together that one still couldn't see that it was mostly dirt and pebbles, would eventually sprout along with dandelions, something that would be in future years regarded as a scourge by the suburban lawn owners. Only the dandelion, half wild, seemed to indicate that neither potatoes, nor the eastern woodland forests that had preceded the potatoes in the field, would ever lie on the spot again. But the dandelions adapted. They were bright and cheerful and they grew without any tending at all.

Elmer drank it in with his eyes and Juliet could see that he was very pleased and somehow soothed by the prosaic scene before him. She fought an unspoken, unnamed resentment and realized it had more to do with Elmer wanting perhaps to live here and not that much about aesthetics. True, she had grown up in her father's Hartford mansion in much more gracious and artistic surroundings, certainly with trees that were two hundred years old, but the cracker box ugliness of the suburban neighborhood was not quite so offensive as the idea that Elmer would prefer to live in a community like this, because she would never fit in here, that she would never belong with him, anywhere.

Looking at it from what she imagined was his point of view, she grudgingly could see a possible attraction. It was new. It was without any history and any caste system. Elmer, so desperate to start his life over, still feeling the long shadow of his prison years over his shoulder, would like to live in a place like this where everything represented starting afresh. All the people who would come to live in this neighborhood would be arriving together. They would all be new together. There would be no older established families to look down on the newcomers. In a way, the entire suburban neighborhood was like a big social experiment. Their children would grow up together, playing here under the open sky in the sunshine. They would all go to the same neighborhood school.

They would all need to drive into town to go to church, those that did go to church. They would all need to drive into town to visit their grandparents, and high school, and for work. They would all *need* a car now, even someone like Elmer, who although he did get his driver's license when got out of prison, still did not own a car. He didn't need one in Hartford. When he needed one, she made it clear he was free to borrow hers.

He loved her Lincoln Cosmopolitan. Was it too posh for a brand-new suburban neighborhood like this?

More to the point, was *she* too posh for a brand-new suburban neighborhood like this? Would he want her here with him in his three-bedroom one-bathroom ranch? Even if he did want her, how could she possibly live in a place like this? Juliet felt her soul would shrivel up and die for the lack of the trees, from the harsh sun, from the claustrophobia of the cookie-cutter ranch house, and from what she imagined might be the dull and uninspiring company of her neighbor housewives.

Suburbia was the promised land for Elmer; for her it was the end of the road.

Robert broke their reverie. "Are we going or what?"

Elmer pulled himself away from the panoramic view of the identical houses lined up with the precision of headstones at a military cemetery and turned his attention back to the car. They all piled back in and they continued south towards the town of Madison on the Connecticut shore.

Jacqueline T. Lynch

Elmer spoke up at last after a few miles of silence and got down to business. "I've filled Robert in a little bit on the case. But I guess the three of us should get together on the basic facts. First of all, we're going to go to Leon's house."

Juliet perked up and emitted a soft gasp. "I'll get to visit with Betty Ann! I was hoping I would get a chance, as long as we were down there. How nice to see her straight away. I'm so anxious to see how she looks." Juliet chuckled and said to Robert, "She is expecting their first baby in three months."

***

Elmer said nothing at first. He gripped the steering will more firmly and brooded out the window. He recalled that Leon had said nothing about his wife being pregnant. Apparently, his missing mistress drove that singular fact out of his mind.

Elmer remarked, "First thing to remember is that none of us knows each other. Not in front of Leon, obviously, but when we get to the playhouse in front of the others. That's how we play this game, Robert. We ingratiate ourselves to strangers by being strangers among them. Juliet, you are to be an aspiring actress."

"Don't tell me I have to be on stage!"

"Not unless one of them is dead or throws up," was Robert's helpful remark.

"I'll throw up just thinking about it," she said.

"She's not kidding. She will." Elmer replied, recalling Juliet's habitual nausea in moments of tension. "Hopefully, she won't have to go on at all."

"Hopefully?"

"Maybe we'll find the lady. Your name is Katie Quackenbush."

Robert burst out laughing, and so did Juliet, but ruefully, as she knew Elmer was not kidding.

"What name are you giving Robert?"

"Robert doesn't really need a name, unless he wants one. He hasn't been written up in the newspapers for the last three years every time we run into a spot, like you have."

She answered, "Your name's been in the newspapers right along with me, pal."

30

"As a solver of crimes, my dear. Right now, I'm *supposed* to be the one with the reputation. The cast is already going to know that I'm a gumshoe of sorts. The reason you and Robert are incognito is because we need you on the inside. It would be normal for me to ask questions, but they may not open up."

Robert asked, "How am I on the inside?"

"You're going to be an apprentice. You're going to be helping out backstage. You'll be painting sets, running the curtain, things like that. That'll get you inside where you can learn as much as you can about the cast."

Robert smiled, shaking his head. "What am I supposed to be doing, asking a bunch of stupid questions? Man, I don't want to be talking to people about stuff that isn't any of my business. We learned to mind our own business in prison, and that's a good rule."

"Eavesdrop. That's the interesting thing about this gig. You find yourself getting really interested in people. I never thought I was. Like you said, in prison we learned to keep to ourselves, but we also learned to keep our eyes open. On the outside is where that really helps. You'll find yourself being curious about things, learning more about people than you thought you could. And feeling sympathy. Everybody's got baggage, Robert. Everybody's carrying a load."

Juliet looked at Elmer admiringly and then back up at the long stretch of highway ahead of them.

Juliet asked "Who's in the play?"

Elmer replied, "The young lady who's gone missing is named Eva Breck. Ever hear of her?"

Juliet answered, "No."

Elmer pulled a piece of paper out of his coat breast pocket and handed it to Juliet. "Here are some of the other names."

Juliet read aloud, "Constance Burch, Guy Norman, Ruth Maguire... I know that name. She's an old character actress from the movies. She's always playing fussy old ladies. Nina Garrett, Bessie Baggs... Oh, Bessie Baggs, I know. She plays a lot of older parts, too. Stephen Grove. Beatrice Longworth—wow, she's famous. She's done a lot of work on stage, Broadway. Been in a lot of movies, she always plays those classy patrician high society types. She's very glamorous. I haven't seen her in any movies in a long time, though. It's quite a coup for Leon to get an actress of her caliber. What's the play?"

Elmer answered, "*Bonaventure*. I tried to get Leon to tell me a little about the plot but he didn't know that much himself."

"It figures that Leon wouldn't know anything about the actual play," Juliet scoffed.

Elmer thought, *He's too busy cheating on his pregnant wife and worried about being blamed for his missing mistress.*

Chapter Three

Leon and Betty Ann Welch lived in a brick colonial house in a neighborhood of Madison, Connecticut, that was called opulent by the dwellers in smaller clapboard cottages on Route 1, also known as the Boston Post Road. Many of the small cottages had been refurbished from nineteenth-century three-season camps. Elmer understood their perspective, shared it himself, but having visited the mansion owned by Juliet's father, Jonas Van Allen, he knew the Welch home was comparatively modest among the millionaire set.

He also compared it in his mind to the new suburban former-farm pioneer land he had admired on the trip down. He noted Juliet had seemed dismissive of it. No wonder. A three-bedroom frame house with only one bath would have no attraction for someone from her world. She didn't grow up in a worker's rowhouse by the factory as he had, with only two bedrooms, and he and his three brothers sharing a bed. She didn't play in the sooty streets as a child. She saw no bright future in a suburbia of green lawns and kids playing in their own yards.

She saw things from a different perspective and that kept them a gulf apart.

The Welches' indifferent housekeeper in a pale blue dress and white apron opened the front door. Her eyes zeroed in on Robert and she appeared visibly startled. Elmer's nerves tightened and he felt full force his old irritation for Leon and all the arrogance—and bigotry—he represented. Juliet spoke up.

"Hello, Annie. Mr. and Mrs. Welch are expecting us."

"Actually," Elmer muttered, "Leon's only expecting me." Juliet gave him a sidelong glance of surprise. Robert, steeling himself against prejudice that was too familiar to be shocking, looked only at the house.

Annie let them into the foyer, and Leon, who emerged from his den just to the right, greeted them with, "Hello, Elmer—thank God—" cut short when he saw the trio.

Elmer said, "Juliet, why don't you take some time first to visit with Betty Ann. We can catch you up later."

Leon recovered in an overly-friendly voice. "Yes… She's upstairs in our room. Why don't you just go on up?"

Juliet, despite a suspicion she was being dismissed, pecked his cheek and scooted past the gentlemen to head up the stairs. "I'm dying to see her."

With Juliet upstairs, Elmer and Robert stepped into Leon's den. Leon closed the double wooden doors. A leather couch and chair were parked below a theater poster framed and mounted on the wall from the Hammonasset Playhouse. His large oak desk commanded the room, and he immediately went and sat behind it, clasping his hands together on his desk as if about to bring a board meeting to order.

"Why the hell did you bring her?" Leon growled, "and who the hell is this?"

Robert yawned.

Elmer answered, "Mind if we sit down?" He sat on the couch without invitation. Robert took the chair.

"Well?" Leon barked.

Elmer asked calmly "Do you have my check?"

"What?!" Leon's voice squealed like a teenage boy's when his voice changes.

"We agreed—$100 a day, plus expenses."

Robert's eyes widened as he gave Elmer a sidelong glance.

Leon countered, "If I thought you were going to get cute with me, I wouldn't have given you this job."

"Get off your high horse, Leon. You called me. I didn't call you. This is Robert. He's going to pretend to be an apprentice backstage. Juliet is going to pretend to be a fill-in you brought in to cover the actress who's taking over the lead. They are going to be my eyes and ears. Juliet doesn't know about your infidelity. I didn't tell her. Just like you forgot to mention your wife is pregnant. I don't like guys who cheat on their wives. I especially don't like guys who cheat on their pregnant wives. Where's my money?"

Leon stiffened, in body and expression, but wordlessly took out an enormous leather-bound checkbook the size of a photo album from the top drawer and dropped it on his desk. He took a ballpoint pen from the gold holder on the top of the desk and wrote a check with a firm hand and too much flourish. He ripped it off and slid it across the blotter.

"This will take you through tomorrow. That's when we open. We had better find her—or her body—by then."

Elmer calmly countered, "And Juliet and Robert get scale for their services to the playhouse for the next couple days."

Leon turned red and a vein bulged along his forehead. "See Kent Murchison about that. He pays the staff."

Elmer slowly stood, walked to Leon's desk and retrieved the check, reading it carefully before he put it into his pocket. Robert sat up a little straighter, his full attention on the proceedings.

"For purposes of this little escapade, Robert and Juliet do not know each other. Neither of them knows me. Juliet is to be called Katie Quackenbush."

Leon's face fell. "You're kidding."

"And I'm going to be introduced by you to the cast and crew as a private detective. We want Juliet and Robert to interact freely with them, but they must be aware from the start that I am suspicious of everybody. Hopefully, we will ferret out some information. Tell me, Leon—did you kill her?"

***

Juliet pulled back from her hug with Betty Ann and placed a gentle hand on her friend's belly over her brightly colored maternity top.

"I've wanted so much to see you like this, darling," Juliet said. "How are you feeling?"

Betty Ann answered, "I'm at the more-energy-than-I-know-what-to-do-with stage."

"And Leon fussing and badgering you to take it easy?" Juliet smiled.

"Lord, no. Leon is the disinterested type. He'll be perfectly happy with a son and heir when it's presented to him after being dressed for a family portrait, but he hasn't the temperament to fuss over an expectant mother, any more than he will be over the baby when it comes." She

35

sounded gaily philosophical, with only a touch of self-pitying irony that Juliet detected was new to Betty Ann.

Juliet responded, "I'm sure Leon will come around. You've wanted this child for so long."

"I have. I'm not so sure about Leon, now that it's really coming. How long can you stay? I wish Leon had told me you would be here. Did you hear—Beatrice Longworth is at the playhouse this coming week. Leon thinks she's washed up since the *Red Channels* thing, but he was so happy to snag her before he realized she was 'damaged goods,' as he said. Oh, Juliet, I'm sorry. I forgot about your own blacklisting with that lot."

"Bless you for forgetting, Betty Ann. I wish I could."

"Still no work?"

"Not yet, but I'm down here with Elmer on a new case. That'll keep me busy for now."

"A new case—listen to you. *Double V Investigators* strike again?"

"What? Oh, that nonsense from that hack Rattinger on *The Hartford Times*. I thought you read *The New London Day* down here, dearie."

"Your fame is spreading."

"Perish the thought. You've heard about the missing ingénue?"

"Leon mentioned something. But then, he gets frantic before every show, as if he were actually directing or producing it, so his hysteria over something being out of place is nothing new. She probably went on a bender. Isn't that the case with many of these actors?"

Juliet sat back in an upholstered easy chair that matched the one in which Betty Ann sat in her large bedroom. The maid must have already been in this room; the bed was made, the curtains were drawn and everything looked neat and orderly, more like a hotel bedroom when one first enters it. It was as immaculate as a magazine picture.

"Isn't he the producer?" Juliet asked, taking her glance away from their double reflection in the large rectangular mirror over the low double dresser. "I mean, along with whoever the board appoints."

Betty Ann pulled a cigarette from the jeweled box on the small table between them and wordlessly offered one to Juliet. Betty Ann lit both cigarettes from a small gold table lighter.

"Jeff Collins really runs the show, ostensibly with Leon's help, but Leon's more of a hindrance than a help. Jeff, however, is only too happy to have the money Leon's family has poured into the playhouse. Leon really just sort of inherited the position on the board from his father. I think his father encouraged it as a means to keep Leon from being too involved in the family business." She chuckled knowingly.

Juliet asked, "His brothers are all still involved with his father's company?"

"They have the heads for it. Oh, Leon has his share of the income, of course, but everybody's happier if Leon has his own pet hobby to occupy him."

"Perhaps Leon doesn't see it as a hobby."

"Oh, no," Betty Ann laughed. "I think he sees himself as the next Ziegfeld."

Juliet smiled. "What has he told you about the missing woman? Let me start this investigation with you."

Betty Ann laughed again. "Oh, me? I feel honored. Oh, the novelty of someone listening to me, and I don't even have anything to offer."

"Do you know anything about her?"

"Eva Breck is the missing person. She plays the lead in the play, a character called Sarat Carn, a woman who is being sent to the gallows for murdering her brother. That's it. I know more about her fictional character than the young lady herself."

"Ever met her? What's she like?"

Betty Ann shook her head, the remaining loose curls from her five-month permanent wave still bouncing as she did. "No. Leon says she's an up-and-coming star who will be snatched up by Hollywood one of these days. Just because of that, I think he's more pleased to have her on board than the old greats in the cast, like Beatrice Longworth. Leon loves the new and shiny."

***

The trio drove to the Madison Beach Hotel to drop off Juliet. It was a former boardinghouse for shipyard workers, now growing into a cozy inn for the growing tourist trade on Route 1. Some of the other actors were lodged here, some at motels and some boarding in private homes. They said goodbye in the car down the road to avoid being seen together. Robert moved over to let her out, and then shot his perplexed attention to Elmer as they drove away.

Robert said, "Elmer, I know you and Juliet must have this unspoken brainwave thing going on between you, but I'm in the dark here. What's going on? What do we do now?"

Elmer answered "I drop you off at the entrance to the playhouse. You go around back to the cottages they reserve for their staff, and you give this letter of introduction I dragged out of Leon to the stage manager. They let you bunk in one of the cottages, probably sharing with another backstage person. I go and check into an auto court on the Post Road. For now, chum, we don't know each other. Keep your eyes open and when I get info for you on the sly, I'll let you know, and you tell me what you've learned. Treat it as a lark, Robert, because that's what it is. You'll get paid, you'll learn something about the theatre, and maybe you will have some time off to go to the beach. Not bad, hey?"

Robert frowned at the dashboard. "And check in with my parole officer every week?"

"We could be done in a few days."

"I don't know if I'm going to like this."

Elmer said to the steering wheel, "You're scared."

"Go to hell."

"You're scared," Elmer repeated, "so what? So was I. Some days I still am, but it wears off. Curiosity gives you courage, pal. Keep curious."

Robert took a deep breath against the slight lurch of the car as they pulled up the gravel drive of the Hammonasset Playhouse.

"You walk from here." Elmer said.

Robert stepped out of the car, pulled his small black gym bag from the back seat that carried the new change of clothes Elmer had purchased for him that morning, and pushed his hat back on his head. He said in a loud stage voice, "Thanks for the ride, stranger."

Elmer smiled. "So long, Bud. Good luck with your new job."

***

Elmer checked into the Wayside Cabins, an auto court close by on Route 1 and unpacked, pulling out his new bathing suit first. With the giddy joy of experiencing something new, something long anticipated as delightful—a feeling he wished Robert could let himself experience, he put on the red swim trunks. He pulled on a navy golf shirt and slipped on a new pair of navy espadrilles. Juliet deftly steered him towards these items on their shopping trip without actually acting like she was "dressing" him. He rolled up a pair of casual white pants in a towel from the motel. It was a short walk to the beach, which was part of Hammonasset State Park.

The word *Hammonasset* was the name of one of the five native tribes that had lived along the shoreline of Connecticut. The word was said to mean "where we dig holes in the ground," because along this area they grew their corn and squash and beans. They fished and hunted from the abundant land as well. Settlers from Europe began to arrive in the year 1639. A Mohican called Uncas married into the Hammonasset tribe and he received part of the land as a dowry. In the 1640s he sold the land to Colonel George Fenwick, who was head of the Saybrook colony of Englishmen, and Fenwick later traded the land to Henry Whitfield of Guilford to use as farmland. The Hammonasset Indians moved over to the Niantic River area and became part of the Mohegan tribe. The land continued to be used as farmland and the vast swaths of salt marsh provided hay for feed for horses and cattle.

In the early 1800s, the present-day Hammonasset Playhouse started life as a barn. Several modifications were required since the turn-of-the-century, not the least of which was the expensive addition of air conditioning in 1950. The old farmhouse, little more than a cottage, was now renovated as the business offices. The little farm was now overrun by a sandy gravel parking lot and surrounded on three sides: by the salt marsh through which the Hammonasset River ran, by Long Island Sound, and by the Hammonasset State Park and its long public beach.

The beach had been used in 1898 by the Winchester Repeating Arms Company as a vast open range to test their new rifle: The Lee Straight Pull Rifle. Curiously, despite the long tradition of beaches for common use in coastal New England, it was not until 1919 that the State of Connecticut began to buy up property that would make up the future Hammonasset State Park to preserve the land for public use.

The park opened to the public in 1920. Reportedly, the first season drew over 75,000 visitors. The commission that had established the park built a grand pavilion and a boardwalk, a clamshell, most of which survived several coastal storms, and the pavilion even survived the horrific Hurricane of 1938, though much of Route 1 was turned into a great nest of fallen trees. The park acquired more land in the twenties and doubled in size. But it was closed down during World War II and leased to the federal government for use as an Army reserve and aircraft firing range. Along the meandering road in front of the future Hammonasset Playhouse, P-47 warplanes shot at targets. At least one of those planes crashed into the Sound. After the war, peace came to the Hammonasset State Park as it did to the rest of the United States, and beachgoers flocked again to the long sandy shore.

Elmer appreciated and mused on the fact that with the tides and each new day, the shore had a timeless quality. The Hurricane of 1938 and P-47 warplanes were things of the past, as were the first settlers, the old tribal communities, the pleasure-bent college kids of the 1920s; but the beach was renewed with every dawn. Such an idea gave Elmer courage and hope, and sadly acknowledging that if he were still searching for such things three years after being released from prison, how much more acute must Robert's pain be now? Elmer marveled that he really was moving past those early agonizing days because he was beginning to forget the pain of them.

***

Juliet had the same idea about visiting the beach and was sitting on her towel wearing a coral-colored one-piece bathing suit. She wore a wide-brimmed straw hat that shaded her face from the late afternoon sun. She saw Elmer, and watched him stand before the incoming tide, the soon-to-be setting sun throwing long shadows and creating that clear, sharp, natural light loved by photographers.

Elmer contemplated the quiet surf, which was really barely small ripples because of the protection offered by Long Island, a thin, gray line on the distant horizon. The determined little ripples rolled up the beach and swallowed his toes. He peeled off his shirt, tossed it onto the towel he placed on the sand, tucked his wallet into one of his shoes, and took a step toward the water.

Juliet indulged in the pleasure of letting her gaze wander from his broad muscled back, his narrow waist, the form-fitting dark red suit snugly against his bottom, his muscled hairy legs.

He looked up and down the beach, and raised his arms above his head, clasping his hands together behind his head in a lazy stretch. She could see he was mentally and physically unwinding. She wondered whether it was from the long drive, the always unpleasant encounter with Leon Welch, or the memory of prison again and the regrets of a lifetime.

She wondered again if he really knew how to swim.

Suddenly, his arms dropped his sides, and he dashed into the water, thrusting himself in a dolphin-like dive, slicing into the sea. Momentarily, his head popped up and he swam long, steady strokes.

Juliet relaxed, relieved to see that he could swim. She wanted to join him, but they were not supposed to be having any contact yet. They were not supposed to know each other.

Later, however, she took the opportunity to innocently sit down next to him at the open-air clam shack on the beach. She gave him the slight perfunctory smile of a stranger merely acknowledging the existence of another person, and then gave her attention to the menu board written in chalk above the wooden counter.

She repeated his order of fried clams and French-fried potatoes. When their food came in paper boats, he casually passed her the ketchup bottle and they enjoyed the nirvana of tasting salt and fried batter and sloshing the unhealthy mixture sipping bottles of Coca-Cola.

He muttered to her, keeping his attention on his food, "How do you keep your figure eating like this?"

"I was going to ask the same of you."

"It's my first time." He bit into a mouthful of fried clams.

She asked, "First time eating fried clams?"

He replied with a full mouth, "Uh-huh."

Juliet forgot the rules of being incognito and looked at him directly. "You've really never been to a beach before?"

He still did not look at her. "Nope. Have a nice evening," he said, and took his food in its paper wrappings and went to stroll on the boardwalk. Juliet looked after him, and then lost him in the small crowd of sunset strollers.

***

Robert, his hands shoved in his pockets, looked back across the salt marsh that stood between Route 1 and the Hammonasset Playhouse. Ed Stiles, the stage manager, came out of a cottage behind the playhouse and whistled sharply, motioning for Robert to follow him.

Robert said, "Thanks for letting me move into your cabin, Mr. Stiles. I hope I don't put you out."

Stiles responded, handing him a script, "That's okay. Don't snore, and stay out of my way and we'll get along fine. You're not the first surprise Leon Welch has sprung on me. I assume you're gentleman enough to give me some space when I've got a lady friend to stay the night?"

Robert asked, "Is that likely to be a nightly occurrence?"

"It'll occur anytime I get lucky, but don't worry, I haven't had that much luck lately. Leon's already beat my time once this month. You can look at this script to get familiar with the show. Come with me inside the theater and I'll show you the ropes. I'm assuming you've had stagehand experience? Leon didn't send me a total greenhorn, did he?"

"I've never worked as a stagehand before."

"Oh, great."

"But I've acted. I've played lots of Shaw, and Ibsen, and Shakespeare."

"Really? Where?"

Robert hesitated. "It's a—a special government program bringing professional theatre to prison inmates. You haven't played Hamlet until you've done it in front of lifers." He neglected to mention he was an inmate himself at the time, clowning for cellmates.

Stiles laughed, "I'll bet. Interesting. So what's with the move to working backstage? Actors love the limelight."

"Not too many commercial theaters are hiring black Hamlets."

Stiles said nothing, but shot him a sympathetic look.

Robert continued, "I figure I'll have a longer, steadier career in theatre if I do backstage work."

"You're right there. We don't get the glory, but the show don't go on without us. You in the union?"

"I'm hoping to qualify this summer."

Stiles led him to the stage, spot-lit by the hard glare of the single standing work light. He turned that off, and turned on the auditorium lights. Robert looked up and around to the stage, to the twenty-eight rows of seating, a spacious barn-like wooden summer theater typical of New England's "straw-hat circuit."

Stiles said, "We open tomorrow night." He did not sound confident. He took Robert on a tour of the actors' dressing rooms below the stage, and then back to the front of the house where the lighting booth perched above the back row of the audience.

They could view the stage set from here. Robert was intrigued. The set depicted the Great Hall of a Catholic convent in England. The canvas flats were painted with various shades of gray textured paint to resemble a wall of stone blocks, with vaulted doorways and recessed alcoves, and large Gothic stained-glass windows depicting images of the Angel Gabriel and the Virgin Mary. A statue of the Virgin stood on a pedestal lit by a small red lamp.

Robert had, indeed, acted in prison, but it was only reading from a book of Shakespeare that had been donated to the prison library. He had never been to a play, save for a school play in grammar school. On that occasion, he had sat on a metal folding chair in the school gym/auditorium with his grandmother, while his cousin Roderick played the lead in a script that the teacher had written herself about good manners. It soured Robert on the theatre for years, until he discovered he could sway his inmate audience and hold them in the palm of his hand with a power like he had never felt before—all the while behind bars in prison. It was a freedom, or at least a sense of freedom, that he had never enjoyed in his life, even on the outside.

He looked at the set. "That's beautiful," he remarked.

Stiles threw a glance towards the set that was still admiring but more critical through his experience. "If you ever want to get into set building, that's another area to make yourself invaluable. The most important thing on that set is the telephone on the sideboard. Audiences are conditioned by now when they see a phone on set, somebody better talk on it at some point." He chuckled. "It can't just be used for set dressing. People are going to obsess on that phone until it either rings, or somebody on stage picks up the receiver and dials it." He shook his head. "It's the damnedest thing. You can put on a great show, but they're concentrating all the while on the damn phone."

Robert laughed. "Yeah," he assured, as if he knew.

***

Each New England summer meant a new season of summer stock theatre, and the coming decade of the 1950s would prove to be the heyday of summer theatre in the United States. Nowhere was this cultural and commercial influence felt more than in New England. Of all the summer playhouses in the country in the 1950s, almost half were in New England.

The rise of summer theatre coincided with the advent of the automobile. Prior to World War II most people lived and worked, if not right in urban downtowns, then certainly close by. Since the 1920s and then through the backwash of the war when the population began to move to the new suburbia carved out of the rural landscape, the actors followed their patrons to the out-of-the-way former barns to escape the summer heat in the cities and enjoy the restorative breezes along the shore or in the mountains.

Connecticut enjoyed that July 1951 with Lillian Gish at the Clinton Playhouse in Clinton in a play called *Miss Mabel*, while George Bernard Shaw's *Candide* starred Olivia de Havilland. Melvyn Douglas starred in *Guilty* with Signe Hasso, and the Ivoryton Playhouse in Ivoryton featured *The Chocolate Soldier*, and *A Streetcar Named Desire* with Claire Luce, and *Rain* with baritone Lawrence Tibbett, and Joan Bennett in *Susan and God*.

The Somers Playhouse up in Somers produced *Light up the Sky*, and *I Remember Mama*. The Show Shop Theater in Canton on Route 44 produced *Out of the Frying Pan*.

Small towns known perhaps only for their summer theaters were the most important destinations on the map in the summer, and frequent Hollywood movie stars trod worn wooden stages, in rambling wooden playhouses converted from barns, church halls, and town halls, and school auditoriums. They stayed in local inns, motels, and often boarded in the homes of theatre-loving residents of the small towns. Many of these big stars began their careers in theatre and loved the opportunity to return to their professional roots.

Some were escapees from Hollywood, where a combination of the Blacklist and the breaking up of the studio monopolies led to many actors' contracts not being renewed. Less films were being made than in the old days, and there were only so many roles to go around. It gave rise to a new legion of acting freelancers.

Some blamed the loss of Hollywood roles on the emerging power of television, but most Americans did not own a television set. Most still left their homes for entertainment two and three times a week, to movies, dancing, and in the summer in New England, to the local playhouse.

Madison, a small town on Connecticut's coast, began as so many did as a tavern stop of the old Boston Post Road that connected New York City to Boston in colonial days. By 1951, its population swelled to 1,950, and its chief attraction was Hammonasset State Beach. The other attraction was Hammonasset Playhouse, founded by Leon Welch's father and some local business cronies who were not so much angels of the theatre as they were men looking for something worthwhile to do for their worthless sons.

The playhouse was perched on a rocky point that jutted out to the sea. On its wooden veranda that wrapped around the gray clapboard shingled building with white trim, one was afforded a commanding view of the great curving crescent beach down to Guilford, the town which Madison had been a part of until the new community was formed and named after President James Madison.

Eastward, the view captured fishing villages in neighboring Clinton. The Hammonasset River emptied lazily into Long Island Sound, after wandering through a vast saltwater marsh.

From the veranda, because of its relatively commanding height of roughly twenty-five feet above sea level, one could see the long blue-gray silhouette of Long Island across the Sound. When lying on the beach below, this distant piece of New York was barely visible with the naked eye, but at this higher vantage point the barrier island was real.

The beaches along the Connecticut shore here enjoyed somewhat warmer water and scant waves, which appealed to some bathers, especially those with small children.

Elmer eyed the playhouse at a distance from the beach as the sun set over the land behind him, and the small theater became a dark shape. Still captivated by his first beach experience, he filled his lungs with the fresh salt-tinged sea air and his mind turned to the mystery of the missing ingénue.

Had Eva Breck simply wanted to leave the show, he could see there were ample avenues to do so: Bus service and car rentals were available in the beachfront towns, taxi service, and the New York, New Haven and Hartford Railroad linked all the towns along the shore.

There were ferries in the summer from Bridgeport to the west over to Port Jefferson, Long Island, and from New London, eastward, to Orient Point, Long Island. She could have hooked up with any local commercial sightseeing boat or private boat as well to leave by sea. There were small airfields, too, at New Haven and over at Essex along the Connecticut River to the east, as well as here in Madison. No end of opportunities and means to leave if Eva Breck wanted out of her contract, or out of her relationship with Leon Welch. It could well be beyond his abilities to find her, Elmer acknowledged to himself, if she had left the area willingly.

Foul play? This was always a possibility, though there was no reason at all yet to assume such an extreme conclusion. Accident? This could be more likely. A swim on the beach could lead to drowning, especially if she had been drinking. A fall from a river bridge on a solitary walk, or struck by an auto on a lonely section of the Boston Post Road?

The saltwater marsh. A wide stretch of soft green grasses swaying slowly, nudged by the gentle slow-as-molasses flow of the Hammonasset River, a haven to marsh creatures, musical with the call of birds—murder or accident, it could certainly hide a body.

The sun set at last as a brilliant orange glow in the west faded to pastels, and then the stars blinked in a darker sky. Elmer changed in the bathhouse into his white trousers and returned to his motel, with his wet bathing suit rolled up in his towel. The motel or auto court was a long single unit of rooms, and courts of small cottages. Auto courts had become popular after World War II, a new innovation along the highways. He had taken himself a cottage.

He went first to the office, where the night desk clerk listened to *Mr. Moto* on the portable radio on the counter. Elmer had missed the virulent antipathy towards the Japanese when he was in prison during the war, but knew enough about it to be impressed that a Japanese hero would be portrayed on the radio these days. The announcer smoothly heralded the intro:

"Coupling his firm belief in the principles of freedom with his acute ability to perceive an enemy, Mr. Moto wages a ruthless war against all men who would extinguish the light of liberty with the foul breath of tyranny." Mr. Moto trailed after communists these days.

His radio fan, a short, balding man in a sweat-stained white button-down shirt and loosened tie kept one eye on the dial with evident concern for Mr. Moto, and slowly turned the pages of the *Sunday Herald* from Bridgeport. Elmer took pamphlets from the rack about the local attractions, and also the local railroad and bus timetables. There was a rack of penny picture postcards. He lingered over them, not thinking of the mystery now, but enjoying the returning flush of feeling like a tourist. He had never been a tourist before, but since his release from prison two years ago, he had learned to enjoy to its fullest every small pleasure.

He took five postcards: one of the state beach and its long wooden pavilion tracing down the curve of the beach; one of the playhouse perched on Hammonasset Point; one of the salt box-style homes in the historic section of town on the Boston Post Road; one of the saltwater marsh with Clinton across the opening of the Hammonasset River to the Sound; and one of the Wayside Cabins Tourist Court.

"You got lots of friends to send these to," the desk clerk jovially offered, rousing from his newspaper and giving Elmer a crooked smile. "You want stamps?"

"Sure, thanks." He gave the man a nickel for the cards. He had intended to keep the cards for himself, but wanted to maintain the normal image of a tourist. He could always use stamps.

Elmer walked next door to a small restaurant with a bar and only a few tables. They were occupied by couples, and a woman sat alone at the bar. A piano player sang "Too Young" to the woman at the bar; though she was far from young and he was far from really being interested. Crooning that they were both too young to fall is love was too silly even for the most flattering drunken fantasy.

The place was not dressy; they wore pastel open-necked shirts and blouses, shorts and deck shoes and espadrilles and sandals.

Elmer closed himself in the phone booth in the corner and called Juliet's hotel, asking the hotel's switchboard operator to be connected to her room.

"Hi, it's me," he said when Juliet answered. "Can you talk?"

"Nobody here but us actresses. Lord, Elmer, the things you get me into."

He smiled. "Likewise, I'm sure. I've got a play program from Leon, but if you could fill me in on the play, the plot, characters, it would help. Have you looked at the script yet?"

"I hope to heaven they don't need me to go on. The next missing ingénue's going to be me if I have to say lines on stage."

"Better you than me."

"I can tell you about the characters," she said, "but I don't have the program, so you tell me who's playing what."

"Okay." He cradled the phone receiver in the crook of his neck and opened the twelve-page program Leon had given him. An illustration of the playhouse was on the front, and there were many pages of ads from local businesses up and down the Post Road, including one from the auto court where he was staying that said they were conveniently located; and finally, the actors' bios and the description of the setting of the play.

Juliet already had her script in hand, which she had been studying when Elmer called. Her mind unrelentingly drifted back to the memory of Elmer on the beach and his form-fitting trunks.

She cleared her throat and said, "Here's the scenario: A hilltop convent in England, isolated during the storm and flood. All the villagers go to the convent to escape the floodwaters. The convent is also a hospital, so the nursing sisters have their hands full. The detective brings a female prisoner and a prison matron to the convent. The prisoner is named Sarat Carn. She's convicted of murdering her brother and she's being sent to the gallows. The storm and flooding have delayed her execution. The real murderer is part of the gathering of townspeople taking shelter at the convent. A nun named Sister Mary Bonaventure and her sidekick, Sister Josephine, are the sleuths. They solve the crime, catch the bad guy, and Sarat is saved at the eleventh hour. Got it?"

"They make it sound so easy. How come it's never that easy for us? Okay. So, says here..." Elmer turned the page of his program, "that the missing ingénue, Eva Breck, was supposed to play Sarat Carn, the accused. That's a leading part."

"Any possibility of her turning up?"

"Beats me." Elmer took care not to mention Leon's affair with Eva. "We've got Beatrice Longworth as Sister Mary Bonaventure."

"Beatrice Longworth! I still can't get over that."

"Big star, huh?"

"Really big. Not so much lately. I suppose she's reached that certain age, as they say, and that may be why the shift from leads to character parts. She's one of the greats, Elmer."

"Bessie Baggs plays Sister Josephine."

"Another old-time favorite. Theatre, movies. Lots of character parts, was never the lead, as far as I know. Well, so far, I must say, Leon's done the playhouse proud contracting those two. Who else?"

"Constance Burch is Nurse Philips."

"I don't know much about her."

"Program bio says lots of theatre and a little TV. Next is Ruth Maguire as the Mother Superior."

"Another old theatre royalty. Probably started with Edwin Booth, for heaven's sake."

"Gary Pirelli as Melling, the police detective."

"Don't know him."

"Willy the handyman is played by Guy Norman."

"Nope, don't know him."

"Nina Garrett is Nurse Brent. If Eva Breck isn't found, then Nina Garrett will play Eva's role of Sarat Carn."

"Please let's find her. Okay?"

He smiled. "If only to save you from having to perform on stage in Nina's old role. Okay. Next is Stephen Grove as Doctor Jeffries."

"Never heard of him."

Elmer continued. "Miss Pierce, the prison matron is played by Paula Miles."

"Probably another character actress."

"And last we have Willy's mother, played by Billie Murchison."

"Oh, wait, I think I remember seeing her in other productions here at the playhouse. I think she a regular minor cast person," she said.

Elmer glanced at his watch. "Don't stay up too late studying. I'll see you tomorrow at the playhouse, Katie Quackenbush."

"Excuse me?"

"Katie Quackenbush. That's you."

Chapter Four

Juliet arrived early to the playhouse the next morning. At first, she sat alone in the audience seating trying to memorize her few lines, sincerely hoping she would not have to perform. For that to happen, Eva Breck would have to be found alive and returned to her role as the lead or she would have to be found dead. Most assuredly, under those tragic circumstances, the show would not "go on." A criminal investigation would likely seal off the playhouse.

No wonder Leon had hired Elmer to investigate ahead of the police; a criminal investigation would possibly destroy the rest of the summer season. The financial health of a summer playhouse could be destroyed by much less.

A few actors arrived, some with coffee in paper cups, cigarettes clasped in their fingers. They were dressed in casual rehearsal clothes. They carried acting edition scripts, but that was for security at this point. They were all "off book," except for herself, Katie Quackenbush.

She recognized Beatrice Longworth, a stately middle-aged woman, tall and graceful, who carried herself like a queen. A glamorous movie star whose roots were in the theatre, she played the lead, Sister Mary Bonaventure.

She arrived with Ruth Maguire, an actress some ten years her senior. Ruth played Mother Superior, but the autocratic and authoritarian stage character was evidently not part of her private nature. She appeared friendly, but quiet, content to sit in the seats that Beatrice chose for them.

Nina Garrett came next, her arm looped through the handles of a brightly colored canvas beach tote. She had been originally cast in the role of Nurse Brent, the role Juliet was now taking. Nina had been promoted to the lead role of Sarat Carn, the convicted murderess on her way to the gallows. She strode into the playhouse with a cheerful bounce in her step, seemingly not merely lighthearted but actually jubilant to be facing the gallows. She wore bright red lipstick and whipped off her sunglasses, placing them to nest on the top of her head.

Ed Stiles the stage manager turned off the bare, bright stage lamp and moved it backstage. Juliet recognized Robert taking a few tentative steps from the wings, looking wide-eyed at the stage, at the lights above, and peeking out at the small auditorium with two hundred wooden tiered chairs that filled the playhouse. A small balcony accommodated fifty more. He glanced among the incoming actors and discovered Juliet. He caught her eye and quickly looked away, careful not to acknowledge her.

Juliet smiled, and thought, *Good, Robert. That's the way.*

Stephen Grove entered the playhouse. He played the doctor. He said good morning to the actresses by name and nodded to Juliet, giving her a curious look. Then he extended his survey to the far back of the theater. Juliet turned around to see who was there. A woman sat alone in the back row.

"Good morning," Grove said, smiling to Juliet, before taking his seat near her.

"Good morning," she answered.

Paula Miles entered, who played the prison matron, Miss Pierce. She snapped gum and waved to everyone, a picture of calm capability. Behind her, Billie Murchison entered, who would play the mother of the handyman Willy, and was the cook in the convent.

Guy Norman, who played the "half-wit" son Willy, walked in, a scowl on his face, without a word to anybody.

Constance Burch, playing Nurse Phillips, chain-smoking, the script and her purse under her arm, entered next with a hello only to Billie Murchison.

Jeff Collins entered and trotted up the side stairs to the stage. He was the director, a lean, energetic man in his late thirties, in white pants and an open-necked pink golf shirt, wearing canvas shoes. Behind him a large, overweight man in an ill-fitting brown suit plodded slowly up the stage steps. He was Kent Murchison, in his mid-fifties, and he was Leon Welch's partner in the operation of the Hammonasset Playhouse. The two men took center stage as if they were a nightclub comedy team. A grim nightclub team.

The actors stopped chatting amongst themselves and gave the two men their attention. Stage manager Ed Stiles stood in the far "stage right" side. Ed muttered to Jeff Collins, "We're waiting on Bessie."

Collins rolled his eyes and sighed, hands on hips. After a moment, he answered, "We'll go ahead anyway." Collins then addressed the actors. "We still have no word about where Eva Breck is. This is Mr. Murchison, whom not all of you have met. He, along with Leon Welch, are managers of the playhouse. The police were notified yesterday, and as of tomorrow, we will be able to officially file a missing person's case. In addition, they have employed a private detective to help us get the ball rolling in the search for Eva. He is Mr. Elmer Var... Var... Excuse me...."

"Vartanian." Elmer called in a loud voice from the screen door to the side of the stage.

He wore a new light tan summer suit that Juliet had not seen before, with the sky-blue-and-yellow striped tie, a white shirt, and a light-colored straw hat. He removed his hat and nodded to the actors, slightly smiling, the picture of the New England gentleman at the summer shore. Juliet mused that he must be the best actor of them all.

Jeff Collins obviously noticed the unnamed woman sitting at the back of the audience. He continued, only slightly distracted, "We're going to proceed with rehearsal today and with the show opening tonight. Nina has generously agreed to step into the role of Sarat Carn, and she's been studying all weekend. Thank you, Nina. We've got a newcomer with us to take over Nina's role of Nurse Breck—Miss...," Collins looked at his notes. "Katie... Quackenbush." His pause and flat delivery of "Quackenbush" made it seem like a punchline and drew a few giggles.

Nice choice for anonymity, Elmer, Juliet thought. *Blend right in, he says. Right.* She blushed. Collins motioned Juliet to stand, and she ruefully did, nodding hello to everyone.

Collins said, "Give these ladies in their new roles, and Mr. Var...the detective, your cooperation, please. We'll start rehearsal in fifteen minutes with a complete run-through. If you're in the first scenes of Act I, the detective will speak to you first. Miss Quackenbush—can I call you Katie?"

"Oh, yes, please."

"You will work with me, since you weren't here and you have no information for the detective. Oh, and this gentleman here is Robert. He's joining us backstage."

Robert waved gamely from the wings, and the elder actresses, who valued backstage crew, clapped for him.

Elmer stood aside for Bessie Baggs arriving late, the elderly actress playing Sister Josephine. Bessie was a short, overweight lady of sixty-five, who stepped gingerly into the auditorium. Everyone watched her closely, and even Collins remained silent until she took her seat.

"Thank you for joining us, Miss Baggs," he said at last, sarcastically. "Mr. Var—here's a cast list in order of appearance. Why don't you follow this to proceed with your questioning?"

Ed Stiles began to instruct Robert on set changes and props. The actors wandered to their places on and offstage. Elmer began his interrogation with Constance Birch.

***

Elmer sat with Constance in the back of the theater on the opposite side to where the unnamed woman sat alone. He leaned closer to Constance Burch and said in a low voice, "First, who is that woman sitting back there? Mr. Collins did not refer to her."

Constance, dragging on her second cigarette since entering, peered back over her shoulder.

"Oh, her again. That some friend of Billie's, I guess. I think she was volunteering to help out the wardrobe mistress, or the box office, or something. Probably got herself a free ticket for helping, you know. A local."

"What's her name?"

She shrugged. "I don't know. She's just starstruck. You run into them."

"What can you tell me about Eva Breck and why she might have gone missing?"

Constance stamped out her cigarette in a small ashtray she carried. "Opening nights always give me the jitters. I smoke too much. Eva? I don't know what I can tell you that anybody else could. She's young, eager."

"Is she a good actress?"

"Fair."

"Beautiful?"

"You must've seen her head shot in the lobby." Constance looked bored.

"Married? Single? Anybody we should notify on her behalf?"

"She never talked about family."

Elmer persisted, "Loner?"

"I *wouldn't say so*." Constance appeared to infer much more from the remark.

"Did she have any particular friends among the cast?"

"Isn't the usual question did she have any enemies?" She smiled a little.

"Only if this becomes a murder investigation. Do you think it should?"

Constance looked at Elmer now, narrowing her eyes and proceeding to light another cigarette. "I wouldn't know."

Elmer paused, considering her. "We could move this on considerably if you come right to the point. Your veiled inferences are discreet, but this isn't a cocktail party."

Constance dangled a leg across her knee, her shapely calves tightly ensconced in pink pedal pushers. "In the interest of moving this along then, I could remark that Beatrice, for one, may know a little more than I do about whether Eva had any enemies."

"Why?"

Constance sighed. "I hate to gossip. But to move this along, as you say, the way I heard it, she messed around with Beatrice's husband. Then he had a heart attack. In her bed."

***

Juliet sat with Jeff Collins in the women's dressing room downstairs, which was shared by all the actresses except for the star, Beatrice Longworth, who, by tradition, had her own private dressing room, which was only a little bigger than a closet. But it had a star on the door.

"I have to confess, Mr. Collins, I don't really have very much experience. I'll try to do my best." Juliet said.

Collins looked up from his script, which theatre folk called "sides," with a grimly sardonic expression. "Miss Quackenbush —"

"Katie, please." Juliet dryly reminded him, "Avoid the last name."

"Yes, of course. Katie... Leon's family has a lot of money, enough to keep this playhouse afloat. That means he's calling the shots. If ingénues come and go because he either likes them or he's through with them, it's none of my business, so neither is how you got this job."

Juliet pulled back, more appalled than annoyed. "You think I'm having an affair with Leon?"

"What ingénue isn't?"

Juliet was stunned. She said nothing, but stared at Collins until his expression softened.

He said, "Look, it's none of my business. I'm just a bit stressed over what's been going on these past several days. I'm sure you'll do a great job."

Juliet recovered herself. "Are you saying as well that Leon fires— gets rid of—an actress because he's been involved with her?"

"I'm not saying you have anything to worry about, dear. I just— look, just do your job, and if you're smart, you'll concentrate on your work and forget trying to sleep your way to the top. It really doesn't work out so well as you might think. If you can't work hard and learn your craft, better get out now, get married and have babies. Okay?"

"Do you think Leon fired Eva?"

"I don't know. Maybe she ditched him along with this show. Now, let's get to work."

***

Nina Garrett was a bundle of energy. Elmer noted her preparedness.

He asked, "I understand summer theaters don't usually have understudies. How do you come to be so well prepared to take over Eva's role?"

"I've learned that to get ahead, you work harder. That's all. I could see the handwriting on the wall as far as Eva was concerned, and sure, I set my sights on her role because I knew it would be up for grabs at some point during the run. I never expected her to ditch before we even opened, but I knew she'd fly sooner or later, probably before we hit Ogunquit. And I wanted to be the one to step in to her part."

Elmer asked, "What made you think she was going to take off?"

"Eva was one of those I'm-too-good-for-this-place types. She was always bucking for more money, or wanting to boot Beatrice out of the star's dressing room, or wanting shorter rehearsal, or wanting lunch to be brought to her on a tray, for heaven's sake. She hinted at having a shot at a role in a show opening on Broadway in the fall, *Saint Joan*. Can you believe it? Not only can I not believe she would tackle such a demanding lead, but I can't believe anybody could see her as Joan of Arc." Nina laughed a high, rippling giggle.

"So you think she left for professional reasons?"

"There's never been anything professional about Eva. But, yeah, I think maybe some contact probably breathed a word to her about a prospect for an audition, and she hightailed it on the train for NYC. If she got the role, we'll never see her again. If she's waiting to hear, we'll never see her again. If she didn't get the role, we'll never see her again because she'll be too embarrassed to show her face."

"Did she fight with Beatrice, over the star's dressing room, I mean?"

"She tried, but Beatrice has a way of dismissing people that makes it hard to fight with her. I guess when you get to be an old broad that's a skill you pick up."

Elmer smiled. "Did Eva fight with anybody else? Anybody who didn't have Beatrice's protective shield?"

"Well, she got Constance's goat more than once. Constance is one of those thin-skinned types, so it's easy to rile her."

***

The director gave Juliet a weak smile and patted her hand that rested on her knee, as she gripped her script defensively. They were alone downstairs, below the stage in the women's dressing room.

He said, "That's all I have time for now. No, really, you've done very well. You know most of your lines. Fortunately, it's not a large part."

Juliet felt as amused by his backhanded compliment as she felt sick at the thought of actually having to perform on stage.

He continued, "I have a million things to do, so I'm going to turn you over to Ruth Maguire to show you the ropes."

Ruth Maguire, as if on cue, appeared in the doorway and gave Juliet a gracious welcome. Collins dashed out and Ruth sat down in the chair he had occupied. She gave Juliet a glance up and down. She was a stately woman with a slight stoop to her shoulders in her late sixties and had let her dark hair turn salt-and-pepper.

"Did you bring your makeup with you?"

Juliet shuddered at her stupidity of forgetting to provide stage makeup. "No. This job came to me so suddenly, I didn't have time to prepare. I only have street makeup with me."

"Well, that's all right, dear. We can fix you up for tonight. Your character is a young nurse. It's not as if we have to age you, or create any special effect. It'll be more a matter of augmenting the street makeup, a little heavier eyeliner around the eyes so we don't lose them in the bright lights. You know what I mean. The playhouse actually has air-conditioning, though it's not on now. Did they tell you? So you don't have to worry about your face dripping off from the heat. I could tell you stories."

Juliet asked, "Does the star have her own dressing room?"

"Beatrice does, yes, but she's a grand girl with an open-door policy. Beatrice is brusque sometimes, but underneath that patrician severity is a kind lady. Here, I'll put you where Eva sat. We all share this dressing room. I'll just move some things off the counter."

Juliet replied, "Oh, please don't bother. I'll take care of myself."

"Sure?"

"Yes, thank you. Ruth, what do you think happened to Eva?"

Ruth considered her own reflection in the long mirror framed by a cluster of brightly lit naked bulbs. "I'm sure I have no idea." There was a kind of finality in the measure of her voice.

Another voice from the open doorway replied, "Nina Garrett probably killed her for her part." Billie Murchison followed up her remark with a snorting laugh. Ruth Maguire shook her head and smiled at Billie.

Ruth said to Juliet, "Don't listen to Billie. Just because she knows where all the bodies are buried."

Billie threw her head back and laughed with a throaty, smoker's rasp. "I think we're scaring this young lady. Don't worry, dear. Eva isn't the first actress who's gone missing in the history of the playhouse, and all the others were due to skipping out because they found better jobs elsewhere or sleeping off a drunken spree. Or, the occasional prima donna wanting a salary increase. But those are few and far between. Most summer theatre players are real troupers. Real troupers, like this lady here." She patted Ruth on the back.

Juliet smiled and asked, "In the history of the playhouse, you said? Have you been here many seasons, Miss Murchison?" Juliet did not mention having seen her in several plays over the years.

"Her brother's Kent Murchison, one of the managers." Ruth said. "Billie's been here as long as those uncomfortable seats."

Billie replied, "Kent is a co-manager with Leon Welch." She stole glances at herself in the mirror. She stood about five feet tall, but being overweight gave her a powerful presence—or perhaps it was just her commanding stage voice which continued offstage. She tended to always sound like she was projecting. "But if you want to know what happened to Eva, I'd ask Leon." She shot a glance to Ruth. Ruth inhaled sharply and gave Billie a severe look shaking her head again.

"With that," Ruth responded, "I will leave you to Billie's tender care. Billie, has that private detective questioned you yet?"

"Yeah. Polite guy, not one of those rude gumshoes who likes to throw his weight around. Not much to look at though." Billie answered.

Juliet bristled at this but said nothing.

Ruth teased, "So I don't need to be afraid of him?"

"Not unless you killed Eva." Billie laughed her own joke.

"Oh, Billie!"

Billie added when Ruth left them, "Ruth's a grand girl. Been in the business forever, paid her dues, you know? Toured every playhouse and vaudeville house in the country, I think, before Hollywood gave her a shot at two leads in the twenties, but that was thirty years ago and now she only gets the occasional mother role. That's how it is. She's real thick with Beatrice, and *nobody's* thick with Beatrice. Queen of the Great White Way, that one." She rolled her eyes.

"I only know Miss Longworth by professional reputation. I haven't met her yet." Juliet answered.

"She's not friendly, at least not to anybody without a theatre pedigree. Which Ruth has."

"Did you say that Leon knows where Eva is? You mean Leon Welch? He brought me on board. I don't really know him."

"Well, believe me, you will." Billie said archly, "or, I shouldn't say that. It's just that Leon has a habit of romancing his discoveries. That doesn't mean he's going to chase you, though. You don't seem to be his type. But that's a good thing. You look like you have too much class for him. Bimbos are easier to chase, and Leon's a lazy guy."

Juliet turned sharply to the counter before the long mirror to pretend to be digging into her purse. She could feel her cheeks warm to a blush. Leon unfaithful to Betty Ann? The thought made her blood boil.

Stephen Grove stepped in the doorway and knocked on the door frame. Juliet jumped.

"I'm sorry, I didn't mean to startle you." He offered a lazy, charming smile and lit a cigarette.

Billie said, "Have you met Stephen? Katie Quackenbush, this is Stephen Grove. He plays the doctor. Katie is our new Nurse Brent."

Stephen Grove shot a lingering glance of discovery over Juliet's body, starting at her groin and ending at her eyes, after a brief pause at her breasts. His delighted smile was disarming.

"Welcome," he said.

Juliet forced a becoming smile. "I hope you don't mind me taking over in this cast shuffle."

"Not at all," he answered, "but we won't be playing off each other. Too bad that you're not taking Eva's role, then I'd have some scenes with you."

"I don't have enough experience for that. That would be like throwing me in the deep water."

"Deep water," Stephen Grove echoed, chuckling.

***

Elmer motioned the woman seated in the back row of the theater to come forward. At first, she seemed surprised, pointed to herself, as if to question, "Who, me?"

Elmer smiled and nodded. As she made her way down the aisle, he said in a loud voice, "Miss Longworth, will you please join me for a few moments?"

The woman coming down the aisle stopped, but Elmer gestured her to continue to come.

Beatrice Longworth moved with assumed boredom and with what seemed to Elmer almost regal bearing. He could see why she had a reputation for being haughty. She took a seat, and looked briefly, dismissively, at the woman in the aisle, when Elmer, who stood as both of them approached, directed her to sit down with them. He wanted to interview them together.

Beatrice Longworth said, "I hope this won't take long, Mr. Vartanian. We have a lot of work to do today." She impressed Elmer with her total recall of his name.

"You're a quick study, Miss Longworth. Vartanian is usually more than most people remember upon first hearing."

She did not respond to him, but knotted a silk turquoise scarf in her hands. "And who is this?" She gestured to the woman with them, who had remained silent.

"You don't know?" Elmer replied, "She's been watching you with rapt attention, you more than anyone else. Who are you, ma'am?"

The woman appeared flustered and swallowed before she spoke but finally replied in a soft voice, "Joan Margolis."

Elmer asked, "Are you involved with the playhouse?"

"No."

Beatrice, becoming interested, noted, "You've been here for days, watching us."

"Watching you, I think, Miss Longworth," Elmer responded in a friendly, conversational manner. He smiled at Joan Margolis. "Why don't you tell us why you're here."

"I don't want to cause any trouble." Joan Margolis took a deep breath and sighed, with a slight nervous giggle. "I'm sorry to appear so strange. I guess I don't really have permission to be here, but nobody asked me to leave, so I just stayed and came back every day."

"You mean you're a vagrant?" Beatrice asked, seemingly both annoyed and amused simultaneously.

"Oh, no. No, I live in Groton. My husband's stationed at the submarine base. He's in the Navy. It's just that I'd read in the paper that you were to be appearing at the playhouse this week, and..."

Elmer asked politely, "And you're a fan of Miss Longworth's?"

Joan Margolis seemed embarrassed, smiling and shrugging.

"Would you like an autograph?" Beatrice asked, as if waiting for the inevitable, and she reached for a pen in her purse.

"No," Joan replied, "I mean, I just—just wanted to see you again."

Elmer asked, "Again?"

Beatrice turned in her seat to face Joan Margolis. Joan stole brief looks at both Elmer and Beatrice, and with a flushed but somehow pleased attitude, she leaned forward and spoke in an almost conspiratorial tone.

"Miss Longworth, we've met before—about twenty years ago. In Hollywood. I appeared with you in *The Storm*."

"*The Storm?*" Beatrice responded, remembering.

"It was back in 1931. I was eight years old. I played the daughter of your love interest, from his first marriage. I only had a couple of scenes. I went by Joanie Kelly back then."

Beatrice searched Joan's face. "I'll be damned. I think that was the second or third film I did when I went out to the West Coast for the first time." She turned to Elmer, "Broadway work had all but dried up after the Wall Street Crash in 1929. A lot of us migrated west just to eat." She turned back to Joan. "Joanie Kelly. I remember doing the picture, but I'm afraid I don't remember much about it. I think I did something like four pictures in that year alone. It was like an assembly line. Essentially playing the same character in different scenarios. The studio system was a swamp. I couldn't wait to get back to the theatre. Now that they've booted me out of Hollywood because of that damned infernal Blacklist, I have only the theatre left. Regional theater, summer stock, at that. Oh, well, no regrets there. The swamp and all its rats can sink for all I care."

Elmer asked, "So you came out of curiosity to see Miss Longworth? Why not just come to a performance? Why have you come here every day to watch rehearsals?"

Joan became thoughtful, at last losing her nervousness. "In a performance, I would have seen Miss Longworth's work—which is always excellent. But I wanted to see her, watch her in unguarded moments, just once more. You see, I was never really a stage-struck person, pining after movie stars and all that. I never even really wanted to be an actress, frankly. My mother pushed me into it."

"God spare us from stage mothers," Beatrice replied.

Joan answered, "Oh, no, she wasn't a stage mother. She wasn't stage-struck, either. It was just the most practical thing to do at the time. We went to California in 1930. We were originally from the Midwest. My father was looking for work as a carpenter. Well, nobody was building anything in the Depression, but he'd heard the Hollywood studios were hiring carpenters, you know, to build their sets and soundstages and back lots. So we went to Hollywood in our broken-down old car—my parents, me, and my three younger sisters. Daddy got a job, and we were thrilled and relieved, of course. But about six months later, he'd had an accident at work. His shoulder and spine were fractured and he couldn't work anymore. My three little sisters were not old enough to go to school yet, the youngest was just a baby, so my mother couldn't go out to work even if she could find a job. They considered putting us all into foster care so that Mother could look for work, but then she saw they were hiring for a series of kiddie B-movies, and she signed me up. I didn't want to do it, but she made me feel like the family was depending on me…

"I'm sorry to be making this story so long."

Elmer said, "No, go ahead."

"Yes, please continue," Beatrice added softly.

"Well, they were casting for *The Storm*, and I got picked out of the kiddie lineup to play the daughter. I was eight years old. I only had a few lines—but it was a big deal for my family. I would be earning fifty dollars a week for two weeks on this picture. Really big money, you understand. My mother was so pleased. It wasn't the fame or working with movie stars, it was only the money. She could have cared less who was in the movie. She never bragged to neighbors or anything like that. It was just to be able to keep the family going.

"I had one big scene in the movie. I was to be drowning in the ocean, and my father, who was played by Ken Rockland, had to save me."

Beatrice smiled and shook her head, "Ken Rockland. We called him Rocky. Nice fellow, but Hollywood spit him out long ago. He had reached his zenith in the silents. The talkies were no favor to him."

Joan continued, "Well, the director called action, and I was put in a tank of dark, freezing water that was being all churned up to make waves. Mr. Rockland saved me every time in seven takes. When it was over, Mr. Rockland climbed out of the pool with a lot of profanity once we'd finally satisfied the director. The tech crew set up for a new shot and everybody wandered away. Somebody fished me out of the drink. And there I stood, in my dripping wet wool bathing suit, half drowned. I never learned how to swim and I swallowed half that tank, I think.

"Children were supposed to be accompanied on set by an adult, a parent or guardian, but my mother could never leave my father and my younger sisters, so they made an exception for me. Working with child stars was more or less regulated at that time. The studio did give me a young woman who was supposed to mind me on set, but she had left to flirt with some grip.

"Now, I had been told by my mother to do whatever I was told to do. She drummed that into me. But for that moment, nobody was telling me to do anything. I just stood there waiting for instructions. Everybody forgot about me. I couldn't help it, I started to tear up and cry. It was an awful experience.

"Then suddenly, someone came up from behind me and wrapped a blanket around me, bundling me in it, and then picked me up." She looked at Beatrice. "It was *you*. I was even more scared. I'm afraid you intimidated me."

"I like to think I intimidated a lot of people." Beatrice smiled.

"Well, you carried me in your arms over to your chair on the set— you know, all the stars had their names stenciled on the backs of their chairs. You sat down, no-nonsense, with me in your lap, and you ordered an assistant get me a cup of hot chocolate. Then you yelled at the director for nearly drowning me and you yelled for someone to find my keeper and get me into some dry clothes.

"All of that took a while. In the meantime, you held up a costly production and cuddled me in your lap. You raked my wet hair off my face with your hands, and rubbing my back to get me warm, you told me that I was a real trouper and a good little girl."

Joan finished and looked down at the floor. Elmer and Beatrice waited for her to continue, but that was evidently the end of the story.

Beatrice asked, incredulous, "And so you've come here every day just to see me rehearse?"

Joan replied, looking back up at her with tear-filled eyes, "My mother never told me I was a good little girl, even when I handed her that paycheck every week." A small gasp like a long-stifled cry escaped her before she resumed silence.

Elmer asked, "Did you make any other movies?"

Joan answered, wiping her eyes, "A few more B-movies, then thankfully, my father was well enough to go back to work—not as a carpenter, he was never able to do that again, but he opened a newsstand on the sidewalk on Wilshire Boulevard. We were able to get by on that, and my mother let me quit the movies."

Beatrice looked at her, not speaking, but taking her in with silence that was more powerful than words.

Elmer broke the silence, "And now, I'd like to ask both of you ladies what you can contribute to this mystery of the whereabouts of Eva Breck."

Beatrice answered brusquely, "A good actress, instinctual rather than trained."

"And offstage?"

"I mind my own business."

Elmer turned to Joan, "Mrs. Margolis?"

Joan obediently shook her head. "I really don't know anything about Miss Breck."

He said, "You had the opportunity to observe more than just Miss Longworth since you've been here. Anything that could help?"

She shook her head.

"I'd like your address and phone number, Mrs. Margolis, to get in touch with you if I need to."

Joan responded, "Do you really think that's necessary? My husband doesn't know I'm here. I feel foolish."

"The police will be involved if Miss Breck doesn't turn up. You'll find working with me a lot less worrisome and a lot less public." He smiled and wrote down her information when she gave it to him.

Beatrice Longworth eyed him and muttered, "If you intend to question Mr. Norman, I suggest you do it soon. He looks like he's already been hitting the bottle—or bottles—pretty heavily."

Guy Norman stood in the side entrance by the stage, brooding, with a sulky expression on his face, watching them. He jerked, apparently startled when Elmer, Beatrice, and Joan all looked his way at once. He rubbed his face and turned and quickly left the playhouse.

Chapter Five

Ruth Maguire, who was playing Mother Superior, changed into her costume for the full dress rehearsal. She passed Elmer on the patch of lawn beside the theater, between the playhouse and the smaller outbuildings that were the box office and the restrooms and the refreshment stand. Elmer had come outside to follow Guy Norman, but Guy had disappeared.

Ruth shook her head when Elmer asked her if she had seen him. "Guy is a bit of a problem; he's been drinking lately. Not to excess, though. Poor Bessie spends more of her time sloshed than Guy Norman. She's a sweetheart, but we have to constantly cover for her. If it weren't for her friends, I don't know how she'd ever find any work as an actress, let alone keep it."

Elmer kept an eye on the grounds and the buildings around them, hoping to spot Guy Norman again. "Miss Baggs plays Sister Josephine?"

"Yes, the convent cook who helps Sister Bonaventure—Beatrice Longworth—to solve the case of Sarat Carn's guilt or innocence." Ruth drew a long puff on her cigarette, which she had pulled out of the wide sleeve of her nun's habit. Elmer gave a short laugh in surprise.

"What?" she asked.

He shook his head, smiling, "The image of a nun smoking."

Ruth threw her head back and laughed. "I'm only a nun from 8:40 to 11 o'clock."

Elmer asked, "Do you always get into your costume this early? The rehearsal isn't until later this afternoon."

"I needed costume adjustments. I'm waiting for Meg the wardrobe mistress. I need her to tack down these beads. In dress rehearsal

65

yesterday, they swished forward in a dramatic moment and smacked Nina in the face." She chuckled, fingering the long line of rosary beads that hung from a cord at her waist.

"What do you think is Guy Norman's problem anyway? Usual jitters about opening night?"

"Him? Guy just strikes me as a morose type. He's always complaining about something. I know he's not happy with his role—Willy the halfwit. His Yorkshire accent is atrocious, by the way, if that's what it is."

"Why doesn't he quit? Too hard to get work?"

Ruth answered pensively, "Guy could probably get work without too much difficulty. He's handsome and he has a good track record, but Constance keeps him on a short leash."

"Constance Burch? Are they a couple?"

"They're married. Constance imagines them as some sort of Lunt-Fontanne duo. Can you believe that?" She snorted and puffed on her cigarette.

"Do you think Guy's chafing at the leash?"

She answered, "Professionally, yes. Personally? You'd have to ask him."

"If I can find him. I think he bolted from me. Maybe he doesn't want to talk."

Ruth said, "Maybe he doesn't want to talk while drunk."

"Was he involved with Eva Breck?"

Now it was Ruth's turned to be startled. She dragged on her cigarette and dropped it to the grass and mashed the butt out with the toe of her shoe.

"Eva casts her line out for any male around—how many or which one she chooses to reel in—I don't know."

Elmer asked, "Who else?"

"I really couldn't say. I've speculated enough already."

Elmer said, "A woman is missing. Suppose she's been murdered?"

Ruth's eyes grew wide. "My God, you don't think *that*, do you? We assumed Eva just ran off, found a better gig, a richer sugar daddy."

"You really thought that? Why?"

Ruth shrugged. "She was flighty and full of herself. She was a talented actress, but so undisciplined. I don't think she cared how she earned a living—or if she earned it, if you know what I mean."

"Who else was seeing her? Or, let's put it this way, who else looked interested?"

"Well... Ed Stiles, the stage manager, for one. I heard him in the wings once mutter that he wished Leon Welch would stop taking the pick of the crop every time a new touring company settled in."

***

Director Jeff Collins allowed Elmer just three minutes, which he timed on his wristwatch as he lit a cigarette. They stood in the lobby where Jeff had gone to escape his cast for a breather.

"How did you come to hire Eva?" Elmer asked.

"Quick study, drop-dead gorgeous."

"Talented?"

"In her way."

"Did you sleep with her?"

***

Juliet tried on her costume so the wardrobe mistress could make alterations, if need be. It was a nurse's uniform and apron, and it fit her perfectly.

"Marvelous!" Meg the wardrobe mistress replied, kneeling on the floor in front of Juliet and tugging at the hem of her dress. "How clever of you to be the same size. What's your name again, I'm sorry?"

Juliet nearly said, "Juliet," but remembered after a beat, "Katie Quackenbush."

"Not really? Great stage name. Did you pick it, or did somebody pick it for you?"

Juliet thought of Elmer and smiled, "Somebody picked it for me."

Beatrice Longworth poked her head into the ladies' dressing room. Her star dressing room was next door.

"Meg, when you have a minute?"

"Sure thing, Miss Longworth. I just thought we could wait with your costume."

Beatrice answered, "My rosary beads are missing."

Meg replied, struggling to get off her knees, "What is this, rosary day? I just heard from Ruth that her beads need adjusting because she bashed Nina in the face with them last time in rehearsal."

Beatrice answered, "Just rig something up."

"All right, look, everybody's going to have to search for them. I'll be there in a minute."

Juliet remarked, "I'm taking Nina's role. Am I to be bashed in the face with rosary beads now?"

Meg chuckled, "We'll see. No, I can put a few stitches so they won't swing around. We only get one chance to practice this afternoon and then it's showtime."

"Nina must be a really quick study. I understand she only just took over the role."

"Quick, my eye. She knew all the lines and the blocking for at least a couple of weeks."

"Oh, she was an understudy?"

"There's no understudies in summer theatre, honey. Nina's just ambitious as Lucifer."

Juliet asked, "What you think happened to Eva?"

"Don't know, can't say. However, if you ask me…"

I just did, Juliet thought.

"… she could have been bumped off."

"Good lord. You're kidding?!"

Meg shrugged. "Well, I guess that's a bit overboard, huh? I've heard actors and actresses say they'd kill for a part, but they never do. They also say they'd slayed their audience—but you know what I mean. It's just an expression. But Eva's the type that pushes the limit."

Juliet replied, "What about Nina? Willing to kill for a part? I wouldn't kill for a part. Now, if Eva were after my boyfriend…" she thought of a name, "…Klaus. I might scratch her eyes out."

"Klaus? What does he do?"

Juliet's imagination took off. "He is…a peanut vendor. At Yankee Stadium."

Meg gave her a quick, dubious look.

Juliet continued, emboldened, "He's six-foot-five and built like Hercules."

Meg smiled. "Oh, well, that makes all the difference, doesn't it? Dick Watson wasn't built like Hercules, but Beatrice didn't appreciate all that scandal about Eva and him."

"Dick Watson?"

"Beatrice's late husband. Only he wasn't really fooling around with Eva—that's what people say, but it's not true. See, he got slammed by those *Red Channels* people. Hollywood—the film crowd went after him because he used to be a communist or something. The pressure killed him. He had a heart attack."

"How was Eva was involved in that?"

"Eva wasn't as interested in men as much as in their money. The way I heard it, it wasn't enough for the red-baiting creeps to destroy Dick Watson's career—he was an agent—one of the best—that they wanted him to rat on actors he knew were communists or union members, which was the same thing to those Hollywood big shots. They hated unions out there. Dick wouldn't, so they—or somebody—got Eva to go along with planting news about cheating with her, being involved in Hollywood orgies, that type of thing. There's nothing rag magazines love better than orgies. Beatrice knew it wasn't true, but she hated Eva for it. When I found out that Eva and Beatrice were both cast for this show, I thought, uh-oh, there's going to be fireworks. Tell you, though, Leon's pleased as punch about it—the box office is doing great. We sold out for all performances. They're thinking about extending the show another two weeks. I think that's why he hired that detective, he needs Eva back for his box office because of the scandal. Have you ever heard of anything like it? For summer theatre?"

"You think Beatrice could have wanted revenge against Eva?"

"She'd have to get in line." Meg said.

"Who else?"

Meg looked around to see if the wooden walls had ears. "Well, in the jealous wife department, you've got Leon's wife, Mrs. Welch. And her being in the family way." She shook her head and tisked. Juliet's heart sank.

Meg continued, "And she seems like such a nice lady. She came to one of our rehearsals and met the cast. She was really lovely. Well, I got to go find Miss Longworth's beads. Some of these actors get very careless. I wouldn't think she'd be the type but there you are. Take this off and hang it on the rack there. You can climb into it again this afternoon when we do the full dress rehearsal."

Meg sprang to her feet and grabbed her sewing kit. She left for the star's dressing room. Juliet could hear the door softly close.

Juliet removed her costume and put on her street clothes again: A light-yellow cotton skirt and white cotton short-sleeved jersey with a bateau neckline. Her thin gold watch was her only jewelry. She slipped on her canvas espadrilles; she wore no stockings. It was a combination such as she would wear for a weekend at the shore. She mused that they were now work clothes. Such is the life of an actress in rehearsal. Such is the life of a private investigator pretending to be one, she thought.

Private investigator? No, that was too much. Sleuth. An avocation rather than a vocation.

Like her painting, Elmer regarded both as professions. He was more serious-minded.

Juliet stopped outside and bumped into Robert just entering the playhouse, carrying a ladder. Both glanced quickly aside to see if they were observed, then Robert asked, "How is it going?"

Juliet answered in a low voice, "A bit of innuendo, not enough to flush out any real leads. You?"

"Hey, you and Elmer are the private eyes, I'm just along for the ride."

Private eyes, there it was again.

Juliet said, "You've got eyes and ears of your own."

Robert glanced around again and leaned closer to her, answering lowly, "Ed Stiles, that's the stage manager, he's mad that Leon nudged him out of line for Eva Breck. I don't think he's mad enough to kill Eva, but if he was, he'd be more than glad to pin it on Leon."

She answered "You've got the hang of this stuff pretty quick, Robert."

He replied, "In the jug, you take it for granted nobody's a saint."

Juliet spotted Betty Ann coming out of the administrative offices. What was she doing here? Juliet wanted to avoid her. She couldn't face her with what she knew about Leon—and yet, how could she not tell her?

Robert continued, "Next on Ed's enemies list is Guy Norman, same reason."

Juliet responded, distracted, "What?"

"He's not too keen on Mr. Murchison, either, Leon's partner. Not for the same reason, though."

"She hasn't captured the heart of every man in Connecticut?"

Robert grinned, "Murchison has no heart, so Ed says. Murchison's fed up with Leon's carrying on, thinks Leon was a fool for spending all that money last year to put air-conditioning in when they're scraping by, and meanwhile, Ed's annoyed about Murchison always putting his sister in every play."

Juliet asked, "Who is his sister?"

"Billie Murchison, takes the small roles."

"Oh, yes. They don't like that?"

"I don't think they care about her; they just don't like Murchison tightening the screws on them all the time."

"Would Mr. Murchison frame Leon?"

Robert answered, "I don't know. So far, he said three words to me: 'Who are you?' And then grunted at me. I can't see a cold fish like that committing a crime of passion."

"Would he pay to have somebody else to do it?"

Robert smiled "You're good at this game, too, aren't you? I don't think this guy likes spending money for anything. Well, I got to go change a gel in one of the Fresnels. That's those big colored lights hanging from the ceiling. Isn't this a great place?"

"You like it here."

"Juliet, I do. It was love at first sight."

Robert took the ladder into the playhouse while Juliet held the screen door open for him. Then she walked quickly around the building along the veranda, to the front. From her vantage point, she saw Elmer in the gravel parking lot, strolling along the line of cars. He had taken his suit coat off and draped it over his arm. His striped tie fluttered in the breeze, slapping his broad chest. She came down off the wooden steps that were dusted with beach sand, and approached him and she said in a low voice, "Let's pretend you want to interrogate me even though I'm new here. That will cover us so I can talk to you."

"Okay. Let's say that."

"Oh, Elmer, I've heard Leon was cheating on Betty Ann with Eva Breck and probably others." She said it in a breathless rush.

He appraised the sick concern in her eyes, her light-green eyes that she shielded from the sun with her hand. He said flatly, "I know."

71

"Who told you? They all know?"

Elmer turned her around so that he was facing the sun so she wouldn't have to squint into the sunlight anymore. He lowered his hat brim against the glare and answered quietly, "Leon told me."

Juliet's eyes grew wide and gasped, "When?"

"When he called me for this job."

Her judgment not just of Leon, but of him, beamed in her angry glare. "You *knew* all along? How could you not tell me? How could you take this job from that pig?! I just saw her over there by the office. I ran over here to avoid her. How do I face her?"

Elmer responded, "I know. I understand. I'm not sure he called me out of real concern for Eva, or because of his involvement with her, or that he knew he would be a prime suspect."

"Maybe he is. Maybe he killed her."

"Maybe Betty Ann did."

Juliet gasped again and scoffed, "Oh my—you, oh, Elmer! Don't say that! You can't be serious!"

"Shh," he said. "Quiet down, please, Juliet. You know I'm no fan of Leon. I never liked him. But we have to look at this calmly and carefully –"

"I can't believe you didn't tell me. Do you realize how betrayed I feel? She's my best friend!"

Elmer wanted to touch her but held back. "I didn't tell you *because* she's your best friend."

"You didn't trust me?"

"I didn't want to put you in the awful position you're in now."

Juliet looked away, mortified, as she always was, by quick tears. Elmer waited another moment, waiting as she pulled a white lace handkerchief out of her purse.

He continued gently, "If she were my friend, I'd hate to tell her, but I have to because I couldn't not let her know. Because if it were me, I'd want to know."

A slight breeze picked up offshore and bounced off the tops the grasses of the saltwater marsh that began along the edge of the parking lot.

Elmer said, "Now you really will have to tell her, like it or not."

She looked up at him. "Because she really is a suspect, if she already knows he's been with her."

He nodded. "I'm so sorry."

"Oh, no. How do I even begin?"

He answered, "It's after you've begun that's important. You can't get caught up in comforting her so much that you forget to be observant of her reactions. You have to spy on your own friend."

"Damn Leon."

Elmer glanced around towards the playhouse to see if they were being observed by anyone. "What have you learned so far?" he asked. Juliet filled him in on her encounters with the actors in the dressing room, and with Meg the wardrobe mistress, and her check-in with Robert.

Elmer smiled. "He's becoming interested in our work?"

"No, he struck me as being skeptical. He said in the jug everybody was suspicious."

"Yeah," Elmer said, his expression clouding over, as it always did when there was a reference to his years in prison.

Juliet continued, "But he's in love with the playhouse. He just lit up talking about it. Elmer, do you think the fooling around with reading plays in prison that you did together meant more to him than you realized?"

"That's one I never imagined. Well, right now we've got enough on our plate. Have you seen where Guy Norman went? He bolted before I could talk to him."

Juliet shook her head. "Do you have any reason to believe Eva's dead as opposed to just having run off?"

He answered, "I'm hoping she's holed up in some local chowder house having a shore dinner and laughing her head off at the trouble she's caused. But why? She has a contract for a limited time. She's not going to get a raise by being difficult. She's here for a couple of weeks for this play and then most of the cast goes on to Ogunquit; others to other plays and other playhouses."

"Blackmail, perhaps? To add to her coffers."

He answered, "Of Leon? Maybe. But that would just give him a motive to kill her."

"The best motive, probably," she said, "but she's run off with so many husbands, Eva's got plenty of enemies."

He filled her in on what he learned from Constance Burch, Beatrice Longworth and her connection. "Thing is, why would he call me in to find a missing person? He's already notified the police. She's not considered officially missing until tomorrow. They have someone already taking over her role. Why not just say he did his best by looking for her and calling the cops, and his responsibility ends there and get another actress in the role and let it go? Why hire me?"

She answered, "Because *he* thinks she's been murdered."

He nodded. "He didn't say so, but if he suspects she's been murdered, he called me to protect himself, to avoid being accused of it. That's Leon."

Elmer nodded to a baby-blue 1951 Cadillac Series 61 convertible. "That's his car there. It hasn't rained down here in over a week, but his car is the only one with mud on the tires and spattered on the undercarriage. See how over on the right of the parking lot there's a line of scrub standing taller in the salt marsh, leading to a stand of trees way out over there? It must be a little bit of high ground, kind of an island in the marsh, or a peninsula."

She replied, "The Hammonasset River is beyond that. The other side of the bay is Clinton."

"The river empties into the harbor over there?"

She answered, "Yes. So what about the mud? Do you think this car has been down that peninsula in the marsh?"

"Leon's pretty fastidious. He wouldn't take his nice baby-blue car off the road unless he had a special reason. Maybe a tryst in the back seat in the privacy of the woods? Maybe dumping Eva's body?"

Juliet closed her eyes.

Elmer continued, "I'm going to pop the trunk, Juliet. Go talk to Betty Ann. Tell her as a friend you've heard that talk is going around. See how she reacts. It's going to be a pretty rotten task, but it's got to be done by one of us. I'd think she'd rather it be you."

She nodded, and left without being able to look at him again.

The keys were in the car. Elmer popped the trunk.

Chapter Six

Juliet spotted Betty Ann, with her pregnant woman's careful waddle, walking towards the playhouse. She waved and motioned Betty Ann to come meet her by the small freestanding booth that served as the box office.

A knot formed in Juliet's stomach, and not just because she had to tell her friend about her husband's infidelity. Juliet had not mentioned to Elmer that Meg the wardrobe mistress said Betty Ann had met the cast and visited them, yet when Juliet had talked with Betty Ann in her bedroom, she had said that she had never met Eva Breck.

Betty Ann whispered, "I thought we weren't supposed to acknowledge each other while you are on the case?"

"I have to tell you something," Juliet replied in a low, soft voice reaching for Betty Ann's arm, pulling her closer. "Please forgive me, but I have to tell you. I just have to."

Betty Ann's brow furrowed, she put her hand on Juliet's arm. Juliet took her hand and grasped it and said, "Let's sit down on this bench."

"Oh, no thanks, hon. I'd rather stand. Getting up is too hard to do. I feel better walking."

"Do you want to walk?"

"Tell me what you have to say. Then we'll walk."

Juliet felt dizzy with anxiety, but looked into Betty Ann's eyes. "Leon has been cheating on you. He's been involved with Eva Breck, the actress who went missing, and it's rumored that he's been involved with other actresses in the past. I don't know about that, but Leon confessed to Elmer that he had a tryst with Eva the night before she went missing. So it's true, darling. I'm so sorry. I'm so sorry to have to tell you, but I couldn't leave you in the dark about this."

Betty Ann laid her hand gently on Juliet's cheek. Wordlessly, she kissed her, and wrapped her in a warm hug, leaning over her belly to clutch Juliet's shoulders. "Sweetie, I know."

Juliet forced herself to take a breath, tears came, but Betty Ann was stoic when she pulled away. "I actually came here to see Kent Murchison. He was out of his office for lunch—oh, but I see he's over there heading back to it. I'll talk to you later." Betty Ann walked towards the office without another word.

Juliet felt a tinge of fear and foreboding. *Betty Ann knew.* She was businesslike about it. At the most emotional time in her life with the coming of her first child, she could be so matter-of-fact about her husband's infidelity.

How long had she known?

Would she have confronted Leon?

Would she have killed Eva?

***

Jeff Collins took the stage and told stage manager Ed Stiles to bring out the actors for the beginning of Act I.

"I just want to run the first nine pages and give some notes before lunch. Katie's got to get her feet wet as Nurse Brent, so we might as well do that before we break. I don't want her thrown into a full dress rehearsal this afternoon without even reading the part once."

Stiles motioned Robert to remove his ladder from the stage, and Robert pulled it down and stowed it off the stage apron, and then looked on with interest from what he learned was stage left.

Ed Stiles called down to the dressing rooms, "Running Act I, pages one through nine! I want Nurse Phillips, Willy, Nurse Brent, Sister Josephine, and Sister Mary Bonaventure!"

Below the stage in their dressing rooms, as if they were firemen who'd heard the alarm bell, Constance Burch stopped digging into her purse, looked up and stood, checking herself in the long mirror, and went toward the stairs. Bessie Baggs, quietly perusing the newspaper, took a quick nip from her ill-concealed bottle, tucked it away and headed up the stairs. Beatrice Longworth, in her own star's dressing room, quickly removed her costume that Meg, on her knees again, was adjusting, and headed upstairs.

Juliet was still outside, when Ed Stiles came out onto the veranda.

"Hey, Katie! Get in here and run the first nine pages!"

Juliet muttered a quiet oath and followed on wobbly legs. She pulled her script out of her purse. "Where do I go?"

Stiles replied, "Well, sweetheart, the script says you enter stage left. No, over there. Phillips—Constance Burch—is already sitting at the table onstage when you enter. You have the first lines of the play. We don't start without you."

Jeff Collins waved her on. "Let's go. It's all right if you're 'holding book,' I don't expect you to know the lines right now—but study them during lunch. I just want you to get the feel of playing off the other actors in your scenes. We'll do the first nine pages of Act I, and then we'll jump to Act II, scene 2, because that's your next part. Got it? Okay. Have we got everybody?"

"Still looking for Guy Norman, boss." Stiles said. "Robert, you seen him?"

Robert shook his head.

Collins swore. "I don't have time for this. Ed, can you read for Willy?"

"Sure, but how about Robert here? He's has some stage experience."

"Really?" Collins said. "Oh, well, fine. Robert, is it? Who's got a script for him?"

Beatrice answered, "He can use mine."

"Fine, fine, let's get going."

"Places!" Ed Stiles shouted.

***

In the trunk of Leon's car, Elmer found a spare tire, a jack, an otherwise pristine trunk with no extra gas can or jumper cables such as a car owner would need to rescue his car on the roadside. Leon was not going to fix things. He would call a cab and get it towed. Or he would buy a car and replace it every two years before it ever had problems.

But being so clean made it easier to spot a few light hairs, and a rust-colored stain on the carpet.

Elmer closed the trunk and walked toward the peninsula, following a wide dirt path that jutted out into the salt marsh.

***

Juliet read awkwardly from her script as the good-natured Nurse Brent, nervous while Constance Burch aggressively played the prickly Nurse Phillips in the story. Bessie Baggs entered as the venerable Sister Josephine, and Juliet could not help but be distracted by the wonder of watching the old veteran actress suddenly command the stage in a way she could never command attention as herself in a room full of others. The shy, even shaky old lady who was known to drink a bit lost all her inhibitions on stage and she spoke as clear as a bell, not fumbling or forgetful.

Then it was time for the entrance of the character Willy, who was referred to as a "half-wit" in the story, a young man of childlike intellect who worked as a handyman in the convent. Robert entered, pretending to carry a load of logs in his arms, as Willy was described in the stage directions.

There were a few chuckles among the other actors, watching from the wings and the audience, and Juliet noted a wry smile from Ed Stiles. It struck her instantly that they did not see Robert as a fellow actor; they saw him as humorously miscast, a black man pretending to be an English half-wit handyman. His jumping into the role, even to help during a rehearsal, was a joke to them.

Then he spoke his first lines, and they gasped in response to hearing his near-perfect mimicry of an East Anglia accent.

***

Elmer walked about halfway down the peninsula in the salt marsh, turned and looked back through tall grasses and scrub pine at the view of the playhouse, with the parking lot before it and the ocean beyond. Weathered wooden fencing as windbreaks, bowed in the wind, held back sand dunes left and right.

It was quieter here, away from the sounds of the beach, the ocean; the stillness and serenity broken by the cry of an egret.

He took off his straw hat and wiped the hat band with his handkerchief. He was able to follow clear tire tracks to this point, but the path grew narrower ahead and would not allow a car. From here, he could discern occasional imprints from a man's shoes. Elmer grew tensely alert, cautious as he proceeded down the last overgrown section of the peninsula as it reached into the most isolated part of the salt marsh.

He froze at the sound of a snapped twig.

***

Robert *was* Willy. His surprising performance shone with utmost empathy with his character, a young man who was excitable, emotional, fearful of reproach in a world in which he was utterly helpless, quick to make inappropriate remarks, quick to lash out in frustration, and soothed in his doglike devotion of Sr. Mary Bonaventure, played by Beatrice Longworth. Beatrice entered and gently coaxed him through "To everything there is a season..." from Ecclesiastes. He strained to say the powerful words, mournful and yearning in his nearly sobbing speech. She was a supportive scene partner, and they played well off each other in a moving, tender relationship. When he made his exit, though the scene was not over, the other actors in the wings and in the house applauded.

***

Elmer continued down the peninsula slowly, walking softly and straining to listen, but hearing only the sound of frogs and the light buzzing of flying insects. He kept a careful watch all around him, not certain that he was alone.

He came to a stand of trees and followed the footprints through them to the muddy shore at the end of the peninsula. From here he could see the salt marsh all around him, with the slow current of the Hammonasset River in the middle, wandering through the tall grasses to the harbor in Clinton beyond. The sun at high noon left a white, almost blinding glare across the glassy water of the marsh.

Then he felt a blow to his head.

***

Director Jeff Collins gave notes to Juliet when the scenes were done that he had wanted to run through, but he only called out briefly to Robert, who had returned to the wings, "Nice job, stagehand."

Ed Stiles patted Robert on the back and said to him quietly, "You weren't kidding; you sure did have some acting training under your belt. Where did you pick up that accent?"

Robert, flushed with exhilaration, replied, "You pick up a lot of stuff in this business, right? You never know when you're going to need it."

"For sure."

Other actors shook his hand and Beatrice smiled. "Well done, young Robert."

Jeff Collins called for lunch and threatened them with death if they did not return on time for the dress rehearsal.

Juliet observed who went where when Collins called for lunch break. Beatrice Longworth, Bessie Baggs, and Ruth Maguire left together, discussing plans for a local restaurant, called the Sea Shell. Beatrice asked Joan Margolis to go with them. Joan was visibly surprised and she demurred, but Beatrice, with a wide smile and a welcoming reach of her arm, insisted.

Beatrice remarked, "You're my guest. You're a veteran of films, too, you know, so you're in the club. You're just not as old as we are."

Joan appeared happy to join them and they filed out of the playhouse towards Beatrice's rental car in the parking lot.

Nina Garrett tucked her bag under her arm and quickly left toward the side entrance that led to the group of outbuildings comprising the box office, the restrooms, and the business office. Paula Miles said she was meeting an old friend for lunch.

Ed Stiles invited Robert for a burger and a beer, and they left together.

Constance Burch went down to the women's dressing room. Billie Murchison, because she lived nearby, went home.

Stephen Grove asked Juliet to dine with him. "Do you like seafood? This is the place for it." His face beamed in a confident, seductive smile.

Though Juliet might have accepted, something more important even than ingratiating herself to him—the better to question him—made her feel she should stay at the playhouse and confer with Elmer. She told Stephen that she wanted to eat a sandwich and apple she had brought and use the time to study her script. He left her with a shrug of implied regret and a wink.

Guy Norman had still not returned.

Juliet went outside to the parking lot. The midday sun sailed high in a bright azure sky. She could hear the sounds of the beachgoers a small distance away, whose dim buzz of laughter and shouts were carried on the warm breeze from the public beach just to the west of the playhouse.

Her car was still in the parking lot, but she did not see Elmer and assumed he was still on the grounds somewhere. She turned toward the outbuildings and wondered if he was in the office with Leon. She proceeded toward the office, a small bungalow covered in gray shingles and white trim, a color scheme typical along the shore. Bright colors tend to fade very quickly in the salt-tinged winds, so weathered natural cedar shakes were the most practical exterior decor for the shoreline and became, over time, the clichéd appearance of shoreline buildings and homes.

The office building converted from the former farmhouse actually contained three offices: An outer office with a long library table that served as a conference room and reception area, and two smaller "executive" offices each held by Leon and his partner Kent Murchison.

As she walked in her mercifully flat shoes on the uneven gravel drive, she noticed a seeming trace of muddy footprints leading toward the office. It started from the grassy edge of the parking lot, suggesting the trail had originated in the saltwater marsh. It led to the business office cottage—but not to the door. It stopped at the side of the building where three metal trash cans stood in a row.

Juliet walked over and took a peek in each one. In the middle can, a pair of muddy men's shoes rested on top a layer of trash.

She heard a crash from the box office building to her other side. It was a much smaller building, just a large shed. Its counter windows were closed and shuttered. The screen door on the side by which one entered the building was not shut completely. Juliet stepped over and pushed open the door, peeking into the darkness.

Guy Norman, on his hands and knees, trying to pick up pieces of broken glass bottle, looked up at her.

He slurred his speech, "I... I made a mess here. Sorry. Sorry. Made a mess. Don't—don't tell Jeff—don't tell Constance. Sorry. I'm sorry."

He was quite drunk. She snapped on the light switch by the door, and he shielded his eyes from the glare with the back of his hand.

"Here, Mr. Norman," Juliet said, "just step aside. Carefully, now. Here, sit on the stool. Let me get this. You'll hurt yourself." She found a broom standing against the back wall and swept up the shards and smaller pieces of the bottle into the corner. Guy tottered on the stool.

Juliet said, "You need some coffee, Mr. Norman. You're in no shape..."

"Don't feel so hot. Felt great before. Not now."

Juliet steered him toward the stage entrance of the playhouse and down the stairs to the dressing rooms. Guy stumbled, shuffled, and advanced slowly in loud moans, until she dropped him in a chair in the men's dressing room. Constance Norman looked in from the hall; she had been alone in the ladies' dressing room. She stared silently, severely at her husband.

Juliet said, "He needs some coffee. Is there some place –"

"Don't bother. I'll take care of him. We have a coffee percolator in here. I'll put him back together. I'd appreciate it if you would keep this to yourself." It was not so much a request as a demand. Juliet silently nodded and left.

She went immediately to Leon's office. Without knocking, she pushed open the door and marched towards his desk. He wasn't there; he was on the couch with Nina on his lap. He scrambled to his feet with a curse, dropping Nina to the floor, which would have been comical if she had not been just in a compromising position with the husband of her best friend. Nina untangled her legs from Leon's and stood, rubbing her bottom. She seemed not as embarrassed as she was annoyed, and perhaps even a little amused herself.

Leon said, urgently, "Nina, will you excuse us, please?"

Nina replied, "What? Well, you just move right on to the next girl, don't you?"

"Nina, please."

Nina eyed Juliet with an arch look of suspicion and left the office with a purposefully undulating gait. She closed the door softly.

Leon said, "I hope you can just forget about what you saw with Nina, Juliet." He lowered his voice, "she's a gold digger—for good parts, I mean. It's something very common in the theatre. We producers have to deal with that a lot. It's very annoying."

"*Your* parts."

"I mean she's been chasing me for starring roles."

"Is that why you picked her for Eva's part? Was Eva's disappearance prearranged?" Juliet asked.

"Don't say that. Nina stepped up to the plate when I needed her. I can't just brush her off."

Juliet answered, "Because you'd been cheating on Betty Ann with Eva?"

Leon swore and slapped his desktop. "Elmer said he wouldn't tell you. I should've known better than to trust that stupid ex-con."

Juliet slapped him hard across the face.

"Ow! What's gotten into you?"

"He didn't tell me. The rest of the cast told me. Your secret isn't very well-kept, Leon."

Leon grasped her arm, "You won't tell Betty Ann! It'll hurt her. For God's sake, Juliet, she's expecting a baby."

"You filthy hypocrite."

"I'm juggling a hell of a lot here! I don't need your judgment. I didn't even want Elmer to bring you with him. I told him not to. The last thing I needed was the stink of your commie reputation bringing scandal onto my playhouse. I deal with a very conservative audience out here. Your type isn't wanted."

Juliet's rage choked her. On the mental checklist of things she could do or say, she chose just to turn and leave. To her shame, it was the easiest.

***

Juliet walked blindly toward the gravel parking lot. She stopped and looked around. She remembered she had last seen Elmer by Leon's car. They had talked about the peninsula out to the saltwater marsh. She decided to go there.

Juliet proceeded down the narrow, muddy pathway, rutted with tire tracks, bordered by scrub pine and marsh, and a few tangled bushes, until the ground rose slightly into a mound in the middle of the salt marsh giving it enough ground to support a stand of a few tall oaks. She could hear the croaking bullfrogs and the buzzing of bees and dragonflies, and a butterfly that nearly lighted on her head. It was warmer here, and quiet;

the sounds of the beach and the sea seemed far away. There was a serene stillness to the place.

She came to the end of the peninsula, where the trees and the scrub obliterated any view of the playhouse from this distance, and she could see all around in three directions the wild salt marsh.

Then she discovered Elmer kneeling in the mud at the shore to her right. He looked disheveled, rubbed the back of his neck, and losing strength to hold himself up, he fell forward, lurching onto his hands, on all fours, and staring into the water like a setter on point.

"Elmer? What are you doing? Are you all right?"

Elmer was slow to respond. "Don't get too close. You'll get all muddy."

"Nonsense!" She moved to help him.

"No! I don't want anybody to know you've been here. Don't get all muddy."

She pulled back fearfully. "What is it?"

"Somebody clocked me. I blacked out."

"Oh, no! How do you feel?"

"Like somebody clocked me."

"What can I do?"

Elmer staggered to his feet and wiped his muddy hands on his handkerchief, waving her off. "First," he said, "don't get muddy. We don't want to tip off the killer that you've been out here."

"Killer?"

He softened his voice, "Steady, Juliet. Over there, by that clump of tall grass. A woman's body."

Juliet risked a quick glance, "Dear lord. Eva?"

"Yes, I think so. I pulled her out onto the bank. She'd been half submerged."

"Time for the police," Juliet said in a shaky voice.

"Yes, but let's wait until showtime."

"You think we have anything to work on?" she asked.

Elmer continued to rub his neck and straightened up, looking around at the vast quiet and peaceful marsh. "Whoever killed Eva didn't take too much trouble to hide the body. Could have killed me, too, but left me here to wake up and get a good look at her. Left Leon's tire tracks almost all the way down here."

She responded, "There's a set of muddy men's shoe prints across the gravel parking lot leading to a trashcan outside Leon's office, where the shoes were left in the barrel."

He smiled grimly. "To be found. Leon's car was the most convenient way to ditch the body, or it was used to point the finger at Leon. Blood stains, I think, in the trunk, and a couple of hairs."

She added, "If the trunk shows evidence, then the body was only left here; the murder was committed elsewhere. Why do you think it's a frame-up? I just left Leon in his office playing a love scene with Nina Garrett. That hypocrite is capable of anything. He got you down here with half-truths."

"I don't know. He could be laying down an elaborate story, yes. But he's never struck me as being that smart."

Juliet crossed her arms, lifted her face to the warm sun and the smell of the sea breeze. She stole another involuntary glance at the corpse. "Curtain is at 8:40. You want to leave her here until then?"

"I don't want to disturb the scene any more than we already did. I'll cover her with something."

"There's an army blanket in the trunk of my car," she said.

"You're kidding. An army blanket?"

"You were expecting Belfast linen?"

He smiled. "Tell me what *you* found out so far."

"Beatrice, Bessie, Ruth, and that camp follower, Joan Margolis, went to lunch together; I believe they said the Sea Shell restaurant on Post Road. I found Guy Norman holed up in the box office drinking to near unconsciousness. I brought him back to the dressing room where his wife took over, trying to sober him up for the opening tonight. I was hoping they'd stick with Robert."

"Robert?"

"He stood in for him in rehearsal. Oh, Elmer, he's just wonderful. You should have seen him. Anyway, I don't think Guy's going to make it. He was pretty far gone."

"Guy Norman is also a suspect—one of Eva's suitors and Leon's rival."

"Perhaps he could be setting up Leon."

He answered, still rubbing his neck, "Could be. I wonder if he's as drunk as he made himself out to be?"

Juliet replied, "Faking it? Then he must have bathed in the stuff, the stench was all over him, his eyes were shot. If he wasn't as drunk as he pretended to be, he was drinking, nevertheless. I'm sure of it. Leon was certainly otherwise occupied. Nina spent her lunch hour in his office attempting to seduce him."

"Oh, fine. Still, that in itself doesn't rule him out. Or her; remember, she stood to gain Eva's role."

Juliet continued, "So either Leon's got some tremendous animal magnetism that escapes me, or Nina is also laying down an alibi. The rest of the cast was at rehearsal. What about Kent Murchison?"

"He wasn't fond of Leon, maybe he had a grudge against Eva, maybe she refused him."

Juliet asked, "Really, are you all right?"

Elmer sighed and took a few steps out of the muck. "Yes, I'll be fine. I have a little headache. I'm going to cover her up, then go back to my room and get cleaned up and then see if I can catch up with the ladies' lunch. Why don't you go back to the playhouse?" He gingerly retrieved his new straw hat, half-submerged in the water and flattened with mud.

"There goes another hat," she said. "You do have a hard time keeping them."

"Yeah, but the hatters love me."

"Poor darling. I'm going to go down to the beach first, get a burger or something at one of the food stands and maybe stop by and check in on Robert again. He might be back soon; he went to lunch with Ed Stiles, and they have to set up for rehearsal."

"Good for Robert. He's done all right so far, don't you think?"

She smiled. "Try not to worry about him too much, Elmer. I know that's a tall order, but I think he senses it. I don't think he wants to be hovered over."

Elmer nodded. They looked at each other a moment, saying nothing, but lingering comfortably until conscience pulled them apart. Juliet turned to walk back up the narrow peninsula, but stopped and remarked, "Suppose Constance knows that her husband Guy's either been with Eva or wanted to? That makes her a suspect, too."

"Yes," he said. "What was she doing in the dressing room? She didn't go to lunch?"

"She didn't appear to have been looking for her husband. She was alone there when I brought him down the stairs. She came into the men's dressing room when I brought him down. We must have made a racket. I could see across the hall into the ladies' dressing room that she'd been sitting in front of the large mirror. There was a sandwich and a thermos on the makeup counter, so I assume she must have been having a quiet lunch by herself. I don't know if she expected her husband to join her. There was one other thing I noticed. She had a string of rosary beads in her hand. It looked like the kind that the ladies who play nuns in the play wear with their costumes, long and dark colored, either black or dark brown. I didn't think anything of it at the time, but now I realize that since she was playing a nurse, she wouldn't have rosary beads as part of her costume, so I don't know what she was doing with them. Maybe she found them and was going to return to them to Meg, the wardrobe mistress. Beatrice Longworth had lost hers. I'm assuming they were Beatrice's. Anyway, Constance started to come over to us, then returned to put them down on the counter when she realized she was still holding them, and then came back into the men's dressing room to help me with Guy. She said she'd take over from there."

"See if you can find time to drop in on her and Guy again just to check up on them."

Juliet nodded and turned again and walked back up the peninsula to the playhouse, comfortably knowing that Elmer was watching her go.

Chapter Seven

Elmer steeled himself to turn the body over. This was the only part of this new career of his that he dreaded.

He examined her more closely. There was a bruise on her forehead that might account for the stains in the trunk, if they were bloodstains, as if she had hit her head on something or had been struck. He could not tell if it could have been a mortal blow, as it seemed fairly superficial. He discovered a lipstick in the left pocket of her skirt. Her wet cotton top lay tight against her skin, and he could perceive a small lumpy formation underneath the wet fabric on her chest. He pulled at her neckline and saw a tangled necklace—no, a string of rosary beads.

They were bunched in a clump lying on the center of her chest, partly caught in her brassiere. He tugged it free and pocketed the beads.

He went to Juliet's car, and retrieved her army blanket from the trunk. Army blanket? That seemed so un-Juliet. He looked all around, wondering if Guy and Constance were still in the playhouse dressing room downstairs, or if Leon was still in his office where Juliet had caught him, or where Kent Murchison had gone. Was it someone else, someone paid, to knock him out in the marsh?

Speak of the devil—Kent Murchison came out of the office bungalow and made his slow waddle to the parking lot. Elmer ducked behind Juliet's car. He did not want Kent to see his muddy clothes, the army blanket. He did not feel obliged to give a report on the case at this time, especially since he was really working for Leon.

Murchison heaved himself into his pre-war auto with a groan, and pulled out. Unless he had an appointment, he was probably, like his sister, going home for lunch. Kent didn't spend more than he had to, and he evidently didn't walk farther than he had to. His house was a quarter of a mile away.

Elmer went back to the marsh, covered the body, and tried to look for more clues on the path, but it was hot, he was dizzy with a headache, hungry, and more than a little disgusted.

Elmer returned to his room at the auto court on the Boston Post Road, showered and changed. He wore gray slacks with a navy blazer, and a tie with wide maroon and gray stripes that he thought would match the outfit when he had labored over it at the store. He felt a little better since the shower and took two aspirin. He had started carrying a small first aid kit since the last job in the past winter when he was searching for Juliet, who been kidnapped, and a series of surprise knocks left him with more than one headache. He reasoned a new crop of bruises every case was going to be a fact of life for a private investigator.

He headed for the Sea Shell restaurant down the street and paused at the bar. He ordered ginger ale to the raised eyebrows of the world-weary bartender. Elmer sipped from the straw and stepped to the edge of the dining room, searching across the tables. He spotted the actresses together, and when the captain asked him if he wanted a table for one, Elmer replied,

"I'm meeting my party—oh I see them. Miss Longworth and the ladies from the playhouse. I'm an advance man for the company doing publicity."

"Very good, sir."

Elmer shot over to the table before the waiter could follow with an extra place setting.

"Ladies, forgive me, but may I join you for lunch?"

They looked at him blankly, and Beatrice, who he and they realized was the leader in any situation, responded, "Can't you continue your investigation after lunch, Mr. Vartanian?"

"Thank you for remembering my name, Miss Longworth. No, it can't wait. Permit me?"

She waved her hand, wafting cigarette smoke in queenly acquiescence.

"Thank you." He pulled a chair from another table just as the waiter arrived with the extra place setting. Beatrice eyed Elmer in such an arch and bemused manner that he believed she knew he had narrowly avoided being caught having lied to the headwaiter.

"Mr. Vartanian," she sighed, "tell me, if Eva Breck's absence is such a concern, why haven't the police been called?"

"There are two reasons, ma'am, that I have at this point." He replied, glancing at his menu "one, the police do not consider a person to be missing until three days pass, in which case they will certainly be notified today. Second, Mr. Welch wanted to protect the reputation, not to say the box office receipts, of the playhouse by making every effort to find her whereabouts before the police were involved."

All eyes were on Elmer as the waiter returned and he ordered a lobster.

The ladies had been nearly finished with their meals, glancing at delicate women's wristwatches to gauge when they should head back to the playhouse. Beatrice Longworth made no move to hustle them in any way. She watched Elmer take another sip of his ginger ale.

"Tell me about the rosary beads," Elmer said. Then he looked at Ruth Maguire.

***

Juliet found Robert on a ladder on the back veranda of the playhouse overlooking the sea. He was taping the end of an electrical extension cord to the eaves of the building with black electrical tape.

"Lighting a gel out here?" Juliet joked.

Robert answered, "Mr. Murchison's borrowing me for the rest of the lunch break. Ed and I got back early, and first thing, Murchison sends me out here. The veranda has to be well lit so the audience can come out here during intermission and drink champagne and talk about how much they love the show. Or how much they hate it."

"I wish they could see you in it. You were marvelous."

He stopped and looked down at her. "No chance, huh?"

"Well. Mr. Norman has been located. A bit drunk, but present and accounted for."

Robert shook his head, "Yeah, that'd be right. They'd keep a drunk white guy before they'd let me go on."

"Tell me, how did you ever learn a Yorkshire accent?"

He grinned. "East Anglia, actually. Guy in the pen was a limey. A grifter, but he could do any kind of British accent you name."

She laughed. "Robert, do you really want to be an actor?"

He dragged his glance to her reluctantly, then determinedly kept his focus on taping the cord. "I don't care what I do."

"In the theatre?"

"In life."

"What was Elmer like when you knew him in prison?"

Robert didn't answer at first. Then he stole another glance at her with something like amusement and understanding.

"Quiet. Kept his mouth shut. Except one time. One time. We had an old fellow died. He'd been in the pen probably since the twenties. They buried him in the cemetery for guys who died in prison, just outside the fence. When they took his coffin—the guards, groundskeepers, the minister they got there to say a few words—some of us were watching through the windows in our cells. When they passed through the fence, some guy yelled, 'Jailbreak!' And we all laughed. Elmer said nothing, just watched. Then as the minister was doing his thing, Elmer starts to sing. He sings something in *Latin*. Beautiful. It was beautiful. We were floored. He's got a great voice, Elmer. Some guys teased him after that, called him choirboy. But he knocked a couple of them flat in the prison yard— which he went to solitary for—and nobody bothered him after that. Nobody forgot about it, though."

She smiled. "Beautiful voice?"

"He could have sung anything. He sings a Latin hymn."

Juliet thought about that. "How did your lunch with Ed Stiles go? Did he say anything?"

"He complimented me on my scene, but even so, he wasn't as chummy as when I first met him and he took me to share his cottage. He seemed on edge, surprised that Elmer showed up to question everybody. I think he's nervous about his turn at bat. Could be he's just worried that he'd confessed to me, and probably others, that he had his eye on Eva, too, and was jealous that Leon won the prize. Maybe he just doesn't want to be connected with her now."

"Could be. I'm off to the beach to get a burger or something. Can I bring you a soda?"

"Yeah, that'd be great. It's hot out here, Miss Quackenbush." He started to snicker when he said it.

***

Elmer's food arrived. He took his time unfolding his napkin upon his lap, surveying the very bright red lobster steaming on his plate. He knew all eyes were upon him. He was more nervous about the lobster; it was his first one.

Ruth Maguire spoke up at last, "You mean when I asked the wardrobe mistress to tack the rosary beads to my costume?"

"Yes." Elmer fumbled with the nutcracker and, cracking the claw in the wrong spot, squirted liquid and meat across the table.

Bessie Baggs downed her cocktail and glanced around the room to see if she might get another from the waiter. The wait staff ignored her.

Elmer's next attempt to dismember the body of the crustacean resulted in another piece of lobster meat flying into the air and landing on his head; while liquid squirted forth and splattered upon Beatrice Longworth's right wrist and her rose gold watch. She glowered at him and dabbed the watch crystal with a napkin.

"You were supplied with a bib, Mr. Vartanian. It is to protect you from your lobster. The rest of us were not given a tarpaulin."

Elmer smiled ruefully, "I've never eaten lobster before."

"This was easily surmised," she replied.

Elmer continued, "Miss Baggs and Miss Longworth, did you both have your rosaries tacked down to your costumes just as Miss Maguire did?"

Bessie shrugged silently, looking more nervous by the minute. "No?"

Bessie fidgeted in her chair. "I—I don't know. My, my... I missed my costume fitting. I'm going to get into costume this afternoon for the first time. But...but I saw the rosary that goes with my costume. They were hanging together in the dressing room where Meg put them."

Beatrice expertly caught the eye of the waiter and nodded to Bessie's empty glass. He came at once and brought Bessie another scotch. Beatrice requested coffee and lit a cigarette. She sat back in her chair and crossed her legs. "My rosary was missing this morning. Young man," she said, pulling a piece of tobacco from her lower lip, "I have been interrogated by fat, stupid red-baiters who, with their ability to kill my husband and rob me of my career, were far more intimidating than you, if that is your intent, to intimidate by insinuation. I suggest you get to the point."

Elmer put down his fork and his dripping nutcracker and wiped his hands on the lobster bib across his chest. He asked, in a softer tone, "Who was your husband and how did he die?"

She took a brief drag on her cigarette. "I have no intention of discussing that with you."

"Please. I'd like to hear about your treatment at the hands of *Red Channels* and the House Un-American Activities Committee. I have a very dear friend who has recently become a blacklist victim."

Beatrice scoffed and drew again on her cigarette. "I believe it. This country has become dangerously twisted. My husband was an actors' agent and an attorney, and worked for the actors' union in Hollywood. That made him an enemy of the studio; the heads felt their employees should not be unionized; they should own them body and soul. After the whole *Red Channels* nonsense started, the badgering became too much. My husband had a heart attack and died. As far as I'm concerned, they murdered him."

Ruth placed her hand on Beatrice's, comforting her. Bessie began to tear up.

"I'm sorry, Miss Longworth," Elmer replied. "And you are a target as well, or only your husband?"

"No, my husband was targeted, officially, for registering to vote as a socialist when he was a young man. I wasn't a target, as far as I know, not until I took out a full-page ad in the *L.A. Times* accusing the committee of fascism. That put me on their hit list."

"You are not a woman I would ever attempt to intimidate, Miss Longworth." Elmer smiled. "Now, if I may get back to my question about rosaries. You three ladies play the only nuns in the show. Miss Maguire's rosary was being tacked onto her costume to keep it from swinging around, is that it, Miss Maguire?"

"Yeah," she said, not taking her eyes, or pulling her concern, from Beatrice.

Elmer asked, "Were all the rosaries that went with your costumes the same kind—long, black, worn from the waist?"

"Yes."

"Were yours attached to your costume as well, Miss Longworth?"

"No," she replied, snuffing her half-smoked cigarette. "It wouldn't be missing now if it had been."

Elmer asked, "You put them on, or intend to put them on at each performance?"

She sighed impatiently, "Yes."

"Do you know where they could be?"

She responded, "Why this interest in our costumes, Mr. Vartanian?"

"Why this reticence to answer a simple question, Miss Longworth?"

"Sister Mary Bonaventure preaches tolerance," Beatrice replied bitterly, "so I suppose I must be tolerant."

Joan Margolis, who had been quietly observing, said, "Constance Burch has her own rosary beads."

They all looked at her blankly. She set down her coffee cup and calmly looked at Elmer, as if waiting for him to question her further. Elmer suspected she might be merely deflecting attention to herself, protecting Beatrice Longworth, whom she clearly idolized. He dipped another forkful of lobster into the melted butter and popped it into his mouth. Bessie Baggs's next drink came.

Elmer asked, glancing at both Beatrice and Joan as he did, "What did Miss Burch's rosary beads look like? The same kind?"

Joan answered, "No. They were a smaller string of beads, white, with colored gemstones separating the white beads. During breaks, sometimes she'd sit in the auditorium holding them, praying with them I suppose, or sometimes before rehearsal started. Once, I saw her walking toward the beach with them, or sitting out on the veranda. She seemed to use them with whatever time she had to be alone. I think she must be very religious."

Elmer asked, "Did any of you other ladies observe Miss Burch with her rosary beads?"

Bessie shook her head vigorously. Ruth shrugged.

"Miss Longworth?"

"No."

"When is the last time any of you saw her with her rosary beads?"

Beatrice interrupted, "Oh, for heaven's sake, who cares? Are you on a hunt for Catholics? Why don't you ask her?"

"Miss Margolis?"

Joan shot a glance at Bessie and Beatrice and hesitated, but answered, "I don't remember, but I've seen her with a brown string of beads as well—I don't know if they were the long costume beads or not—they were bunched up in her hand."

"When was this?"

"Saturday afternoon during the lunch break. I thought she might be just holding them for one of these ladies, or the wardrobe mistress, but then she appeared to be praying with them. She was sitting out front in the audience. Some of the costumes were out on a rack to use for that afternoon's dress rehearsal, and she took it off the rack."

Beatrice replied irritably, "Any other questions, Mr. Vartanian? We are due back at the playhouse."

"Just one. What's this?" He poked at the green blob in the middle of his lobster.

Beatrice replied, "That is the tomalley. The liver of the lobster. It is edible."

Elmer mumbled, "Yecch. Not by me, it isn't."

***

Juliet brought her burger wrapped in paper back to the playhouse veranda. She handed Robert, who came down from the ladder, a bottle of Coke. He sat down next to her on the top step, where they could look westward toward the beach.

He said, "Appreciate this. It's hot. They gave me a twenty-dollar bill when I got out of prison. That's all I get till payday here. My one payday. When you and Elmer," he lowered his voice, "I mean, when this gig is over, I'm out of a job again." He chuckled.

"Elmer and I are in your corner, Robert. We'll help you all we can, you know." She bit into her burger.

Robert said, "I get him, he's my buddy. Why you?" He took a long gulp of his soda.

"Elmer is my buddy, too."

He smiled. "That's all? Jeez, he's a slow mover."

"We've both got our baggage. Right now, I'm Katie Quackenbush and we don't know each other. Did Ed Stiles say anything more about romantic triangles—between Eva and Leon or with any other member of the cast?"

"Maybe." He took another long swig from his Coke bottle. "That's good. I was thirsty." He looked around, and picked up a screwdriver. He said in a low voice, "Gary Pirelli—he's the actor who plays the detective—and Stephen Grove, the guy who plays the doctor—they went out for lunch together. They came over to us in the parking lot and asked Stiles what was going on with the private eye, meaning Elmer. Apparently, up until then they thought this was just a ruse by Eva, acting like a prima donna. They never thought she might be in danger. They want to know what's going on. Pirelli laughed a little and kidded the other two, saying he never thought he'd be happy to be the only guy around who wasn't involved with Eva. I guess that means Stephen Grove might have been, too."

Juliet momentarily considered telling Robert that Eva's body had been found in the salt marsh, but she wondered if having that knowledge might compromise his parole. It was one thing for her and Elmer to take a chance by not alerting the police immediately; it would be a much more serious offense for Robert to be accused of withholding evidence of a crime scene. She decided not to tell him. She blotted her lips with a paper napkin and smiled at him and patted his shoulder.

"With any luck, this will all be over in a day or two. When they do their dress rehearsal this afternoon, we should find out a lot more just by being able to watch their movements. That will narrow down considerably who was where when all this was happening, and the actors will be able to show us that without realizing they're revealing their movements. Eva was first discovered missing during the Friday rehearsal when she didn't answer her cue."

Robert laid the dripping cold bottle against his cheek a moment, thoughtfully. "I guess you two know what you're doing. I know this must sound crazy and probably morbid, but I'm not looking forward to ending the scheme. I kind of like it here."

"Even with a murderer on the loose?"

He looked at her in surprise, and she realized that she had said too much.

Juliet stood, smoothing her skirt, and rumpled the paper wrapping from the hamburger into a ball. "Put it this way, the case is open until it's closed."

Juliet noticed a car moving slowly down the long road that split off from the main entrance at Hammonasset State Beach and led to the playhouse. The car proceeded at a leisurely pace, sometimes made briefly invisible as it disappeared behind a sand dune with windbreaks of wild grass or fragrant wild beach roses, and Juliet could imagine the occupants of the vehicle enjoying the restful scenery as they progressed towards the playhouse.

At last the car pulled into the gravel parking lot in front of the building and Juliet recognized Beatrice climbing out of the driver's seat. Ruth Maguire climbed out of the passenger's seat and helped Bessie Baggs out of the rear passenger's seat, though whether her girth, her age, or her libation was what made her unsteady, Juliet could not guess. Another woman stepped out of the rear driver's seat. It was Joan Margolis, the woman who would been watching from the back of the auditorium. She walked with Bessie and Joan to the front entrance of the playhouse. Beatrice, however, looked at Juliet and Robert sitting on the steps together. She stopped only momentarily, the summer breeze ruffling the pink silk kerchief that protected her new permanent wave. Instead of going in the front way with the other ladies, Beatrice walked straight towards Juliet and Robert at the back of the building, determined and decisive.

She was a tall, trim woman, someone who likely exercised or played golf to keep so, and inevitably watched her weight, Juliet thought. As she approached the steps, Robert stood politely and Juliet began to stand as well, but Beatrice motioned with her hands in traffic cop's style for them to sit.

"There's no need to treat me like the Queen Mother. Sit back down. We have a moment before we have to go in, or at least I do. Young man, your name is Robert, isn't it?"

"Yes ma'am."

"And young woman, what is your name again?"

"Katie Quackenbush."

"Yes. Never try to be too cute with a stage name, especially one that's too long for the marquee." Beatrice fished in her light straw summer purse for her silver cigarette case and a matching lighter with her initials on it. She briskly lit a cigarette and blew a puff of smoke into the breeze.

She added, "Robert, you're quite good. Frankly, I hope Guy Norman continues to take his leave, because you're much better in his part than he is. What experience have you had? On stage, I mean, not backstage."

Robert hesitated a moment and then to Juliet's surprise, he told her the truth.

97

"Only as an amateur, ma'am. I've never had a paid acting job in my life. But it's what I'd like to do. But if I can only get jobs working backstage, I'll be happy. See, I've just been released on parole from prison. There's not much future in any line of work for me, not now, not when people know that. And very few people do know that. I'd like to keep it that way. Is there any advice you can give me?"

Juliet realized Robert had learned to "size" people up in "the pen." He evidently thought he could trust Beatrice Longworth.

Beatrice regarded him silently a moment. She rested her hand on the wooden railing of the steps and flicked her cigarette ash into the sand. She turned her head and cast a glance out over Long Island Sound. Here, on the slight rise above the beach, one could see better the thin, gray line of Long Island as a protective barrier to the Connecticut coast. Though the playhouse perched on a rocky outcropping, bolstered by a sand dune, from the flat perspective of the coast it might as well of been built on the top of a mountain. Even twenty feet in height could make a hill seem like a mountain on the shoreline. Perspective was entirely different in a lot of ways on the seashore. Time seemed also to have a different meaning here.

Beatrice Longworth said, "Robert, I have some friends up at the Bushnell in Hartford. They're beginning a new actor journeymen program. Likely, many of the participants will be younger than you, but that's not a requirement. The program starts in late August and will run through the winter stock season ending next May. They have training in stagecraft and acting and you'll work backstage but they'll have you take minor roles onstage in several plays during the season. In that way, not only will you get experience but you'll get contacts and you'll also be able to earn your Equity card. The Actors' Equity is, of course, the union to which we belong. You'll need that if you want to pursue a career. The pay is minimal, but I think it would be a good program for you. I'll write you a letter of introduction and I'll call the artistic director myself and set it up for you. But I would suggest you not mention prison to anyone. I won't. Not that it would prohibit you from getting a job—we in the theatre tend to be pretty open-minded about the vagaries of life. But at some point, your career might lead you into television or even the movies where they tend to be a bit more hypocritical."

Robert stood again, slowly hoisting himself up on the railing as if he were suddenly weak. "Miss Longworth, thank you so much. I can hardly believe it. Thank you so much. Thank you."

Beatrice smiled slightly and patted him on the shoulder. "We actors have to stick together. It's a cold world out there. Besides, I would not get involved if you weren't as talented as you are, so you really have only yourself to thank." And then she turned to Juliet and gave her what Juliet thought to be a more critical appraisal.

Juliet decided, for what it was worth, to follow Robert's example and present Beatrice with a sliver of truth.

"Miss Longworth, I have a rather different predicament. I don't expect my acting career to continue much longer. Actually, my problem is of a peculiar nature. You see, some years ago when I was a college student, I was involved in a student activity supporting the Republicans during the Spanish Civil War. For that one single act, I find myself on the Blacklist."

Beatrice closed her eyes and held up her hand up, traffic cop style again. "Say no more. I completely understand. It is my hope that that problem will, eventually, go away for all of us. But I have no ready answers for you, or for myself. It's because of that damned Blacklist that I've returned to theatre and am now plying my trade in summer stock. But you know something? I think it's been the best thing for me. I really love it."

Juliet sprang up from her seat on the top step quite suddenly and her tone of voice changed, becoming conspiratorial, and she looked over her shoulder and said in sotto voice, "Miss Longworth, I just want to say that we feel, most of the cast that is, are very much on your side over the whole mess about Eva Breck and your husband. I can express my sympathy there, personally, because, you see, I used to be married and when I found out about my husband's affair, while that almost killed me, I can tell you..."

Robert looked up at her, a quizzical expression as his brows furrowed and he glanced back and forth between Beatrice and Juliet.

Beatrice stiffened and interrupted Juliet. "The only thing more prevalent about the camaraderie and the open-hearted acceptance of theatre folk, is the accompanying gossip. I suggest you pay attention to your script and leave my private life to me." Beatrice then stepped between them and marched up the wooden stairs to the veranda and entered the playhouse through the rear door. Robert took a final sip of his soda and stood regarding Juliet.

"I don't know if you're a good actress or a good detective, but that change of scene was intended, wasn't it?"

Juliet blushed a little, as was her habit when even slightly flustered, and answered, "Getting information in this business is a bit trickier than just going to a library card catalog file."

"What did you learn?"

"It's hard to say what anything means until you put it all together. She's a very controlled woman, very proud, and very intelligent. It's possible she could have long-plotted some sort of revenge against Eva, but I somehow doubt she's capable of a crime of passion. Even her work on stage is controlled."

"She's playing a *character* who's controlled. Who's to say she wouldn't be bouncing off the walls if she wasn't on stage?"

Juliet smiled and patted his arm, "You're not a bad detective yourself, Robert, and you sure do know this play."

***

Everybody returned to the playhouse from their lunch break, filing in all the entrances in couples or one by one, ready to go back to work, but there was an air of expectancy far beyond the normal tensions of the final dress rehearsal. The actors found themselves unable to ignore Elmer and watched him more than they watched each other or their director. Stage manager Ed Stiles, prepping in the wings, noticed. The director, to his annoyance, noticed as well. He glared at Elmer once or twice, huffed and muttered and slipped out briefly while the Act I scene was being set. He returned with Kent Murchison, who, wearing his habitual scowl, was, Elmer surmised, brought to keep Elmer busy so as not to interfere too much with the rehearsal.

Murchison, moving with difficulty because of his large girth, picked his way carefully up the aisle to where Elmer was seated about halfway towards the back. Elmer watched him approach, but he did not stand.

Murchison took his time making his way up to speak with Elmer. Elmer knew that Murchison was carving out some time to talk to him, rather than just observing the afternoon rehearsal, and he marveled that he had not solicited the interview, and that Murchison, a man who hardly left his office, would make the effort. At last, Murchison stood before him, sweating, breathing heavily, and looking down with a disdainful expression.

Elmer said, unnecessarily, "Do you have a moment for a chat, Mr. Murchison?"

Murchison inserted himself in the seat next to Elmer, the seat on the aisle that Elmer had left open for anyone who might want to talk to him. It took a moment for Murchison to wedge himself into the wooden theater seat, not without grumbled complaint.

"I hate these seats. I don't know how the manufacturer of these things thinks they can possibly be comfortable. If I had my way, we would have used all that money we wasted on air-conditioning last year and put it in new seating, bigger, padded," he coughed.

Elmer replied, "I imagine air-conditioning is pretty deluxe for a summer theater, might be an attraction, though. Seems like everybody's putting it in these days; stores, movie theaters. Before you know it, people will start having it in their houses."

"In a pig's eye. It's too expensive, and in New England, we'll only use it for a few short weeks. I suppose I can understand why a lot of summer theaters are wanting to put it in if they could, competing with movie theaters, but most can't. I don't happen to believe that we need it all. Here we are sitting right on the ocean. It's cooler here than pretty much everywhere else in town. Sure, we have our heat waves, but our shows, except for the Wednesday and Saturday matinee, are always in the evening when it's cooler anyway."

"Whose decision was it to put in the air-conditioning? Do you have a board of directors?"

"We have a nominal board, but most of the decision-making is left up to Mr. Welch and myself. Mr. Welch, as is sometimes his habit, overruled me by simply not discussing the issue with me. Well, we'll see if the audience numbers go up this season, and if they don't or remain the same, then he won't be able to tell the board that the air-conditioning is bringing in more patrons. Frankly, I'm more worried about television than I am about the heat. People are starting to stay home."

Elmer remarked, "Theatre is special. You can't get that in a little box in the living room. When movies came along, we still had theatre. When radio came along, theatre didn't die."

"That's true, Mr. Var...Mr. Var..."

"Vartanian."

"But I feel people are becoming a different sort of animal now. You know, summer theatre really came of age with the automobile and the ability to get to out-of-the-way places. People started building summer theaters along the shore, in the mountains, in resort areas where people went especially for relaxation and enjoyment. But now everyone's moving out to the suburbs and you'd think that would make summer theatre more accessible with all these cars we have now, and the highways they're building, but it isn't. People aren't leaving home to relax anymore. They're finding ways to do that at home. They're building their barbecue pits and their recreation rooms, they've got their console television like a holy altar set up in their living room. Oh, sure, Mother and Father still go to their garden clubs and their Rotarian meetings, but it's the kids that are really leaving the house now. You know, when I was a teenager, I had to help support my mother and my sister. I couldn't go off on my own to have fun."

Elmer answered, "I was told that Miss Billie Murchison, who plays the role of Martha, the mother of the character played by Guy Norman, that she is your sister."

He answered, "Yes. I like to reserve a role in most of our plays, if I can, for my sister. I honestly don't know how good an actress she is, but she has a passion for acting, and obviously, I like to take care of her. The roles she plays are only minor; they have a line or two, oftentimes they're just walk-ons. I know that this is been a bone of contention between Leon and me, but there are so many other bones of contention that this really seems unimportant. I hardly think a charge of nepotism, particularly with such small roles, can compare to being frivolous and imprudent with the playhouse resources, with him showing otherwise very little interest in the running of the playhouse except for whatever blonde bimbos he can hire as actresses."

Murchison had spat out these words, his breath increased, his agitation increased, and he actually became red in the face. Elmer marveled that Murchison was almost like a cartoon character in that every emotion was so evident in his facial expression and his body language. This was a man, he thought, who if he had anything to hide, would not be able to hide it very well.

Murchison's large sausage-like fingers drummed on the wooden arm of the seat between them. Elmer asked, "Mr. Murchison, what do you think happened to Eva Breck?"

Murchison's face became stony again. He took a deep breath, and then a wheezing sound when he exhaled as if all the air was being slowly let out a beach ball. He merely glanced at Elmer and then looked away when he answered, "I don't know."

"Would you care to speculate?"

"No."

"Since you've already inferred that Mr. Welch has more than a fiduciary interest in the actresses who play here, would it surprise you if he were involved in her disappearance, and perhaps even—murder?"

Murchison stopped fidgeting and became very still. He looked ahead, staring at the descending rows of seats in front of them. Beads of perspiration began to form along his receding hairline.

There was movement as the actors began to assemble on stage and discuss notes with the director and start filing down to the dressing rooms to get into their costumes. Murchison might not have ever been interested in that aspect, the creative aspect of putting on a play. Perhaps the only thing that interested him was the cash box. And keeping his sister happy.

Murchison said softly, almost in a whisper, "I'm not accusing Leon of anything, you understand. But no, I would not be surprised if he were involved with Eva Breck, as far as that goes. In fact, I know that he was. They left together sometimes after rehearsal. Once, I—I even followed them to a motel on the Post Road. It sounds shabby of me, I know. I just wanted to see for myself. I guess I wanted to—to hang something on him to bring to the executive board. Truthfully, I'd like to see him removed. It's so frustrating working with him. He's really a do-nothing and his independent streak, putting in that air-conditioning without asking me, well it's just very difficult working with a person like that. He doesn't do anything else around here, none of the real administrative work. I even arranged for the programs to be printed, and wrote some of the copy. He picked them up from the printer; that was his sole contribution on this production. But he didn't even bring them into the playhouse; I saw him get Guy Norman to do the heavy work of carrying the boxes inside!"

"Can you think of why, if he was involved with Eva, he would want to see her disappear, or possibly kill her?"

"No, I can't." Murchison responded, and then seemed to grow thoughtful. "Leon's appetite is such that I can't imagine he would care if she moved on with the play to the next playhouse somewhere and he never saw her again. To him, there is always a fresh new batch of prospects with each touring company."

Elmer asked, "What did you think of Eva?"

Murchison again looked at Elmer, briefly, as if wanting to make eye contact to prove his sincerity, and yet not wanting to prove anything at all. "She was a very beautiful woman, but undisciplined when it came to her work on stage. I mean, she was late a lot of the time. I really can't say how good an actress she was except that she was certainly very beautiful and that always helps."

"Do you know if Leon Welch was the only person in this company to be romantically linked to Eva? Do you know if anyone else was, any other actors, stagehands…or perhaps yourself?"

He answered as one pained, "No, I was not involved with her. I've never been involved with any of our actresses. Don't think me a prude, Mr.—or more self-disciplined than I really am. As you can see, I'm a very large gentleman, I'm middle-aged, and I've never been handsome. There is no reason for a starlet to be interested in me."

"Maybe you underestimate yourself, Mr. Murchison. Could it be you underestimate your wealth and the charms *that* has for some starlets?"

Murchison replied, "I was not born to wealth, which makes me something of an outsider in this company among the board of directors, most of which are Leon's family. And what security I have managed to accumulate through my life has been modest, I assure you. I live in a cottage on the Post Road that has two bedrooms, a kitchen, a living room, a bath, and a crawl space for an attic. There is no basement. There is a very small yard where I grow roses. It would hardly tempt anyone except me, perhaps. Because I am close enough to work, I am close enough to see the salt marshes and the ocean and I'm happy here. Running the playhouse is the only glamorous aspect to my life, and even that is tucked behind a mechanical adding machine and a ledger book. I like control, Mr. Vartanian. And I have obtained a small, comforting measure of control of my life. The only thing I cannot control is Leon Welch."

Guy Norman and Constance Burch were in heated discussion at the stage curtain with the director and the stage manager. Ed Stiles, who cradled his script in his arms like a baby and would not let it go for the remainder of the evening, appeared to be making a few points, but the director seemed adamant. He poked Guy in the chest a couple of times but Guy did not return his anger. Constance Burch returned the anger in her voice as it rose. There were comments about contracts. The director threw his hands up, patted Guy on the shoulder a couple of times and waved them off. Apparently appeased, Constance Burch led the way downstairs to the dressing rooms and her husband followed her.

Elmer remarked to Kent Murchison, "It seems Guy Norman has turned up and I expect he's going back into his role tonight, replacing that young fellow who read for him during rehearsal. Too bad, everybody's seems to think that guy was pretty good."

"I wouldn't know, I didn't see him. But we certainly can't have a colored man playing the son of my sister."

Elmer looked at him calmly, "Why?"

"Don't be ridiculous."

Elmer replied, standing as he did so and looking down upon Murchison, "The theatre creates its own realities. Most of it is illusion that just works. If you can't make a guy like that fit in your play just because of his skin color, you are either not creative, not logical, or you're just a damn bigot."

Murchison looked glowering and remarked, "The theatre world is full of liberal progressive types, but I had no idea that the world of private detectives was also."

"I guess everybody is taking sides these days." Elmer stole a quick glance at Murchison's shoes. They were worn, inexpensive shoes he probably wore every day with his dark-colored suits, and there was no mud on them.

Elmer asked, "Do you attend the performances, or at least the opening night show?"

"I'm here supervising the box office and I put the receipts away in the safe during every show, but I usually only peek in briefly to watch the performances, a bit at a time. By the end of the run, I've managed to see most, if not all, of a show."

"How about Leon?"

"He attends every one. Loves greeting the audience and making a speech at the curtain to request people to become 'angels' and thanking the local businesses for donating a couch or some such thing. He likes mingling on the veranda during the intermissions with a glass of champagne in his hand. He likes to dress in his tuxedo on opening night."

"He'll wear one tonight?"

"Undoubtedly. He keeps his tux in his office. He has his black dress shoes shined for every production and calls it a business expense."

Chapter Eight

The dressing rooms under the playhouse were abuzz with activity. Meg the seamstress made adjustments and fluttered around the actors, eyeing their costumes critically and proudly. Juliet, who had never been witness to communal undressing among strangers, even in the boarding schools she attended, mused that this was a new adventure, indeed. She went to the corner reserved for her and found her costume on a hook on the wall. She removed her skirt and folded it neatly on the wooden counter that was supported by wooden two-by-fours. On one wall above the counter was the long mirror where the actresses were already putting on their makeup.

It suddenly occurred to Juliet that she did not know how to apply stage makeup, and watching them as she unfastened her stockings from her garters, it suddenly hit her that she was going to have to actually go on stage this evening, and a ball of the lead formed in her stomach. It was her habit during stressful moments to relieve the tension by thoroughly vomiting at the most inopportune moments. She hoped, this time, she could master some self-control. She ruefully mused at the irony that she was able to play-act in everyday life in order to track down a murderer, but to play-act on stage to entertain an audience scared her to death. She had never done well in school plays, and even reading once that the great Helen Hayes and the great Ethel Barrymore were also stricken by stage fright in their long careers, never comforted her. It only made her think that one really had something to be afraid of; they must know because they were the greats.

Bessie Baggs was helped into her costume by Meg as well as a teenage girl who was hired as a dresser for the evening. More apprentices turned up in the course of the afternoon, and people would come later to hand out programs or to help in the box office. It was unlikely that any of them would have known about the murder even if they had heard rumors about the disappearance of Eva.

The actresses playing nuns wore blue habits and each struggled with an impressive white cornet, of which the seamstress was particularly proud. Some costumes could be rented for each production but occasionally Meg had to create them from scratch, and she always felt each show was an exhibition of *her* work.

Juliet dressed quickly and meandered over to the long lighted mirror, and observing the other actresses and their makeup, tried to duplicate what they were doing in applying her own. She outlined her eyes more heavily because they did, knowing that stage lighting called for a different effect to keep the actors from looking washed out. She used her own street makeup and marveled at the intricate makeup kits the size of fishing tackle boxes used by the other actresses. All she had was a small, if chic, cosmetics bag.

Ruth Maguire, smearing cold cream on her face that would make removing her makeup easier later on, remarked to Juliet, "You haven't been at this long, have you?"

Juliet replied, "Nope," and left it at that.

Billie Murchison, who had much experience in the playhouse and yet as a player of minor roles was not relegated to a seat of importance in the dressing room despite her brother's being one of the managers, took Juliet aside.

"Here, sit down. I'll give you a hand. You're not dressing to go to the Stork Club. You want people in the back row to see you." Billie began to remove Juliet's makeup and then to reapply it.

Juliet said, "Thank you very much, Miss Murchison."

"Billie, kid. It's just Billie. I know it's a pain in the ass for you to have to be brought on like this so quick, but enjoy the ride. Even if you have to have your book in hand for this dress rehearsal try not to look at it too much on stage. The thing is, when the performance starts you've just got to fly. So if you can't remember your exact lines, then you just have to say something, anything so that the other actors can pick up their cues. So in this rehearsal, don't worry about not being off book or knowing all the blocking. You haven't had weeks to do that, but you've got to know what your character's supposed to be doing. Listen to what the other people are saying and whatever your line is, if you can't remember exactly, at least try to have it make sense in the context of the play so that the other actors can hit the ball back. You know what I mean?"

"Yes, that makes sense. I'm glad it's not a big role."

"Most people your age clamor for the bigger roles. Me? I learned to take the crumbs and make them work. I enjoy the smaller roles. It's all I'm going to get, anyway, but I make do. You know, when you're a character actor you can pretty much fit in anywhere. It's the stars that have to worry about getting older, staying pretty. That's what's such a shame about somebody like Bessie Baggs," she whispered. "She's got the chops to play every kind of auntie-washerwoman-society-tugboat captain that comes along; she's golden. She could get a job anywhere, but she drinks. Her friends have to hold her up, get her dressed, and whisper lines in her ears." Billie tisked and shook her head. "What a waste. I would have been in the chips if I've had the opportunities she had and not just stayed at this playhouse."

"Have you ever worked at any other playhouse?"

Billie shook her head. "My brother needs me. Besides, I've got it good here."

Nina snorted in derision from the next chair.

Billie rolled her eyes for Juliet's benefit and answered in Nina's general direction, "Not everybody is ready to take on a part at the drop of a hat. Not everybody is letter-perfect in parts they were never assigned. That certainly raises some questions about you, Nina. How come you were off book in the starring role when you came here to play a minor part? Yes, that certainly did raise some questions. Maybe you knew Eva wasn't going to be here very long?"

Nina pulled away from the absorbing sight of herself in the mirror and turned in a flash on Billie, "That's called foresight, dearie. It was no secret how Eva was coming on to Leon."

Juliet flinched as Billie accidentally jabbed a bobby pin into her scalp, intending to fasten the starched nurse's cap to Juliet's short "bubble" cut. Billie answered, "That's an old story in theatre, *dearie*, and there was no reason for you to expect that she wasn't going to be around to play her part."

Nina looked around the room for support, but the other actresses were as determined to continue to dress and apply their makeup as they were determined to listen.

Nina replied at last, "Maybe I had a little more information to go by than the rest of you dumb clucks. I keep my ear to the ground. This is a dog-eat-dog business, and there's no pretending it isn't. We're forced to dress together, but we don't need to get personal; we don't socialize together and we don't pair off together when the show ends, except maybe for the ingénue who's sleeping with the boss." She threw a shaft to Juliet. "Especially when there's more than one going after Leon."

Juliet felt that was her cue. She asked, "I'd like to know what's really been going on here. That detective was grilling me as I suppose he was all of you, but I don't have the advantage of knowing what's been going on. Just because I wanted a few words with Leon in his office, Nina, doesn't mean you can accuse me of being his new conquest. You're the one that fell off his lap when I walked in."

A few chuckles escaped the other actresses.

Juliet continued, "It seems to me you're the one who's opting for the new role as his mistress and leading lady. Maybe that *is* how you got the part."

Nina swore and poked Juliet in the arm with a long and well-manicured red fingernail that otherwise wouldn't have belonged on her character of a convict being sent to the gallows. "Don't pin this on me. I heard plenty, too. That afternoon Eva and Leon were fighting in his office, I could hear them shouting about Eva being pregnant."

The ladies dressing room erupted in a series of gasps.

Ruth Maguire put down her eyeliner and spoke up. "That's enough. We have the show to do. We're professionals. Whatever happens in the private lives of our castmates, and Lord knows the theatre is for telling stories, when it comes time to work, we work. We open in several hours. This isn't helping."

Nina turned on her, now that she seemed to have the floor and enjoyed it, "Maybe some of our castmates are more professional than others. I'm not suggesting Leon made Eva disappear; we all know there are any number of us who wouldn't have minded seeing her leave the show. Your pal Beatrice more than most. We all know Eva was having an affair with Beatrice's husband, pretty much everyone on the Coast knows that when he had his heart attack, he died in her bed. And Beatrice joined the cast three weeks ago. This tour group was set up in California back in March, so where did the great Miss Longworth suddenly come from? Beatrice probably killed her."

Bessie Baggs said, "No, she didn't." All eyes turned to Bessie in a manner to which, as a character actress her entire career, she was mostly unaccustomed. Her role was to support the stars, not to upstage the star—unless a convenient opportunity presented itself.

Nina answered, "And how would you know? You're always drunk."

Ruth Maguire stood this time. "That's enough, Nina."

Bessie replied, in a shaky voice, "I have nerves. I'm nervous and I take a drink. But I'm never drunk. I see, I hear things that I remember. The last time I saw Eva, she was coming into the playhouse from the stage right entrance at the same time that Beatrice was leaving out the main entrance. Beatrice was heading for her car in the parking lot go to lunch. Ruth and I, we were going to meet her. We spent Friday afternoon together, so Beatrice wasn't anywhere near Eva the last time we saw her. Maybe it was that woman—that Joan Margolis woman, the one who sits up in the audience watching us for days. Today she told us that she was a former child actress Beatrice worked with out in Hollywood and she just wanted to see Beatrice again. Maybe she thought she was avenging Beatrice by the killing Eva."

Ruth put her hand on Bessie's arm and patted her, "That's enough Bessie. We don't know what happened to Eva and we're not here to speculate. Leave that for the police."

"Why should we need the police? Do you know something we don't?" The voice came from Constance Burch, who had been silent through this interchange, sitting before the makeup table, dabbing at her face in small, light movements, slow and then still as a stone. She had been listening intently. Suddenly, she announced to her reflection, "I went to lunch with my husband."

Nina sneered at her. "So you now think you've got him back on a short leash?"

Ruth said, "Nina..."

Nina persisted, "Guy's been chasing Eva like a puppy dog for weeks, ever since we were in California for our first read-through. Eva joked about it."

Constance said flatly, "You have a filthy mouth."

Nina remarked, "You have a filthy husband. Maybe you know that and maybe that's why you keep acting holier than thou. You with your 'Is there a church in this town where I can go to Mass every morning?' You with your prayer books. 'There are none so blind as those who do not see.'" Nina laughed. Suddenly a loud voice called from the hall and they jumped.

Stage manager Ed Stiles yelled again, "Places for Act I!"

That was the call that usually had actress scrambling. But in the ladies' dressing room, they were frozen, anxious, and watching each other's next move.

Juliet felt Billie pat her shoulders. "That's you; you and Constance are on first. You make your entrance on page two." Billie told Juliet. "It's only rehearsal, but break a leg."

Chapter Nine

Elmer stepped over Kent Murchison, who was still tightly plugged into his seat, and with some difficulty stood in the aisle. Murchison never took his eyes off him. Though it was not usually his custom to watch dress rehearsals, he remained to watch Elmer, not the show. Elmer glanced around the auditorium. Joan Margolis was in her customary seat near the rear of the house. The director was also sitting in the far back of the house. His assistant, a woman in her thirties who followed him slavishly carrying a clipboard, made notes for him. She had been given the morning off and had not been here, but returned to a tense and surreal rehearsal.

Ed Stiles walked across the stage, spot-checking everything: The lights, the furniture and set, the props. In the tradition of the theatre, Ed was making the transition to become the most important person in the playhouse. When the show opened, the director's job, technically, was over, and the stage manager was the person in charge. In a few hours it would be his baby. His eye was critical.

There were two teenage boys who were going to serve as stagehands. The head carpenter came by for one last check and examined a flat with Stiles. Elmer walked to the back of the house and stepped into the lobby, where a small group of new people came to work, a few middle-aged men and women and a few teenagers. They were cutting open boxes and lifting out the programs, putting inserts in the programs and getting their assignments to serve as ushers. It took a lot of people to run a playhouse. Most of them would never step on stage. Most of them would never be in the limelight.

A signboard with headshots of the actors stood by the entrance. Elmer's eyes wandered on the professional, air-brushed black-and-white studio portrait photos, some of which, for the older actors, had been taken years before. He lingered on Eva Breck's photo. She was a stunningly beautiful woman, with large eyes and a practiced seductive pout. He tried not to think of her face as he had last seen it when he pulled her body from the marsh.

Someone had placed a piece of paper across the bottom of her picture, "Not Appearing This Evening."

He went back into "the house."

The rehearsal had begun.

Beatrice Longworth as sister Mary Bonaventure called to Willy from offstage, admonishing him for an outburst, and then entered. Beatrice, like Bessie Baggs, was clearly at home on stage. Her patrician command offstage, though still evident in Sister Mary Bonaventure, was toned down. Sister Mary's humor and interest in others shone like a light that Beatrice had turned on. Sister Mary was not as aloof as Beatrice, and Elmer marveled that she could change her personality as easily as someone might change his shirt.

If that is what it means to be an actor, to be a good actor, then how much acting did actors do offstage to protect themselves?

Guy Norman as Willy exited the stage via the fake staircase that led nowhere. The convent ended in the wings and abruptly became a dark backstage of unfinished wood, prop tables, folding chairs, the stagehands dressed in black, a well-thumbed script left on the floor to be thumbed through again just before the entrance—just in case. A small pinhole poked into the canvas flat so an actor could peek at the audience.

Juliet stiffly said her last line on page nine and then exited the stage. Halfway down the page, she reentered briefly and told Constance Burch—Nurse Philips—that a phone call was for her. Then the two ladies exited together. Elmer found himself being relieved for her sake. She was a stiff as a board.

Only Bessie Baggs as Sister Josephine and Beatrice Longworth as Sister Mary Bonaventure remained on stage, continuing the dialogue. Elmer smiled to watch the two old pros, the two old friends. The saying goes "like a well-oiled machine," and he smiled at the thought of it. On the next page, Stephen Grove made his first entrance as Doctor Jeffries. Then on page eleven, Ruth Maguire entered as the Reverend Mother and

Bessie Baggs exited the stage. The doctor and then Ruth Maguire both exited, then only Beatrice Longworth and Ruth Maguire were on stage, and like the combination of Beatrice and Bessie, Elmer admired the two old pros, ladies in their fifties and sixties whom Hollywood had jettisoned, still working in their careers, perfectly at home on the stage. In a moment, Bessie Baggs reentered and the trio was a picture of the indomitable spirit and the unusual independence of middle-aged actresses.

Elmer went backstage and wandered slowly around. The actors who stood in the wings and the stagehands gave him brief, curious glances but otherwise continued to pay attention to their work. It was dark backstage, with only a few penlights pointed on the scripts that were being read or flashlights pointed to the floor when an actor had to make a quick exit so he would not be stepping off into the darkness.

Elmer saw a pinhole of light through a canvas flat and, as the actors and stagehands do, curiously put his eye to the pinhole and peeked out at what was called "the house." It was dark out there with the lights lowered, but he could see Betty Ann and Joan Margolis watching intently from their seats, and somewhere away in the back was the director and his assistant. Everyone was quiet backstage just as they would be during a performance, walking on tiptoe, whispering if they had to speak at all, mostly ignoring each other to be able to concentrate on the separate jobs they had to do, all separate pieces of a large puzzle that magically came together and would come together every night during the run of the show.

Elmer stepped down the stairs to the dressing rooms. Gary Pirelli was in the hallway clearing his throat, mentally preparing himself to make his entrance. Juliet stood in the doorway of the ladies' dressing room dressed in her nurse's uniform, taking peeks into the men's dressing room, trying to observe all that went around her.

Elmer had to smile at her briefly and then he approached, speaking softly, "When it gets to be the point where Eva made her entrance, I'm going to stop the show. I noticed Leon isn't here. I never thought to ask him but I suspect he's the kind of guy who probably doesn't really watch the rehearsals, although I did half expect him to be backstage, chatting up the current actress of his choice. You have any idea who that might be?"

Juliet noticed Nina watching them. Juliet put her fingertips lightly on Elmer's chest and gently and seductively gripped the lapels of his coat and pulled him a step closer to her as she lifted her face to him and whispered in his ear, "Nina's curious about us. We're not going to have any privacy to talk unless we look like we're looking for it."

Elmer rested one palm against the wall behind Juliet's head and with his other hand he began to caress her upper arm. "Okay. For the moment let's let her think we're flirting. We only have a short time to trade notes. I found a string of rosary beads on Eva's body. They were tucked below the neckline of her top as if they had been put there, or tucked into her brassiere. I don't know if she put them there, or if someone else did. They're not the kind of rosary beads that the actresses playing the nuns are using; they're a small set, white. I took them in a handkerchief and have them in my pocket. They look very old and ornate. There's been talk about Constance Burch making a habit of saying the Rosary daily. Unless Eva has the same habit, perhaps they're Constance's."

"I heard that, too." Juliet asked, stroking her finger along his face for Nina's benefit, "Do you think someone could have planted them on Eva to implicate Constance?"

He whispered, "It's possible. But to put them on that part of her body would suggest that they did it in a hurry. Why not put them in her pocket? She had patch pockets on her skirt."

"It looks like there was no time to bring Eva's body out of here during the short space of people making exits and entrances."

Elmer said, kissing her hair, "At last Friday's rehearsal, Eva doesn't make her entrance, and the show stops for a few minutes and everybody goes looking for her, but nobody finds her."

Juliet said, nuzzling him, "She either walked away off to Leon's office, which would be pretty strange in the middle of a rehearsal unless she was particularly upset about something and wanted to throw a fit and complain or—and he killed her and put her in the trunk of his car."

"No, because when they broke for lunch, Guy Norman helped Leon put boxes of programs into the playhouse, taking them out of the trunk of Leon's car. He would have seen the body."

Juliet countered, nuzzling Elmer's neck, "Leon could have temporarily hidden her somewhere else, maybe he left her body in his office and then brought the car over to the playhouse. Guy removed the programs, then Leon drove back to his office and put Eva's body in the trunk, then took her out to the marsh."

Elmer said, kissing her fingertips, "It's possible. Especially as Nina said that Eva and Leon were fighting."

Juliet kissed him on the lips, and pulling apart, "But what about those muddy shoes in the trashcan outside his office? That was just too obvious a clue. It's really seems like someone is trying to implicate Leon."

"Or Leon's trying to throw a smokescreen by implicating himself in such a phony way."

Juliet touched his lips and drew her finger down his chin, down his neck slowly and seductively, "Yes, I suppose that's possible."

Elmer touched his lips to her cheek and facing away from the now openly gaping Nina as he spoke softly into Juliet's ear, "But there's still Guy Norman. Something about that bothers me, about you finding him drunk in the box office. About him rumored to be having an affair with her, and being pushed out by Leon."

"Nina also suggested that either Beatrice Longworth killed Eva out of revenge for having an affair with her husband before he died, or perhaps it was the mystery woman in the audience, Joan Margolis."

"Mrs. Margolis is pretty small, thin person. I don't think she could have bested Eva. Beatrice Longworth might have physically been able to kill her as well as hide her body, but she's middle-aged compared to a twenty-five-year-old woman, and even though she plays against Eva on stage, she really doesn't have any time backstage with her. They wouldn't have been alone together."

Juliet answered, "We're going under the assumption that Eva was killed at about the time she failed to show up for her cue? Not that she wandered off in a huff to be alone and later at some point in the course of the weekend was murdered?"

Elmer replied, "Only a medical examiner would be able to determine the time the death, or at least make a better guess that I could, but I would say it was likely she was killed Friday. Without going into any of the gory details."

Juliet put her head on his shoulder and glanced at the dim yellow glare of the naked light bulb in the ceiling, listening to the rumble of voices from the stage above them as Act I continued and Gary Pirelli, standing in the doorway to the men's dressing room, prepared to make his entrance as Detective Melling. As he passed them, Elmer reached out and grasped Gary Pirelli's arm. Pirelli stopped, flustered, anxious to make his cue.

"Going on!" he whispered urgently.

Elmer asked, "Did you ever see Guy Norman drinking backstage in the dressing room or anywhere down here?"

Still flustered, Pirelli shrugged and shook his head and pulled away from Elmer, more concerned about missing his cue and suffering the wrath of the director than he was about not cooperating with the detective. Elmer let him go.

He asked Nina, who was trying not to stare at them so obviously, "During the Friday rehearsal, were there people down here waiting just as they are now to make their entrances or was anyone sitting in the wings or sitting in the audience more casually as they were at the rehearsal this morning?"

Nina answered, her eyes constantly flicking back to Juliet, "There might have been someone down here, I don't know. I was out in the audience watching. A lot of us were. It's not until the dress rehearsal we're required to stay backstage. The early rehearsals are pretty loose; as long as we make our cues, we can watch from the house if we want to." She sidled past them and went up the stairs after Pirelli to make her entrance as his prisoner.

Elmer said, pulling away from Juliet now that Nina was no longer there to spy on them, "Guy Norman is standing backstage on the far right."

Juliet answered, smiling, but regretting the loss of their clinch, "In theatre parlance, it's called stage left. The direction is when you're facing the audience, not from the audience facing the stage. I've learned that much today. In fact, I got yelled at it about it once or twice."

"He's not supposed to go on for a while. He could probably just come back down here but he's probably avoiding me. But where was he on Friday's rehearsal? Was he in the house, watching; was he here with Eva? We know Eva wasn't in the house or out in the wings or out on the veranda because nobody saw her; they only saw her in the dressing room. Pirelli walks up to make his entrance figuring she's going to follow when it's their turn, but he's not actually down here; he's standing in the wings backstage. He notices she's not there, so he goes down to look, but she's not down here and neither is anybody else. So where's Guy Norman?"

Juliet said, "All right. He had a former affair with Eva that she broke off. Let's say they had words, maybe he killed her in a fit of jealousy. He doesn't seem the jealous rage type, somebody who's been on a tight leash by his wife for so many years. But let's say he killed her and left her body somewhere down here. She doesn't show up for her cue, the director gets upset and decides to break for early lunch. Nobody's around, so Guy can drive his car to the marsh and get rid of the body."

Elmer said, "Kent Murchison told me that Leon had boxes of play programs in his trunk, and that Guy Norman unloaded them into the playhouse. Did Guy leave for lunch or did he drive Leon's car out to the marsh?"

"Why would he murder her? Jealousy? And put his wife's rosary on the body? Why?"

"I don't know. The rosary must have belonged to Constance, because she was later observed by Joan Margolis to be praying with the long brown one used in the play."

"Beatrice Longworth was missing hers."

He nodded. "So if Constance was using them, she had lost her own beads. But the point isn't just to get rid of the body; it's to implicate Leon because the murderer figures the body will be found and it's better to lay down a trail early to point the finger to Leon, who's a logical suspect. Leon, like most people, leaves his keys in the car, so it's an easy matter to take the car, but when? How long is the body in the trunk? Does Leon leave for lunch and come back? What about Betty Ann showing up? I hate to say it, but she's still a suspect. If she knew about the affair, that makes her a suspect."

"I'm not sure if she knew about the particular affair with Eva Breck, but she did know Leon had affairs. She intimated as much. She didn't seem surprised when I told her." Juliet answered with a pained expression. "But she's six months pregnant. I really don't think that she would physically be able to overpower Eva and get rid of her body, even if she had the temperament to do it, which I don't believe, either."

"It makes the most sense that Leon had the motive and the opportunity to do it himself, and then try to implicate himself in that phony way through a smokescreen."

"I agree," Juliet said.

"If it just weren't for the rosary beads." Elmer muttered.

Juliet searched his face, thinking of the Latin hymn Robert said Elmer had sung years before at the funeral in prison, "Do you really think there's an implication to Constance Burch?"

He pulled the beads out of his pocket, opened his handkerchief and showed her, "This is something that someone maybe received as a gift for a special occasion—First Communion, Confirmation, or a wedding—or maybe it's a family heirloom, something that belonged to her mother or grandmother."

She could not help but ask him, "Do you have rosary beads?"

He seemed startled, but muttered, "A long time ago."

She felt she had strayed into a too personal memory, and diverted herself. "Assuming that Eva is not the kind of person who would own these beads or say the Rosary, why would they be tucked under her top and not in her pocket?" Juliet put her hands in the patch pockets of her nurse's uniform and took a step or two away, padding softly on the rug that had been placed down on the concrete floor to diminish noise. The carpet was several seasons old, and had not been cleaned since the beginning of the season. The maintenance staff vacuumed it every week, mainly because of the beach sand that was always tracked in on the shoes of the actors. It was a brown carpet, ugly and utilitarian. The wooden stairs were also covered with a piece of carpeting tacked down for serviceable use rather than for looks.

Juliet had been gazing at the carpet absentmindedly, trying to think. Elmer wondered if she saw something and he brought his attention to the carpet as well. He knelt down, took out his penlight and flashed on the carpet to examine it more closely. Juliet realized the spots she had absently stared at on the dark brown carpet might been blood, or may been paint or even theatrical makeup. There was another spot on the stairs, easier to see because the rug was lighter.

Juliet said, "It still doesn't seem possible that someone could have killed Eva and carried her right out of here right under everybody's noses."

Elmer replied, "I know. It just seems like Leon would have had more opportunity in the privacy of his office, unobserved by the rest of the cast, who were rehearsing. But that would mean she would have left and gone over there. But if so, there wouldn't be blood traces here. What's back there at the end of the hallway?"

"Small storage area, and the little space where the seamstress makes last-minute repairs. There's a workbench and a light." Juliet led the way to the partitioned area. The crude wooden wall that separated this area from the men's dressing room held a rack of costumes covered in plastic, a workbench with tailoring supplies and another workbench in the corner that had odds and ends: tools, electrical tape, lengths of rope and extension cords, slim wooden shims; in one corner there was a couple of old flats that were not being used and a roll of muslin which was used to cover the flat frames that made up the walls on the set. There was no carpet here, just the bare cement floor. Elmer looked closely with his flashlight for more blood spots and found another dark spot on the bare cement that, again, could have been blood or paint. He pulled the unused flats from against the wall and peered behind them. There was a larger splotch on the floor.

Juliet said, "I don't think that's paint. There would be more drops of different colors, there would be paint cans of the same color, there would be something to indicate that someone was storing paint here or painting at this spot for that to happen. Look at the dust back here; this corner is rarely used."

Elmer replied, "You could be right. It's dried. There's no telling how long that's been here. That's going to take a police lab to determine what it is."

"At least we know it's possible Eva could have been killed here, hidden here until everyone broke for lunch and then the body put in Leon's trunk after the boxes of programs were removed. Later that evening, he could have moved it to the swamp."

Elmer nodded. "It's possible. But why the rosary? It's like there are two different scenarios here that don't match."

Juliet said, "So far, we've got Constance, we've got Guy, and we've got Leon. The only other person is Nina, because like me, she would have been downstairs or could have been downstairs when Eva went missing, although we can easily find out if she was out of the theater with the rest of the actors because they could corroborate that."

Elmer said, "I think it's time we brought the curtain down on this or at least made what they call a curtain speech."

She nodded, grasped his hand and squeezed it, and muttered, "Break a leg."

They went up the carpeted steps, scanning the steps for more traces of blood. Elmer took another look around the men's dressing room for any signs of evidence, and the women's dressing room, and went back up the steps to the stage. He walked out into the house.

***

Gary Pirelli, playing the detective Melling, entered with his prisoner, now played by Nina. They were followed by Constance Burch.

Elmer yelled, "Stop!"

Jeff the director swore loudly from the back of the house and the actors on stage jumped with confusion. Bessie even gave a little shriek of surprise. The actors froze and stared out at the empty blackness of the house, the bright stage lights on them like suspects in a police lineup.

Elmer shouted again, "Turn on the lights in the audience, please."

Jeff hopped up from his seat at the back of the house and ran down the aisle. "What the hell do you think you're doing? We're rehearsing!" He said it as if had just Elmer had interrupted the creation of the world.

Elmer continued to shout in a loud voice as if he were now directing the show.

"At this point in the play, the character Sarat Carn makes her entrance. Eva Breck is supposed to enter with Gary Pirelli playing the role of Detective Melling, and then the prison matron."

Gary Pirelli and Nina stepped out from the wings, looking quizzically at Elmer and at the director.

Before the director could voice his annoyance bordering on hysterical fit, Elmer continued.

"When you started Friday's rehearsal, this was the point at which Eva Breck was supposed to make her entrance and did not. Did somebody go downstairs and look for her?"

Jeff exploded, "Of course, we did! We searched all over the playhouse, the lobby, the ladies' room, we went outside. She was gone. So Nina stepped into the role for the afternoon. When Eva never came back, we gave Nina the role."

"Eva did not have a car of her own in the parking lot?"

Jeff threw his arms up in the air and walked around, pacing back and forth like a metal duck at an arcade gallery. His fit was wordless, yet eloquent. The actors mumbled on stage and those that were still

122

downstage in the dressing rooms took a few tentative steps up the stairs to listen to what was happening.

Elmer demanded, "Well, did she?"

Bessie Baggs, Gary Pirelli, Nina, Beatrice Longworth, and Ruth Maguire, who began to cluster together in a group on stage out of nervousness, quietly affirmed that Eva did not appear to have a car.

"And if no one saw her walking away, walking down the long gravel drive, walking down the long access road to the Boston Post Road, then she never left the playhouse. Juliet! Juliet!"

Jeff sputtered, "Oh great. Now he thinks were doing *Romeo and Juliet*. What's next, *Hamlet*?"

***

Juliet, who had become so used to being referred to as Katie Quackenbush, almost forgot to answer to her name. She came out of the wings and took a few tentative steps out onto the stage. The other cast looked at her as if she were, indeed, Hamlet's ghost, wondering why she would answer to the name of Juliet. Only Robert smiled from behind the flats. Ed Stiles came out on stage and threw a quizzical look at Robert, but Robert avoided meeting his glance. He just crossed his arms in a bored manner and looked down at his shoes.

Elmer said, "Juliet, could you please go over to the box office and get Leon?"

Juliet answered, "Time for the grand finale?"

"It looks that way. If these people actually want to have the show tonight, we'd better get a move on." Juliet nodded and exited the stage.

Jeff shouted, "At last! He actually realizes we have the show to do in a few hours. Look, what is going on here? Who is Juliet?"

Elmer announced to the cast, "Katie Quackenbush is working with me. Her real name is Juliet Van Allen. She is not an actress."

Nina huffed, "I could have told you that."

Elmer ignored her remark. "It is sometimes necessary to have an inside person get to know the suspects of the case because quite often people are reluctant to simply spill the beans. Even if it's in their best interest. And let me assure you all," Elmer began a long, slow pacing back and front across the stage as if he actually were the director, "it *is* in your best interest to be completely candid.

123

"Ladies and gentlemen, it's time for a little curtain speech. That's what it's called, isn't it, when the director comes before the cast just before the play opens, just before the curtain rises, and makes a little pep talk for the cast and crew? Well, this isn't going to be a pep talk. Eva Breck has been murdered."

There were a few gasps from the cast, from a couple of the young stagehands who were new to the plot, from the house manager who dropped an armload of programs on the floor with inserts that said "appearing in the role of Nurse Breck will be Katie Quackenbush," and from the technician in the lighting booth who dropped his coffee all over the lighting board and cursed.

Elmer continued, "I found her body on the edge of the salt marsh. There was a bruise on the side of her head, which could have been the fatal blow, or not. A medical examiner will determine that and her exact time of death. I'm going to bring the police in now and it will be their investigation. It's going to be very messy and very public. And I doubt very much that the show will continue, in fact, the playhouse may have to close down for several weeks. Unless, that is, I get more cooperation from you. It is possible to turn the case over to the police with a murder victim and a murder suspect, to hand them their case and their investigation will cause only minimal disruption to the activities of this playhouse and your careers. Your show will go on, and the playhouse will continue. That will be up to the police. What's up to you is how messy you want to make this."

Director Jeff, open-mouthed, slowly backed away and sat down in the front row seat, clearly overwhelmed. He said no more.

Elmer continued. "Those of you who have no knowledge of the murder and who are understandably upset by it, will obviously want this to be settled quickly and expediently. But the murderer wants to stall and dodge as much as he or she can. That's what happens when you commit a crime. You don't want anyone to find out and you'll drag your feet and do almost anything to avoid being discovered. That is human nature. So the only one I don't expect complete cooperation from is the murderer. Or perhaps an accomplice, a loved one who may want to protect the murderer."

From the side entrance of the playhouse, Juliet reemerged with Leon. He looked around sheepishly, as if despite being a manager of the playhouse, he really had very little business being here, and seemed like a confused guest. Juliet cast a glance up at the house at where Betty Ann sat stoically.

Elmer said to Leon, "Eva Breck's body was found on the edge of the salt marsh."

Leon said nothing but looked down at the floor in contemplation and then looked up again at Elmer, an expression of dread in his eyes and something as well of defiance.

He said, "Well, now what?"

Elmer replied, "I'm going to be very blunt. If this case continues beyond today, the newspaper headlines are going to be far more cruel. And I'm assuming, Leon, that you called me in on this case even though you supposedly did not know that Eva had been murdered but suspected her only as missing, because you feared scandal and you wanted it handled quietly and quickly. You were having an affair with Eva Breck."

Leon's eyes burned through him as he replied hoarsely, "I didn't hire you for this."

"You hired me to find Eva. I found her. If you wanted me to cover up a crime for you, you should've been more explicit in your instructions. Then I could have spat in your face."

Leon's indignant expression broke out over his face like a case of measles and he swiped his hand through his hair, glancing nervously up at his wife in the audience.

"What am I supposed to say to that?"

Elmer asked, "Did you kill her?"

"No!" Leon shouted.

Elmer looked over at Nina, who was standing on stage between Gary Pirelli and Paula Miles, who played the prison matron, almost as if she were still playing the part of the convicted murderer. All the actors froze in their positions.

"Nina says that you and Eva were having an argument just before the Friday morning rehearsal started. She could hear you shouting from your office. What was the fight about?"

Leon said, "We should have this discussion privately."

Kent Murchison called from the audience, sitting across the aisle from Betty Ann Welch, "I say we have it right here and now."

Leon called to him, "May I remind you, Kent, that my family owns seventy-five percent of this playhouse. And of the remaining twenty-five percent, you control exactly one percent."

"You're assuming, Leon, that the remaining twenty-five percent won't complain to your father and brothers at your management, or I should say, lack of management in this playhouse. You're also assuming your father and brothers will stand behind you. You've taken a lot of risks in your personal life. You might discover that the people around you are more averse to risk."

Leon fumed but he had no answer. He shot a look up at his wife again.

"What was the fight about?" Elmer asked.

"None of your business!"

Elmer looked at Nina, "Nina? What was the fight about?"

Nina glanced at Leon and then his wife, so the actors on stage began to take a step or two away from Nina and all attention was diverted to her. She was, as those around her suspected where she usually wanted to be, center stage.

Juliet offered, "You were given the lead role after this conversation between Eva and Leon. You have no experience as a lead in a play. There usually are no understudies in summer theatre. Yet you walked into the role having already memorized the part. Either you knew you were going to get the lead role, or you suspected there was a way for you to take it. It seems there are three ways for an actress to get lead roles in this playhouse. You either slept with Leon, or you murdered Eva, or you knew something that would incriminate Leon and you blackmailed him, and when the time was right, you put your plan into effect having already memorized the lead role. You know what the fight was about, Nina. And even if you are not the murderer yourself, the police could still find you an accessory after the fact." Juliet, as if to emphasize the fact that she was working with Elmer, slowly and deliberately as she spoke, unpinned her nurse's cap and placed it on the edge of the stage. If none of the cast had paid much attention to Juliet before, they most certainly did now.

For the first time the smirk and sneer on Nina's face melted away, and after a few flickering images of uncertainty, it was replaced by a look of abject horror.

She sputtered, "Listen, I had nothing to do with Eva's disappearance, or murder. I didn't know any of this. At the time Eva even went missing during the rehearsal, I was sitting out in the house watching. I wasn't anywhere near her."

Elmer said, quietly, "But earlier you were near enough to Leon's office to hear what they were shouting about. You either know, or you don't. If you know, I suggest you say what it was. If you claim you don't, I suggest you prepare yourself to testify in court."

Nina said, in a loud voice jacked up by her excitement, as if it were a climax in a play, "Eva was pregnant! She told Leon that she was pregnant and she wanted to know what they were going to do about it."

Elmer noted a few more gasps and looks of surprise exchanged among some of the cast members, and the few I-told-you-so looks from others, as he noticed Juliet involuntarily glancing back at Betty Ann in the house. Juliet looked as though she had been punched; there was no stirring from Betty Ann.

Nina continued, "But Leon laughed at Eva. He just laughed and said it wasn't his."

Leon remained standing by the edge of the stage. He clasped his hands in front of him like a church usher, and looked down at the floor, burning a hole in it with his eyes.

Nina continued, "Eva didn't believe him and said he was a rat and— other things. She kept cursing him, and then he shouted over her that he couldn't be the father because he'd had a vasectomy. Well, that stopped her in her tracks. She didn't say anything after that, she just walked out. She was furious."

Leon remained like a statue, not looking up.

Elmer said quietly to Leon, "Your wife being six months pregnant, I'm assuming you had the vasectomy at some point in the interval? Or were you lying to Eva?"

Leon glanced up in a slow perusal of Elmer, a quick peek over at his wife in the audience, then he answered Elmer in a thick voice, "I was in Los Angeles for six weeks back in March, arranging for some packaged shows, some performers to come for this summer season. That's where I hired Beatrice Longworth and Ruth Maguire, and arranged for the show to come here. While I was there, I saw a doctor and had the procedure done. When I came back here, I guess it was the middle of April by that time."

Elmer said, "And while you were in California, you first met Eva as well?"

127

"I met her at a party in March. I offered her the role in the play. And...I also saw her when the play toured...in Ohio...in June. I went for the weekend."

Elmer said, "And you may, obviously, be required to submit documentation, proof of this medical procedure, if the medical examiner determines that Eva was pregnant at the time of her death."

"I can."

A voice boomed from the audience; it was Kent Murchison, "You had better not have put that vasectomy on your expense account!"

That remark brought a few nervous chuckles to the cast, though Murchison was serious, and Elmer and Juliet both caught each other's eye but refused to smile.

Elmer asked "When was this cast first assembled and when did the roadshows begin?"

"I think in May. I forget where. Different actors joined along the way, others left."

Murchison hauled himself out of his seat and made his awkward waddle down the auditorium. He said, "Rehearsals for that company began the third week of May and there were three bookings before the play came here. The first was in Ohio, that was the first week of June and the cast was completely assembled with the principal actors Beatrice Longworth, Ruth Maguire, Bessie Baggs, Constance Burch, Guy Norman, and Eva Breck. They played in upstate New York and New Jersey. From here, they to go on to Ogunquit and the Cape Playhouse in Dennis."

Elmer said, "Miss Burch, when Eva did not return to make her entrance during that morning rehearsal Friday and you broke for an early lunch, did you and your husband leave the playhouse as well?"

"Yes, but..." Constance glanced at her husband Guy. Dressed as Willy, the village idiot, as if channeling his character, he wore a look of abject confusion and stuffed his hands in the pockets of his worn, baggy pants. He truly looked like he did not know what to say.

Elmer said, "Miss Burch, where were you during Eva's entrance?"

"I was downstairs in the dressing room."

"You weren't watching from the house?"

"No, not at that time."

"Then you were alone with Eva?"

She answered, "For a moment. I came down after making my exit. Eva was in the dressing room. I think she was fixing her makeup. But I didn't pay attention. Oh, I know—I went down the hall to the lavatory. Yes, that's where I went."

Elmer said, "We suspect that Eva was killed in the ladies' dressing room. She was alone for a few moments, except for the killer, and due to the abrasions on the side of her head and her face, it seems there wasn't much of a struggle. The dressing room could not have been much messed up or you all would have noticed; the person either hit her with an object or possibly pushed her and she fell against the counter in front of the long mirror where the actresses sit and make up. There are only small bloodstains on the carpet leading down the hall to a small storage area in the back where there are some old flats against the wall. That's what you call them, 'flats?' The set pieces that make up the walls? That area looks as if it been disturbed.

"It's possible the body was immediately taken there, perhaps her head was wrapped in a towel to avoid excessive bleeding on the floor, she was dragged to that back room and hidden behind the flats temporarily. As the rehearsal continued, the time came for her and Mr. Pirelli to make their entrance. Pirelli was already at the top of the stairs, standing in the wings. He looked back to see where Eva was and then he came down to the dressing room to get her. He did not find her, so he went back up and announced that she had gone and then the director, Mr. Collins, stopped the rehearsal. Mr. Pirelli, are you certain you *heard* no signs of struggle?"

All eyes were on Gary Pirelli, which is something that rarely happened to him in his stage career, being a player of small character parts. He did not look happy with the attention.

He stammered, "N-no, I swear I didn't hear anything. Or, if I did hear anything, it didn't sound like anything unusual; there's so much going on during the rehearsal. If I'd heard footsteps behind me, I might have assumed it was Eva, but I never heard anything that would make me think there was a fight going on."

Elmer turned to Constance Burch, "And from the washroom, you did not hear any signs of struggle, any noise that made you suspicious, coming from the dressing room or the hallway?"

"No."

Elmer said, "At some point, the body was removed from behind the flats and taken to the salt marsh. There is evidence to believe that it was put in the trunk of Leon's car and driven there."

All eyes reverted back to Leon. He raised his glance from the floor, finally looked up and fussed with his tie and brushed his hand through his hair and swallowed audibly a few times. "I, I didn't put her in the trunk of my car. I didn't kill her, and I had no idea she was put in my trunk. I didn't have anything to do with that. You have to believe me."

Elmer continued, "It was just about this time, just before the lunch break, that you drove your car to the side of the playhouse because you had boxes of programs in the trunk and you had to unload them and carry them into the playhouse. Isn't that right?"

Leon said nervously, "Yes, yes, I pulled the car up to the side entrance, but I didn't put her body in the trunk. It was full of boxes from the printer, and I was carrying them up—and Guy, it was Guy Norman who actually brought the boxes in, not me!" Leon brightened, and looked as though he were suddenly breathing easy, "Guy took the boxes out of the trunk. He volunteered to do it for me, because I had a call to make in my office. *He* finished the job and then he closed the trunk and when I came back later and saw my car still there, I just drove off, not realizing anything was in the trunk. I went to lunch."

Guy Norman looked around, anxious, seemingly dumbstruck.

Kent Murchison offered, "You didn't have a call to make. You just saw someone else taking over some work you didn't want to do, and you let him do it. That's your way."

Leon said, "Shut up, you fat old loser!"

Murchison responded, "You should've been kicked out a long time ago, you with your shenanigans."

Leon hollered shrilly, "You putting your no-talent sister in every stupid play we do –"

Elmer said, "All right, that's enough. So Mr. Norman, you brought the programs into the building, and when the trunk was empty, what did you do?"

Guy answered in a small, soft voice, "I closed the trunk. Then I went to lunch with my wife."

Elmer said to Constance Burch, "And when you emerged from the ladies' room and you saw the play had stopped and there was a fuss about trying to locate Eva, the director decided to stop the rehearsal and continue after lunch; what did you do?"

"I went up on stage to listen to the director and when he said we could break for lunch, I went downstairs to get my purse. I got it and I went out to our car to wait for my husband. We rented a car for the week. When I was looking for the car keys in my purse, I noticed that my rosary beads were missing. They were not in my purse. Guy was taking such a long time because he was helping unload the boxes—I didn't know that; I was on the other side of the playhouse—I started to go back to look for my rosary beads. Finally, Guy came around the playhouse and walked towards the parking lot. I told him I had to go back to look for them, and he said he would help me. So we went to the dressing room and I couldn't find them. He looked around the stairs, the hallway, we couldn't find them anywhere, so we went out back to the parking lot and looked around the parking lot to see if I had dropped them in the gravel somewhere. We decided to go to lunch and come back later and ask if anyone found them."

Elmer asked, "Did any of you other ladies go down to the dressing room before you left the playhouse for lunch? To retrieve your purses?"

Beatrice, Ruth, Bessie, and Nina all nodded.

Beatrice Longworth spoke up, "My purse was in my separate dressing room. I saw nothing unusual downstairs."

"None of you saw any trace of a disturbance, anything that would make you suspicious?"

They shook their heads.

"What about the men? Did any of you go back to the men's dressing room before you left?"

All shook their heads, but Stephen Grove spoke up, "I went back briefly for my windbreaker. But I didn't see anything, either."

"Mr. Stiles, what about you and the technical staff?"

Ed Stiles remarked, "That morning we ran a skeleton crew. There was just me and Bobby from up in the lighting booth, and Clarence, one of our high school summer interns. I think Bobby spent the whole time up on the ladder adjusting some troublesome gobos. Isn't that right Bob?"

A voice from on high in the lighting booth responded, "Yep, that's right."

They all looked momentarily towards the shadow in the booth; that's all Bobby ever was to them, a silhouette.

Kent Murchison asked Juliet, "Would it be all right if they continue the rehearsal? Is there any chance that we might open tonight?"

Juliet replied, "That depends. If we determine who the murderer is and we get enough information, we may be able to suggest to the police that you be allowed to continue with this performance. If not, that'll be up to the police. If they're not comfortable with the information we give them, they'll shut down the show for tonight and for the rest of the run. Maybe even for the rest of the season."

Murchison muttered, mopping his face with his handkerchief, "The playhouse can't survive this."

Juliet remarked, noting his perspiring, "You haven't turned the air conditioning on. Leon was so proud about it."

"No, I only allow that to be put on during the show, to save money. I was going to do it soon, to get ready for tonight. Guess it doesn't matter now."

Elmer motioned to Constance. "Come with me, please, Miss Burch, to the business offices."

Guy said nothing.

Leon made as though to go with them.

"No, Leon. I want to talk with Miss Burch in private. She was in close proximity, by her own admission, to the deceased at the apparent time of her disappearance. This makes her our prime suspect." He glanced back at Juliet, telegraphing a look that had no meaning for anyone else.

The director finally spoke up, musing, "Well, I guess if the police do let us go on, we could just fill in for Constance. Sally, one of our interns, she might be able to handle it. We could let her use the book on stage."

Sally, who had been standing in a small cluster on stage with the other apprentices seemed undecided whether to be horrified or enormously delighted.

"Of course," Jeff Collins continued, "that's if you agree to continue to play Nurse Brent," he said to Juliet.

Chapter Ten

Elmer brought Constance into the cottage with the offices. He looked around the outer office first and then decided they should use Leon's private office. They entered and he flipped on the lights. There was a modern-looking desk with an expensive leather chair behind it, a leather couch against one wall, a single file cabinet and photographs on the wall of previous productions. Perhaps not so coincidentally, they were all portraits of only young actresses who performed at the playhouse. Elmer and Constance exchanged sardonic expressions.

She muttered disgustedly, "His Hall of Fame of conquests?"

Kent Murchison's office was a jumble of paperwork, several file cabinets, inboxes and outboxes both bursting, a scene associated with someone who actually works in his office, while Leon's office was immaculate.

There was a small refrigerator in one corner and a minibar in Leon's office. He had a telephone on his desk but not even a pen or pencil. Elmer sat down at his desk and began to look through the drawers. He did find a pad and a pencil. On the coat rack in one corner was a garment bag. Elmer unzipped it and examined the tuxedo that Leon would have worn to the opening night performance. There were no dress shoes to go with the suit. Elmer surmised they were muddy and lying in the garbage can.

He said to Constance, "I'll be one moment." He retrieved the shoes in an old piece of newspaper from the trash can. He brought them into Leon's office and laid the shoes on the newspaper on top of Leon's very shiny desk. They were caked with mud.

"No one would wear expensive Italian handmade shoes out to a salt marsh unless they were being chased by somebody. This was obviously a plant."

Constance said, "Maybe he planted them against himself. Maybe he wanted to look like he's being framed."

"Miss Burch, does your husband have a drinking problem? Has he ever gotten drunk during a rehearsal or performance?"

Constance stiffened, "Certainly not."

"He did this time. He got drunk during rehearsal today and needed to be replaced by the stagehand. Who, I understand, was quite good." He said it with a little pride.

"Guy's always a little nervous just before opening nights. Most actors are. I wouldn't attribute this slip-up to anything more than forgetting how many drinks he'd had. It was a stupid mistake and I'm very upset with him. But this is not his habit and it won't happen again."

Elmer replied, "I'm not your employer, Miss Burch. I don't really care whether Guy has a drinking problem or not, or whether this will ever happen again. I only want to find out why it happened now. Where was Guy Friday evening?"

She looked irritated, and as if she was trying to remember. "After rehearsal that night, we went back to our motel. We bought some food in one of those little clam shacks they have all along Route 1—they call it the Boston Post Road here—and we brought it back to our room."

"Were you there the rest of the night, both of you?"

"Yes, of course. We were soon asleep. It had been a long day. I'm not the sort of person who would lie, Mr.—what was your name again?"

"Vartanian."

"And I very much resent the idea that not only have you considered me a suspect, but you're calling me a liar."

Elmer reached into his coat pocket and pulled out the rosary wrapped in his handkerchief. He opened the little bundle carefully, not touching the beads with his hands and showed it to Constance Burch. For the first time the frozen expression of disdain crumbled off her face, and she stood up and took a few steps, trance-like, towards him, her eyes wide and intent. He held up one hand in a policeman's gesture of stop, to let her know that he was not offering her the rosary beads. She stopped and looked up at him quizzically.

"Where did you find them?"

Elmer asked, "Do these belong to you?"

"Yes. Where did you find them?"

"On the body of Eva Breck."

***

Jeff Collins jumped from his seat and paced, now seemingly over his shock and having entered a new state of agitation. "Are we going to be allowed to put on a show tonight or what? We can't just sit here. Are the police being called? This is crazy." He fumbled with lighting a cigarette and walked back and forth with his hands on his hips. Some of the cast began to stir on stage, tired of being at attention.

Nina asked, sarcastically, "Are we supposed to be prisoners here?"

Juliet said, "I suggest you all come down here and sit in the seats in the first row. Make yourselves comfortable. But you need to stay here and you need to stay together."

The actors slowly began to file off the stage and they did she asked, sitting together in the first row of seats. Juliet motioned for the technical staff to do likewise, and the stage manager took his script and directed his crew to do likewise. He, Robert, Clarence, and few other apprentices came out from the wings, along with Meg the wardrobe mistress, and all sat in the second row. Juliet glanced up at Bobby in the booth. "Would you come down, too, Bobby?" she called.

Bobby growled from the booth, "Yes, ma'am."

In a few moments, Bobby came down from the booth, walked down the center aisle and took his own place in the third row, a solitary figure in the theater, used to being solitary and preferring it. The actors glanced over their shoulders to look at him. For most of the production he had been only a voice and a silhouette in the booth. He was a short man in gray gabardine slacks and a turquoise bowling shirt that said "Bobby" on one pocket and "Kingpins" on the other. He did not look so omnipotent in this light.

Juliet stood in front of the stage, resting the small of her back against it, the center of attention for all of them. She had since taken off her nurse's cap, but she continued to wear her costume and looked rather like a school nurse addressing an assembly of students about hygiene or first aid. She kept the feeling of ridiculousness to herself.

135

"We believe that the body, when it was hidden behind the flats, was probably wrapped up or at least the head and shoulders, in some of the old muslin that is stored back there. Where the body was found in the marsh, there was no muslin covering it. This suggests that the person used it to avoid leaving a trail of blood from the dressing rooms to where it was put into Leon's trunk, and disposed of it afterward. There were a few traces of blood on the carpet of Leon's trunk, but that's all, only a few traces. So the blow to the head might not have been what killed her. And leaving traces of blood in the trunk might have been on purpose."

"Hey," Bobby the lighting booth man roared, "I remember where I heard your name now! Juliet Van Allen, Elmer Vartanian—you guys are the Double V Investigators! I read about you guys in the paper!"

Juliet replied, ignoring him, "Can anyone here tell me if anyone saw a lot of old discarded muslin or canvas used for flats in a trash can or anywhere on the grounds?"

No one responded at first, then young Clarence raised his hand as if he were in school. He had only just graduated from high school the month before, so was a natural reaction.

Juliet patiently asked, "Yes, Clarence?"

Heads turned to look at Clarence in the second row. Clarence, used to being a techie and not being the focus of attention for actors, appeared a bit unnerved. "Well, on Saturday morning, Mr. Stiles told me to get rid of a box of trash that was backstage. It was just some paper and cut up lighting gels, some scraps of wood, pieces from the carpenters. It was just stuff that had been sitting around backstage for a while and we were starting to get the area ready for the performance, so we had to clean up. I went out to the trash barrels in the back of the playhouse and they were all full, so I went over to the ones by Mr. Welch's and Mr. Murchison's office, and those were full, too. Mr. Stiles was walking by and I said the barrels were full, what should I do with this trash, are there any more barrels, and he told me to walk down to the beach and stuff it in one of their public trash barrels there."

All eyes looked to Stiles and he shrugged and said defensively, "We've done that before. I don't think the state beach likes it too much, us stuffing our trash in their barrels, but it gets taken away all the same. It's not like we do it every day."

Juliet asked, "Where did you find the piece of canvas, Clarence?"

136

Clarence answered, now warming to the attention and feeling braver, "When I went out to the barrel on the beach, it was in there. It was sitting on the top of whatever regular trash was there. I remember it because when I saw that, I knew it was from the theater. Nobody else would throw away a big piece of canvas like that, and I thought, well, I guess everybody knows to put trash out here and I didn't, so now I know it's okay."

"Did you look at the cloth? Did you see if there was any blood on it?"

"No ma'am, I didn't really take it out and look at it, but from where I could see just noticing it in there, there was a big splotch of brown paint on it, as if paint had been spilled on it. It looked sort of dry but you could still smell the paint. So I just put my trash on top of it and I came back to the playhouse."

Juliet said, "I discovered Leon's muddy shoes in the trash barrels by the office today—"

Leon looked up, "My shoes? My dress shoes? I was looking for them!"

"Sure, you were." Murchison answered.

"Murchison, you fat slob, I'm going to—"

"You're going to what?" Murchison answered, "Kill me?"

The showdown ended in cold silence.

Juliet continued, "The shoes were all that was in the barrel, except for newspapers. When is the trash emptied here at the playhouse?"

Murchison said, "Monday morning."

Juliet asked, "Does anyone know when the trash on the beach is emptied?"

Murchison again responded "The beach is maintained by the state. I imagine it's probably emptied every day or at least every other day in the summer."

Juliet said, "If Clarence put his trash there Saturday morning, it's not likely to be there now. We'll have a look just the same. Has anyone noticed a can of brown or black paint moved from where it normally would be or has anyone noticed a splotch of paint on the ground?"

Stiles asked, "Why would someone pour brown paint on this piece of canvas?"

"To cover the blood should the piece be found."

"Why not just throw it away?"

She answered, "Because someone like Clarence might come along and see a blood streaked-piece of cloth and start asking questions. Obviously, if he sees a piece of cloth with paint on it, anyone would assume it was used as a rag."

Robert offered from his seat, smiling, "You're very good at this, Miss."

She answered wryly, "Thank you, Mr. Forde."

***

Constance looked genuinely stunned, even sickened. She reached out for the rosary, but Elmer pulled it away from her and would not let her touch the beads.

Constance said, "They were found...on her body?"

"They were tucked into her clothing, under her top. Either she put them there herself or someone put them on her. Do you know any reason why she would have taken these rosary beads and hidden them on her person? I understand that you and Eva did not particularly get along, that she frequently taunted or mocked you. It is also known among the cast that your husband had an affair with Eva."

She snapped, "That was all over before we came here."

"Whether it was—or wasn't—you and Eva had animosity for each other. Do you think it's possible that Eva would have taken the rosary to tease you or to play a trick on you? To harass or annoy you?"

"I believe she was capable of anything."

"Your beads went missing around the time Eva went missing. Did you and she have an altercation which would have caused her to take the beads?"

Constance crossed her arms in a defensive posture. She hesitated and then announced, "Yes. It was during the rehearsal, at the very beginning. I was in the dressing room. I had just come down after exiting the stage after I made my entrance at the beginning of Act I. I came back downstairs to grab a couple of tissues and sit out in the audience until it was my turn to come on again. Eva was down in the dressing room because she hadn't yet made her entrance. She was fussing and fuming about something, pacing back and forth. There is a scene on stage where she and I have angry words and her character, Sarat Carn, pushes me to the floor. My character is a very angry and unpleasant woman. She's not exactly wrong, in fact, she's a rather righteous person but she comes on a little strong and in an excitable moment, pushes Sarat Carn to the floor. Well, every time we practiced this Eva was a little rough, I thought, so as long as we two were alone backstage—I really don't like to make scenes in front of the other actors or take every little problem I have to the director, it's unprofessional. But as long as we were alone together, I told her to please not be so rough, that it wasn't necessary, that we are only acting."

Elmer asked, "Was she only acting?"

Constance gave a sarcastic laugh, "Not entirely. Eva was a very childish woman, high strung and seemed to feel very entitled. Of course, she had the starring role and stars often feel that way, from what I've noticed in the business. But she hadn't been in the business very long. In fact, as I understand it, this was her first starring role on stage. She started in Hollywood and was working her way up, I think by the casting couch, but she had never done any stage work or at least not much of it. This whole run has been a challenge for her. At any rate, as far as being a theatrical player, Eva was a little rough around the edges. She could also be ruthless, as you may have heard."

"How did she respond when you asked her to be less rough?"

Constance replied, "She became very insulting and she said—she said she knew things about my husband that I didn't know. Frankly, I'd had enough. I hate to admit it, but my temper got the best of me and I told her to leave me alone. I said the next time she pushed me around on stage I might be inclined to push back. And I actually, well, I pushed her right there. I pushed her and she stumbled back, in fact, she fell."

Elmer asked, "Show me. How did you push her, and how did she fall?"

"Well," Constance started, suddenly feeling awkward, "In the heat of the moment I—I shouted something and I stepped towards her and I pushed her." Constance raised her hands and made a couple of steps toward Elmer, her eyes suddenly focusing on the rosary beads in his hands again. She did not touch them but she made as though to raise both hands as if to push them against his chest. She stopped after a moment, still focused on the rosary beads, which he would not let her touch.

"And then?"

Constance's voice grew weak and somewhat shaky as she lifted her eyes to Elmer's.

"Well, she stumbled back. She's a little shorter than I am. I should not have done it. She stumbled back and as she fell, she bumped her head against counter where we apply our makeup. The makeup table is one long counter against the wall, as I think you've seen. She cursed me using such foul language that I will not repeat. She rubbed her head and she said that I would be sorry for that. I said, 'I doubt it.' Well, I was so upset, I walked out. I went down the hall to the ladies' room, that was the last time I saw her."

"What happened when you came out of the ladies' room, was anyone down there at that time? Did you just go upstairs to the house?"

"Stephen Grove was just coming down the steps. He said that Eva was furious and stomped up the stairs and he wondered what happened. I didn't tell him, of course, I didn't think it was appropriate to talk about it, so I just—I don't remember what I said, something like what else or what do you think or something like that and I went upstairs and went out to the house and sat there until was my turn to make an entrance again. Then I went backstage and entered from backstage. But a few moments later it was Eva's turned to go on and she wasn't there. As you know, the director called for lunch and we assumed that Eva would return, that she was making some sort of diva's trick of making the cast wait. I really don't think anyone at the time thought that she had been murdered."

"Except the murderer."

"You think it was one of us?"

Elmer didn't answer. He folded her rosary beads carefully in his handkerchief and demonstrably put them back in his pocket.

She asked, defiantly, "You think it was me?"

***

Juliet watched Stephen Grove light a cigarette for Guy Norman. The rest of the cast were restless. She continued her questioning.

"Mr. Grove, where were you just before Eva was to make her entrance?"

He looked up at her, put his lighter back in his coat pocket and in a gentlemanly way, like the doctor he played on stage, he gave her his patient attention. "I think I was backstage. I can remember standing far back against the wall or at one point, I think I was standing on the top of the stairs leading down to the dressing room, listening to the action. You see, I didn't have to go on for some time, so naturally I wouldn't have stood in the way of the other actors who had to make their entrances and exits. When it's not your turn to go on, you hang back a little and give the others some room to come and go. Sometimes I'm downstairs in the green room—or in the dressing room—during a show. Some people choose to sit in the house and watch until it's their turn. On that day, I did go out to the audience but I don't think I was there at that point. I think I was still backstage. I remember seeing Constance walk past me and go downstairs after she'd made her exit. I assumed Eva was already down there because I heard loud voices, Constance and, I assume, Eva having words with each other. Because I was listening to what was going on onstage, I couldn't quite make out what they were saying but they seemed to be having an argument. Of course, that wasn't unusual for Eva, she was known to blow up quite often. But it was unusual for Constance, so that's why I remember it. After that, I don't really remember what happened because I was moving forward to make my entrance."

All eyes, except Guy Norman's, were on him.

Grove continued, "Well, I made my entrance first. The only people on stage were Beatrice and Bessie. I say my little bit and I exited stage left, and I was followed by Ruth. After I exited, I went down into the house and sat there, watching the others."

Juliet said to Gary Pirelli, "After Miss Baggs leaves the stage briefly, she comes on again as Sister Josephine, shortly after that you follow playing Melling and you are supposed to bring Eva on stage."

Bessie Baggs spoke up nervously, "I never left the backstage. I was right there, I didn't go back down to the dressing room or out into the house. Mr. Stiles can tell you I was standing not too far away from him."

Nina spoke up, "Of course not. She stashes her nip bottle by the flat. She's never too far away from it."

Jeff Collins glared at Nina, "Shut your mouth, Nina."

Nina flashed an unrepentant smile.

Juliet asked, "Mr. Pirelli, where were you before you had to go on? Had you always been in the wings, or were you downstairs in the dressing room before you went up?"

"I was out on the back veranda grabbing a smoke. Usually, I'm downstairs making up, of course, but we weren't doing makeup. I was right outside the screen door so I could hear how far they were getting in the play and I was just going to toss my cigarette and go on for my line. I just figured Eva would be there, ready to make her entrance with me."

"So you didn't see Eva at all?"

"Oh, well, I saw her about fifteen minutes before that. She came out of Leon's office and she was really mad, sputtering and I just turned around and didn't look at her. Eva goes after anybody who gives her the slightest bit of attention. So I paid her no attention. I was digging out my smokes and trying to get my lighter to work. I eventually did, I just busied myself with it. I guess you could say it's a bit of 'business.' That's what we call it on stage for fumbling with the prop: a bit of business. I was doing that so she would avoid me. I didn't like her very much. I don't guess anybody here did, except for Mr. Welch that is, but I'll say it out loud."

Leon shot him a disgusted look.

Juliet continued, "And then you went backstage to wait for your entrance, which happens on page fourteen. So by the time you got there, Miss Maguire, Miss Longworth and Miss Baggs were on stage. Mr. Grove had already made his exit and he was already off stage left and sitting in the house. All the other actors were watching from the house except for Constance, who was downstairs, and Eva, who when last seen, was downstairs. Mr. Norman, where were you when Eva and Constance were downstairs?"

Guy Norman dragged deeply on his cigarette, visibly nervous.

He said in a quiet voice, "After I did my bit on stage, I exited left and I went out on the veranda just for a minute or two. It was a nice day. You know, the sun was shining and I just looked out over towards the beach and just looked at the people for a while. It's tough being inside on such a nice day, you just want to be out in the sunshine. It's pretty dark inside the theater."

"Did you see Mr. Grove exit stage left a couple of pages after you did?"

Stephen Grove looked up at her as if suddenly surprised to be a focal point. He glanced at Guy. He spoke up, "No, I never saw Guy. I must've gone into the audience before he came out."

***

Elmer crossed his arms across his chest and looked critically down at Constance, who sat on Leon's leather couch, "Did you kill Eva Breck?"

She looked up at him, appalled more than angry, "Of course not! I wouldn't kill her, I wouldn't kill anybody."

"But you did have a physical fight. You pushed her, and she fell to the floor."

"And after that I left. I couldn't have pushed her hard enough to kill her. In fact, when she fell down on the floor, she swore at me, that's how much life was in her miserable body. I wasn't going to take any more, that's why I left. She was alive when I left her, Mr. Vartanian. I swear to God."

"And there was no one else downstairs that you knew? No man in the men's dressing room?"

"Not that I know of. At the time, I believe that there was no one else down there."

"All right, Miss Burch. I don't think you killed Eva. Eva's neck was broken."

Constance gasped, put her hand over her mouth and looked away.

Elmer continued, "But someone purposely took your rosary beads and put them on her body. It's possible she took them herself to tease you. And then someone killed her, not knowing that she had the beads on her. It's also possible someone put them there as a clue pointing toward you. Your husband had a relationship with Eva. Yes, yes, I know, that's over. Can you tell me for certain that he wouldn't kill her and try to frame you? You've heard that moments before Eva came into the playhouse that morning, she confessed to Leon that she was pregnant, insisted he was the father, and demanded his financial support."

"You mean blackmail him."

"But Leon is not the father. So she leaves his office and storms back into the playhouse. Someone else is the father."

"It could have been anyone. Eva played fast and loose with anyone she thought could advance her career."

"Could your husband be the father of her child?"

"And are you accusing my husband of killing her and then framing me for it?" She attempted a brief sarcastic laugh but choked on it instead. "I don't know. I don't know."

"You and your husband do not have any children, do you?"

"What does that have to do with it?" She looked away from him, "I'm not able to have children."

***

Gary Pirelli said, "I knew Eva was down there when we started rehearsal, because I could hear shouting. I had started halfway down the steps and she was having some sort of battle with another actress in the dressing room. Not unusual for Eva. I couldn't really hear Constance's voice that much, she wasn't as loud, but I knew it probably was her because Eva was shouting Guy's name. I figured they were fighting over Guy, which wasn't a surprise. I guess pretty much like everybody else, I knew that Guy had been seeing Eva—at least before we came to Connecticut. I gathered from the gossip that was off and it was all about Leon now. So like I say, when I heard this, I figured, no sir, I'm not getting in the middle of that—and I started back up the stairs to wait for our entrance. I figured, and hoped, she would come up in time for her cue. But she never did. Frankly, I sort of forgot about it. You know, when you're standing backstage and you're looking onto the set at the other actors and listening for your turn to jump in, it's kind of like being a racehorse at the starting gate. You just focus on when it's your turn to jump in. At the moment we come on, I turned around expecting her to be there and she wasn't there. That's when I ran back downstairs to go get her. But I didn't see anybody but Constance. She was marching right upstairs. Steve was backstage at that point, Stephen Grove, I mean, who plays the doctor. He said that Eva dashed out and he wondered what had been going on downstairs, said he'd heard it, too."

Juliet asked, "But you hadn't seen Mr. Grove until that moment?"

Gary said, "No, I guess not. I don't remember seeing him before that, but he could have been around and I just wasn't paying attention. People generally pace around before their time to go on. For instance, Guy ended up down there, too, but I never noticed him pass me, unless he had been down there since the start of rehearsal."

Juliet said, "Mr. Grove, you said you had exited stage left after your scene was through. At what point did you come back to stage right and tell Mr. Pirelli that Eva had gone off in a huff?"

Stephen Grove hesitated, and then offered, "Well I... I don't know. I thought I had gone down into the house at that point to watch. Oh, that might be when I started back to the dressing room. I was going to get my cigarettes. I left them on the counter in the men's dressing room. I crossed down in the front of the house and then went backstage right. I was about to go down the stairs but then I saw Eva leave very angrily. I wasn't going to be the one to tell her to stay. I figured maybe she was just going to march over to Leon's office again for some reason. She was impulsive."

Juliet turned around and called toward the back of the house, "Mrs. Margolis, on that day, did you ever see Mr. Grove enter the house from the left at that point, cross over, then enter backstage right? I presume you were here for that rehearsal on Friday morning. Do you remember?"

Stephen Grove said, laughing, "Look here..."

Joan Margolis called from the back of the house, "No."

Juliet asked, "No, he didn't cross the house, or no, you don't remember?"

"No.... He never entered the house. I remember because I was very interested to see who was coming and going. I didn't know actors sometimes watched each other during rehearsals in the theatre. I hadn't realized it was so informal during the early rehearsals. It was interesting for me to keep track of who was making entrances and exits, and from where they were doing it. And if they would make it stage on time. I guess it got to be quite a game with me."

Kent Murchison volunteered, "I can vouch that Eva and Leon were fighting in Leon's office that morning. I was in my office and I came out to the reception area. Nina was out there, evidently waiting her turn to have a word with Leon and we both heard Eva announce that she was pregnant and that Leon was the father of her child. When Eva stomped out, Nina was still there smirking at me, somehow triumphant, and then she went in to see Leon. I heard nothing else after the door closed. But I did see that Eva went to the playhouse. And she was obviously upset. At that point, I was so disgusted I went to lunch. I figured fireworks would occur when I got back. I knew that he was probably going to be casting a new leading lady."

145

"Murchison, you're through here," Leon growled.

"Tell that to the board," he answered.

"Excuse me, Miss?" Joan Margolis called out. All turned to face her. "Mr. Norman was also in the audience, sitting in the last seat near the exit down front, and he went backstage moments before he was to make his entrance, just as others had done. Mr. Grove passed him as he went back first."

Juliet answered, "Thank you, Mrs. Margolis."

***

Elmer asked Constance, "And when you came out of the restroom, who was the first person you saw?"

Constance replied, "I saw Stephen Grove. He was standing in the hallway looking up the stairs, then he turned back to me and he said, 'Eva's just gone off in a huff. She just took off.' At that point, I didn't really care. Her unprofessionalism didn't surprise me, and I was still upset by my encounter with her, so I was glad she was gone. When we all came back from lunch and she still hadn't returned, Jeff put Nina in Eva's role. Even though I was surprised that Nina had the role memorized, I was glad she it took it over and that we could move on. I'd hoped that Eva had been fired, but nobody said anything to that effect and I certainly wasn't going to poke my nose in it."

***

Juliet said, "Mr. Grove, you had been backstage before you made your entrance, you had been in the dressing room and then after your entrance you say you went into the house to watch. Mrs. Margolis says you did not. There we have a discrepancy."

Stephen Grove replied, "Well, I was wandering around a lot. Maybe she didn't see me. I don't really remember exactly everywhere I went all that morning. Except that I believe I went to sit in the house."

Juliet continued, "Mr. Pirelli was standing backstage about to make his entrance when he realized Eva was not with him, so he walked downstairs to the dressing rooms and did not see her; he only saw Constance Burch standing at the bottom of the stairs."

To Gary Pirelli she said, "Guy Norman, who you said could have passed without you noticing, was in the men's dressing room and his wife was talking to him through the doorway and Constance told you that Eva had left in a huff, is that about it?"

Pirelli nodded, "Yes, that's what she said. I didn't really look everywhere downstairs, I just poked my head into the dressing room saw Guy sitting in there, which was nothing unusual about that, even though I didn't see him go there. Nothing looked wrong."

"And you never saw Eva pass you backstage to leave the playhouse?"

"No, I never did. Of course, that doesn't mean she didn't. I was watching the show behind the curtain. She could have come behind me and I never would have seen her, like I never saw Guy pass me. Although Ed was behind me at his podium, he might've seen her."

All attention went to Ed Stiles. He still had his script in his arms like a baby he would not put down. He answered, "I never saw her pass me. Frankly, it's my job to notice everything that's going on backstage as well as onstage, but I don't think she left the playhouse or at least not at that moment or I would have seen her. A few moments later on we couldn't find her and Jeff said we should break for lunch, then she could have left without my noticing. I mean, if she was still downstairs, she could have left after that but I don't know where she would have hid. The dressing rooms were empty, there was no one in the restroom. There's the small storage area where the seamstress works and a woodshop underneath, but as far as I know she wasn't down there either. I really don't think she could have got past me but I'm not saying it's impossible."

Juliet turned to face the house. She glanced up involuntarily at Betty Ann Welch, who was still sitting, as if frozen, in her seat on the aisle about halfway back. She seemed not to have taken her eyes off Leon, who rested his rear end on the edge of stage, his legs crossed, his arms folded, looking downward at the floor. He would not look at her.

Juliet said, "Robert, could you please go over to Leon's office and give a report to Elmer and Constance? I think they could use an update."

All eyes turned to Robert quizzically. "Sure thing," he said and walked out of the playhouse.

Nina called out, "Why does he get to go and we have to stay here like we were criminals or something."

147

Beatrice Longworth answered, "Because he only just joined us today. So he's not a suspect, and we all are."

Guy Norman continued to look visibly upset. He sucked on his cigarette and finished it quickly, throwing it to the floor and mashing it out with his shoe. Now he had nothing to do with his hands, so he folded his arms, his hands tightly under his armpits and sat on the edge of the stage, leaning against it as he observed what Leon was doing and he tapped his foot repeatedly, nervously jangling his leg on the floor.

***

Elmer spoke gently to Constance Burch, as one reasoning with her rather than accusing her. "Rosary beads are a very personal article."

He held them up again, careful not to put his fingerprints on them, but using his handkerchief to grasp the loop. The crucifix dangled gently from the graceful strand. "And to one of the faith who is particularly devout, using them in any manner except in prayer would be unthinkable. Have you said the Rosary today, Miss Burch?"

"Not yet."

"Today would be the Joyful Mysteries."

She brought her gaze from the rosary to his face, his rough, not handsome but not unpleasant face. "Are you Catholic?" She asked curiously as if the very idea was impossible.

He looked at the beads. "Yes." He did not mention that he had not been to Mass in years, not since before he'd gone to prison. "And you borrowed Beatrice's beads that went with her costume on Friday afternoon because it is your habit to pray, and because you never did find your beads. Isn't that it?"

"I don't know what to say, Mr. Vartanian, except I hope you believe me when I say I had no idea what happened to those rosary beads. I did not put them on Eva, that is not something I would have done."

He answered, "But someone did, and if we find out the reason why, then will find out who did it. Now, if Eva took those herself, she could have meant to tease you, was killed and had those on her body without the killer knowing it. Or the killer put them on her body in a way to implicate you. Since probably most of the cast and crew were aware of your habit of daily prayer, pretty much anybody could have been the one to do it."

There was a knock on the office door. Elmer turned, and said, "Yes?"

"It's Robert. Miss Van Allen sent me over to give you an update."

"Come on in."

Robert stepped in and glanced around Leon's office. Elmer could see him taking note of all the beautiful starlets on the walls.

Robert said, "Juliet's covering a lot of ground. It's like watching another play. Upshot is, Gary Pirelli was waiting to go on at the point Eva was supposed to make her entrance. She wasn't there, so he went downstairs and saw Miss Burch standing in the hallway talking through the open door to Mr. Norman, who was sitting in the men's dressing room. He didn't see anybody else down there. Guy Norman says he never saw anything. Stephen Grove says he never saw anything, went on to do his scene, came off and then went into the house to watch the show, only Joan Margolis, the mystery lady who likes to watch the rehearsals, she says she never saw him in the house. That's pretty much where we stand except Guy Norman looks like he's about to have a nervous breakdown, if you ask me. Stephen Grove looked like he was trying to calm him down."

Constance replied, "But Stephen Grove *was* there. He's the one who told me that Eva had left a huff. When I came out of the restroom, he was standing at the foot of the stairs as if he had just been coming down and he said Eva had left angrily and asked me what that was all about, and I said I didn't know except that we'd had a few words before I went into the restroom. According to Stephen, she walked out on her own two feet, so she couldn't have been hurt, and she couldn't even have been feigning being hurt if she walked off in a huff, could she?"

Elmer remarked, "Is there a possibility that Guy would want to kill Eva? Perhaps she was framing him, perhaps the child she was carrying was actually his and she confronted him and he killed her? And if Stephen Grove says she walked off, maybe he was lying. Maybe he was covering up for Guy. But why would he do that? What was in it for him? Do you have any answers?"

She shook her head. "Guy couldn't be the father…oh, I can't even think of it."

Elmer said, "I need to talk to your husband now. I'm going to bring him here and ask that you step into Mr. Murchison's office and stay there."

She answered, "Why don't you let me speak to him. I can get to the bottom of this. He'll tell me the truth."

Elmer replied, "If you think there's a chance he won't tell me the truth, then he won't tell you the truth. He deceived you when he had an affair with Eva."

She interrupted, "That's all in the past."

"The past inevitably has repercussions into the present. You seem to be a person who's very interested in right over wrong, truth over lies. Are you not?"

She answered stiffly, "I should hope I am."

"Now I'm asking you to add one more golden quality to your repertoire. I'm asking you to trust your husband's answers and trust me to do the right thing. I'm not going to browbeat the man. I just want to separate him from Mr. Grove."

"What do you think Stephen Grove has to do with all this?"

"I'll know that better when I hear your husband's version."

He led Constance into Murchison's office and asked her to take a seat. Murchison's office had a quite different décor than Leon's. There were no stunning photographs of leading ladies on the wall, and, also unlike Leon, no pictures of himself, either. He had a plain steel desk unlike Leon's polished oak desk. There was a painting of a sailing ship on one wall and a painting of a different schooner on another wall such as might be found in any auto court room on the Boston Post Road. His tastes looked simple and did not outwardly appear as if they included theatre. His inbox was full of papers and his outbox was full of even more of them. He doodled on his desk blotter. Mostly circles and squares and spirals. Elmer left her there, sitting erect on the metal folding chair, composed and staring off out the window at a scrub pine that blocked the ocean view.

He closed the office door gently and said to Robert, "Could you stay here in the outer office and just keep watch on things? Guard her, keep her here if she wants to wanders off. Okay?"

Robert put his hands in his pockets, shrugged and said, "Okay. If I can. You know what you're doing, Elmer?"

"I never know until the end of the story."

Elmer walked over to the playhouse and all eyes turned to him as he entered. He walked down to the front of the house and exchanged only a brief glance with Leon, who preferred to stand by himself in petulant self-absorption and isolation. Elmer approached Juliet, pulled her aside and whispered in her ear, knowing all eyes were on them.

"Any more conflicting stories about Stephen Grove?"

She touched her cheek to his and she whispered into his ear, breathing in his aftershave.

"None, except that he's extraordinarily calm and confident, where the rest of the cast are fidgety and nervous. None more so than Guy Norman."

He whispered back into the blonde curls above her ear, "I'm going to bring Norman back to the office with me to talk to him privately. Constance seemed shocked about the rosary beads. She didn't know. We'll see what he knows."

She asked, "Who are you leaning towards?"

"I don't know. Guy's a strong contender, but with two people—Leon and Constance—that look like they're being framed for this, it makes sense that possibly two people were involved in the cover-up and maybe didn't know what the other was doing. Stephen Grove?"

She responded, "Maybe, but I don't see a motive yet. Here's what I would suggest: Bring Kent Murchison back with you, too. Have him go in another office and dig up either in his files or by calling out to L.A. about Stephen Grove's background. Maybe he and Eva were involved in California before they came here. The cast doesn't seem to know anything about it, and they're hardly closemouthed; they should have known something by now and no one said anything. I'll keep questioning here. But maybe there's something else going on that Eva found out about and was using as blackmail."

He answered, "Good idea. I'll give it another half-hour before we bring in the cops."

Elmer announced in a loud, and what he hoped would be an authoritative, voice, "Mr. Norman, I'm going to ask you and Mr. Murchison to come back with me to the office."

Stephen Grove's eyes darted to Guy. Guy looked suddenly haggard, more defeated than nervous, and he stood frozen at his spot. Kent Murchison followed Elmer and glared at Leon as he passed him, but Guy needed Elmer to actually put his hand on his arm and lead him out before he would move.

***

The last row of the back of the house began to fill with silent but captivated volunteers—ushers and concessions workers, the boys who directed cars in the parking lot, apprentices.

Juliet announced to them, "I'm going to ask you support personnel to please wait at the box office until you're given further instructions."

No one moved for a moment, not sure who the strange woman was and what authority she had. Ed Stiles spoke up, "We'll call you when we need you."

The house manager took her cue from him and turned on them and shooed them away. She led them to the box office where they grumbled about a mystery but hoped they would not be sent home before they knew what it was.

"Mr. Grove," Juliet said, "after you made your entrance and then left the stage, when is the last point that you saw Guy Norman?"

He said nothing at first, but furrowed his brow, and busied himself with cigarettes again, like a bit of business on stage, as Gary Pirelli had described earlier. "Well, I don't think I saw him until we all broke up the rehearsal, when we realized Eva was gone. I can't remember seeing him before that."

"Where were you when the director announced that the rehearsal would break early for lunch?"

"I don't remember exactly. I thought I was here in the house, even though our mystery guest claims she never saw me." He looked over at Joan Margolis, no trace of good humor left in his voice, and Joan shifted uncomfortably in her seat.

***

Elmer walked out of the playhouse with Kent Murchison and Guy Norman in tow. He had to slow his pace for both gentlemen, as Murchison labored under his extra weight and did not walk fast as a consequence, and because Norman just seemed to drag. His extra weight at the moment was purely emotional. He perspired, fumbled for cigarettes again and dropped them on the ground. He appeared to be breathing heavily. Elmer surmised he was in the early stages of a panic attack. They walked past the box office building where a small crowd of support staff were gathering and stood staring at them.

Kent Murchison muttered, "What a circus this is turning out to be."

They went into the offices and Elmer brought Guy into Leon's office and asked him to sit on the couch. Guy looked around at all the photographs of the women and sat forward and put his head in his hands. Elmer left him there a moment and stepped back into the outer office. He asked Mr. Murchison to go into his own office, and brought Constance Burch to the outer office where he asked her to have a seat. He said quietly to Robert, "Stay here with her and make sure she doesn't leave, but don't chat with her, keep it quiet. I'm going to tell him that the cops have taken her away."

Elmer said to Kent Murchison when they were in his office, "I'd like you to go through whatever files you have and make whatever phone calls to the Coast you need to tell me more about Stephen Grove. He hooked up with the group in California; how did that go? But I want to know everything you can find out about him. Were he and Eva connected? Were they lovers, or did she have some sort of secret on him?"

Kent Murchison replied, "You suspect *him*?"

"He's a contender."

Elmer closed the door and went back into Leon's office where Guy sat looking miserable. Elmer sat on the edge of Leon's desk. He said quietly, "Mr. Norman, we have some serious evidence against your wife."

Guy looked up at him, "Where is she? I thought you took her here."

"She's in police custody."

"Already? Cops came and they didn't want to talk to anybody else?"

"These were plainclothes detectives. We didn't want to cause a stir. They wanted to talk to her in more official surroundings. Tell me, when you went back looking for your wife's rosary, did you ever find it?"

"No."

"I have them now." He held it up, "Your wife's rosary was found on Eva's body."

Guy Norman looked up confused and horrified. "That can't be!"

"Either Eva took them to tease Constance or someone else took them to implicate Constance as the murderer. They were tucked inside Eva's clothing. Did you do that?"

Guy Norman sat upright, and looked around as if his mind were racing. "No. I didn't do that."

"What *did* you do?"

"What do you mean?"

Elmer said, "The only other people down there before Eva made her entrance were you and Mr. Grove. Mr. Pirelli states that you were both down there earlier but that he did not see either of you at that point, and when it was time for Eva to make her entrance, only Constance was down there alone, apparently. We know she and Constance had a fight and that Constance pushed her and she fell to the floor. Constance states that when she came out of the restroom there was no one else there except Mr. Grove, who told her that Eva was angry and left."

Guy asked, "She said that? She said he told her that Eva left?"

"Yes. He says he wasn't there. She says he was, and that he told her Eva left. Eva's body was found with her rosary beads planted on it, yet there is evidence that Eva's body was put in the trunk of Leon's car, that the car was driven out to the salt marsh where her body was found, and that a pair of Leon's shoes were left in the trash barrel all muddy. It becomes an interesting game of who was lying and for what reason. At least one of you is."

Guy stopped shaking. He stared away as if trying to add up a situation he could not understand.

Elmer continued, "Perhaps Constance hadn't realized that in causing Eva to hit her head that she killed Eva, and Stephen Grove was trying to protect her by telling her that Eva walked out when she hadn't. But why would he do that? Why would he protect Constance? Did Constance have some information on him? Where he and Eva lovers and she knew?"

Guy said, "I don't know. You mean Leon isn't a suspect?"

"I suspect Leon of many things, but it actually appears that he was being framed. It appears that both he and Constance were being framed and one would think they were being framed by two different people who didn't know the other person was planting evidence."

Guy's gaze meandered among all the photographs of the beautiful women on the walls. Several of them had Leon in the photo, his arm draped around the women. They were publicity shots, if not for the theater then for Leon's own personal need for self-publicity. He and the actresses smiled at the camera invitingly, but that arm of his placed across the shoulders skewed the image into making one think there was more going on the second after the photo was taken. For most of these photos that was probably not true. Leon talked a big game and thought himself a big man, but it was quite probable that he did not sleep with *all* these actresses. He only liked to think so, or perhaps liked to make others wonder if he did.

Guy's eyes followed an imagined story of the photographs as he listened to Elmer.

He finally said, "Yeah, we weren't here more than a day for us to pick up on the kind of person he is."

Elmer asked, "You are aware he had an affair with Eva even before the company arrived in Connecticut?"

"I'm aware of it now."

"But you were involved with Eva in California?"

Guy Norman looked down at the floor. After a moment he said, "Yes."

"But not here?"

"No."

"You break up with her or did she break up with you?"

Guy answered, weariness in his voice, "I'd like to say it was mutual. I must've been an idiot. She's not the kind of person who would stay with anyone who couldn't do something for her. No, I guess she broke up with me."

"Your wife found out about it?"

Guy answered, "Yeah. But it was over by the time she found out about it. Eva had a way of lording it over people once it was over, like she always had something on you. I guess she did. She must have lorded it over Constance."

"With your wife's rosary beads hidden on the murder victim, someone has obviously inferred that your wife is the killer. What do you think?"

Guy Norman finally looked Elmer in the eye. "Absolutely not. Constance isn't a killer. I mean…"

"And how do you think her rosary got placed on Eva's body?"

"I don't know."

Elmer said, "Well, I'll tell you, Mr. Norman, I don't think Eva put those beads there like that. For one reason, they are quite ornate and the crucifix is rather large and I think it would be a very uncomfortable thing to have them against her skin there. Even if she might have briefly, teasingly taken them, I don't think she would have just dropped them down her shirt. Of course, they may have been valuable enough to steal and if a person wanted to steal them, they might conceal them in any way possible, but I don't know that Eva was a thief, at least not for objects. For husbands perhaps, but not for anything else. Also, when I found her body it was on the edge of the salt marsh partly protruding out of the water. If someone really wanted to get rid of the body, they would have taken her farther out into the marsh, then she might never have been found. Maybe the current from the river might've taken her out into the Long Island Sound and she would never be seen again."

Still sitting on the edge of Leon's desk, he loosened the light bulb from the desk lamp as he spoke as an irresistible prank on Leon. "The person who put the body there wanted it to be found. That person wanted these muddy shoes thrown in the garbage to be found, too, and wanted the evidence to point to Leon. Leon didn't put that body where it could be found; it was someone else who wanted to frame Leon, and a second person wanted to frame Constance, and neither of these conspirators knew what the other was doing. That second person was the one who killed Eva. When I found the body, it was positioned such that I could tell even after a couple of days of lying there that the neck had been broken. There were bruises on her neck as if she had been choked and her neck snapped."

Guy Norman's eyes grew wide and he gasped a curse.

Elmer continued "The person who did that to her not only would have to be strong enough to do that, but would have to know how. He might have to know some sort of commando move to be able to do that. Did you serve in the military, Mr. Norman, in the last war?" Elmer leaned crossed his arms in front of him, aware of the irony of his asking the question about the war, for it was a question that deeply embarrassed him when people asked him—because he had spent the war years in prison and felt guilty about that.

Guy remarked, "No, I was 4-F." At this moment, there was a knock on the door. Kent Murchison entered with a notepad.

Elmer said, "Do you have any information, Mr. Murchison?"

Kent's eyes darted back and forth between Guy and Elmer and then, involuntarily, at the photos on the walls. He muttered, "You have no idea how I avoid coming in here. Anyway, I called out to the West Coast. Stephen Grove started in the pictures using the name Sonny Kerry. A few B-movies, an undistinguished career, and then he was drafted. He spent the war years in the South Pacific, saw action, and when he came back, he started over, got himself a new name and began in minor roles at the Pasadena Playhouse. He appeared with a few touring companies and Leon picked him up out there. His last job was a cattle call with Republic Pictures. Was working on a movie about atomic bombs destroying the world or some such nonsense. Eva Breck was also in the cast."

Elmer said, "Was Eva's role more prominent than Mr. Grove's?"

Murchison replied, "Yes, in a manner of speaking. He only played a scientist. She played a victim of a death ray. I think she had about five minutes in the movie, but she's the one people remember."

Elmer turned back to Guy, who was trying to take this in.

Elmer said, "Mr. Norman, Stephen Grove says he saw you coming out of the dressing rooms and leaving a hurry, that you seemed flustered. He suggested that you were down with Constance and Eva. Now, your wife says that Stephen Grove told her Eva left the building after their argument. So as far as your wife's concerned, Eva walked away still alive when she left the basement. I found drops of blood in the storage area where I believe her body was hidden behind the flats. All this would have happened when Constance was in the restroom. When she comes out, Stephen Grove says Eva's gone.

"So maybe Stephen Grove killed Eva and hid her body. But he's not the one that took that body out to the salt marsh. You did that, didn't you, Guy?"

Guy Norman mumbled, trancelike, "I wasn't there when—He told Constance that Eva walked out?"

"What did he tell you, Mr. Norman?"

"He must have had it set up before I even got there! It was all acting..." Guy's voice trailed off as he waved his cigarette in the air, a gesture of futility.

***

Juliet responded, "Suspicious?"

Stephen Grove hesitated and sounded like he was hedging his bets. "Nervous. Guy's always been rather a quiet fellow for as long as I've known him with this group. A little henpecked, I should say," he looked around at the other actors and smiled as if cueing them for their approbation if not their shared amusement. Either they did not agree but were too smart to allow themselves to be pulled into this mystery any deeper, or they were the best actors in the world, because no one gave anything but a stone-faced response. It appeared as though he could have been speaking some foreign language and they, disinterested strangers, only stared.

Stephen Grove continued, "Well, be that as it may, Guy's been especially nervous since Eva's disappearance, distracted and irritable. Of course, just today, he missed the morning rehearsal, went out and got himself sloshed. Wasn't even noontime."

Juliet said, "Are you suggesting that he knows something more about Eva's murder, or that he murdered her?"

Beatrice Longworth responded, "Yes, Stephen, why don't we cut to the chase? It's growing unlikely that we're going to perform tonight, or even perform the show at all this week. Don't drag this out or be coy. If you have something to say, say it."

He turned on her sharply, "I have no connection with Eva. Your husband had an affair with her. You have more to do with this than I. You may be the *grande dame* on stage, Beatrice, but at the moment you're just another suspect. So shut up."

***

Elmer said to Guy, bringing him a glass with a splash of bourbon in it from Leon's private stock, "Even if you were never in the service and trained as a soldier, you're still strong enough so that if you knew how, you could have broken her neck. You were seeing her, you were infatuated with her, and you could have been angry enough at her taunting you to hurt her. Particularly, she may have taunted you with the notion that she was pregnant and you were *not* the father. Although, being told you're not the father would also bring some measure of relief, wouldn't it? Unless you are prepared to leave your wife for her. Were you?"

"I don't know." He said it with a shaky voice and messily slurped the drink, holding the glass with both hands. He looked up imploringly at Elmer. "I don't know. I don't think so. I love my wife. I just... Things got out of hand. If Eva was interested in you, if she wanted you, you couldn't help it. I don't think any man could."

"Did you love your wife enough to want to protect her? Did you think that she murdered Eva? Did you hide the body in the marsh to protect Constance, and did you try to plant evidence suggesting that it was Leon who did the murder?"

He said nothing but searched with his eyes again the glamorous photo gallery on the wall. Finally, he muttered, "He's such a rat, Leon. When Eva started seeing him, she flaunted it, and he sure didn't keep it any secret."

"You did try to pin the murder on Leon, didn't you?"

Guy answered, "Yes."

"You left the body at the edge of the marsh so that it would be found, when you could just as easily have gotten rid of it."

"Yes."

And you didn't know about your wife's rosary beads that were found on Eva's body?"

"No!"

"Somebody else wanted to pin the murder on Constance just as you wanted to pin the murder on Leon. It's possible Constance could have murdered Eva. But I don't think so. Now the thing is, Constance has told us that Stephen Grove was in the hall after she came out of the restroom and he told her that Eva was alive and that she stormed out of the building. Constance didn't know Eva had been murdered, and it did not seem strange to her that Eva ran off. But why would Stephen Grove say that to her?"

"She told you that?"

"That's her story, that she didn't kill Eva and she was told Eva ran off. Grove told her."

Guy Norman rubbed his eyes, and downed the rest of his drink. Elmer could see his mind was working feverishly.

"What did Grove tell you, Guy? You talked to him, didn't you?"

"Can I have another drink?"

"No."

"Was my wife really arrested?"

Elmer lied, "I don't think they've formally charged her yet, she's just in custody for questioning, that's all. And she's talking a blue streak. You know your wife."

159

Guy licked his lips and rubbed his face. He seemed on the verge of speech, but could not untangle in his mind what was the safest thing for him to say.

Elmer said, "Stephen Grove told you Constance killed her, didn't he? Did he help you to hide the body?"

"No, I did it myself." Guy replied, and then his words came in a rush, "He—he told me what happened, that Constance fought with her and Eva fell, struck her head. I said, what do I do? I begged him to help me. And he said hide the body back there behind the flats. We'll say that Eva ran off. Maybe you could dump her in the marsh later when no one's around and then no one will ever find out. We can just say she ran off. He said he didn't think Constance even knew that Eva was dead. So it would be easy to protect her. I said yes, I'll do that. And I said you won't say anything will you? And he said no, of course not. I thought it was all spur of the moment."

Elmer said, "He seemed pretty willing to be an accomplice to cover up a murder, and for what reason? Just to be a nice guy? Doesn't that seem strange to you?"

Guy answered, breathless, "At the time, I didn't think. I was just in a panic. Wasn't until I brought the body out to the marsh and I realized just having Eva disappear wasn't enough and I thought, well, why not pin this on Leon, he's such a rat. Everybody knew he'd been seeing her."

Kent Murchison, tired of standing, sat in Leon's leather chair behind his immaculate desk. He helped himself to a drink at Leon's private bar.

Elmer continued, "And Stephen didn't know you were going to come down the stairs at that moment. He was probably prepared to leave the body there and set it up so that Constance would be implicated. How did you find the body?"

"The door to the ladies' dressing room was closed. Grove opened it and showed me. Couple of chairs were overturned, Eva was lying on the floor. She had that bruise on her head. I thought maybe it could have been an accident but I didn't know her neck was broken."

"And Stephen planted the rosary beads on her body."

"I had no idea. He was lying to me. He set me up. He set Constance up. But why would he kill Eva?"

Murchison answered, "His career was starting to take off. After he left this play, he was headed for a role on Broadway."

Elmer added, "And *he* was the father of her baby, I think."

160

"Oh."

Elmer continued, "When Eva couldn't attach herself to Leon anymore because he, obviously, could not have been the father of her child, and since he was not going to have anything more to do with her now that she was pregnant, she decided to see how far she could go with Stephen Grove. She had already dumped him once, or he had dumped her, seeing what kind of opportunist she was. And he wasn't going to fall into that trap again. I suppose he could have merely suggested to her that he wasn't the father and that she couldn't prove it. She evidently chose not to pin it on you."

Guy admitted, "I wasn't as good a meal ticket as Stephen Grove, and I was married and not about to get out of it."

"Exactly. You weren't of any use to her."

Elmer stepped into the outer office. Constance and Robert looked up expectantly.

"Miss Burch, would you come in here, please? Robert, I've got a message for you to bring to Juliet."

***

"Why would I want to kill her?" Stephen Grove almost laughed as he said it. He put a hand in his pocket, gestured with a cigarette in his other hand, leaving a trail of smoke in the air and looking as relaxed and as self-superior as an art critic in a gallery. "Why don't you ask Nina where she was and what she was doing? And what she might've had cooked up with Leon. She joined the show in a bit part and now she's got the lead, apart from which, she already memorized her lines. I saw her script marked up for Eva's part *last week*. Eva's out and isn't that a little too convenient?"

Nina angrily responded, "I didn't kill her. Lots of understudies go on for actresses, they don't kill them to do it."

He said, "You were never her understudy. That's the point."

Nina said, "I wasn't even backstage at the time. You ask her," she pointed to Joan Margolis at the back of the house, "ask the mystery lady. I came out front here, I was watching the show."

Stephen Grove continued, "For that matter, why don't we ask that woman what she's even doing here? She's been spying on us the entire week. What's her part in all this?"

Beatrice Longworth answered, "Her name is Joan Margolis, and she and I used to work in pictures a long time ago. She's only here to see me and renew old times. She lives in Connecticut."

Grove scoffed, "Oh, wonderful, more refugees from Hollywood."

The director muttered, "You're a refugee from that sinkhole, too, Steve."

Grove answered, "I'm opening on Broadway in October, Jeff. I'm not a refugee from anything, I'm going places."

At that, half the cast grumbled in derision, and half remained in silence with that attitude customary to out-of-work actors and losing gamblers—why is it other people always have the luck?

Juliet looked around at all of them in the rustic little playhouse. Summer theatre was beginning a new and vibrant era, and refugees from Hollywood helped make it so. The other component was the audiences, increasingly made up of young couples, returning vets and their wives, people who could never afford to attend a play when they were growing up in the Great Depression but who now not only could afford it, but could actually appreciate it. The returning vets had seen entertainers at the USO canteens and at their camps and bases. They had seen movie stars and theatre greats, they had seen musicals and Shakespeare. They were probably the best prepared and educated audience to sit before this new vibrancy in summer theatre.

"Mr. Grove," Juliet said at last, "I don't think Nina killed for the role. And I don't think Beatrice killed out of jealousy. And I don't think the killing was planned. In fact, the cover-up was sloppily done. There is evidence to suggest that Eva's body was hidden behind the flats in the storage area underneath the stage, then removed at some point to the trunk of Leon's car and then transported out to the salt marsh, but the body was not dumped into the marsh in an effort to hide it. The person who did that left the body half on the shore purposely to be found and purposely planted evidence that would lead to Leon."

Grove's eyes narrowed, his cigarette burned low, forgotten in his hand.

Juliet continued, "Some evidence was planted this morning when Guy Norman stole Leon's dress shoes, put them on and walked out to the marsh where the body was, got plenty of mud on them and walked back right to the side of Leon's office, where he took off his shoes and put them in the trash can. And he hid in the box office to avoid detection while Mr. Vartanian and I were roaming about. He was not drinking, at least he was not drunk. That was an act. Guy Norman is a better actor than you give him credit for. He had to find a way to excuse his absence to do all this and so he created the story about going off to get drunk. In the meantime, the body was also found with Constance Burch's rosary beads planted on it."

Robert entered the theater and all eyes were on him as he motioned for Juliet to come. He spoke to her quietly, and nodded, looking grim. Then she turned back to her audience.

"The rosary beads," she continued, "Guy didn't put them there. Someone else did. So one person tries to implicate Leon and another person tries to implicate Constance. And neither one knows what the other did. That's an unfortunate mistake for the killer."

Stephen Grove's face went expressionless as his cigarette burned to the end. He finally noticed the heat encroaching upon his fingertips and he dropped it quickly and snuffed it out with his shoe.

Juliet said, "Eva did suffer a bruise on the side of her head from the fall, and you are right when you told Constance that she got up again. But you lied when you said that Eva had left the building. At the moment that you told her, Eva was dead and her body was hidden behind the flats in the storage area."

All eyes were on Juliet. She continued, "Eva's neck was broken."

There were soft gasps.

"Were you in the service, Mr. Grove, in the war?"

He answered "What has that got to do with anything?"

"I think you know. Only a person trained to snap a person's neck could have done it so quickly and so silently, without any apparent struggle."

"Why me? Why not Guy?"

"Why did you lie to Constance and tell her that Eva had left the building? Guy Norman has already confessed that when he arrived in the room, Eva was dead and you told him that Constance killed her, and in a panic, Guy asked you to help him hide the body so he could protect his wife, because he believed you. Then he took the task on himself to get rid of the body and, without you knowing it, he came up with the plan of trying to pin it on Leon. He didn't know you told Constance that Eva had already left; your plan was that she be missing and never found, but his plan was that she be found and Leon take the blame. You were both at cross purposes. But neither Guy nor Constance was the killer; you were."

"This is ridiculous."

She answered, "I agree. The truth is sometimes quite ridiculous."

"Why would I want to kill Eva? I'm going to Broadway in the fall. Why would I mess that up for myself?"

"I suppose the short answer is you lost your head when she surmised that the child she was carrying was actually yours. Unless she had more on you than that…Sonny Kerry.

***

Elmer said to Kent Murchison, "Sorry, Mr. Murchison, no show tonight, obviously. I'm going to bring the cops in now."

Murchison nodded. "I'll contact the local radio stations and ask them to announce cancellation of the show due to unforeseen circumstances. Is it okay if I have one of the apprentices make a sign and bring it out to the main road?"

"That's a good idea. Better have a couple of them standing out on the access road as well."

"Yeah." Murchison walked over to the box office, where the entire nonessential staff were huddled like hamsters in a cage, all speculating on what was happening.

Elmer brought Constance together with Guy in Leon's office, where the husband and wife regarded each other silently and nervously. Elmer said, "Miss Burch, I believe what happened is this: You got into an argument with Eva and pushed her and she fell to the floor. You went into the restroom. Stephen Grove had been in the men's dressing room and he heard this commotion. When you were down the hall, he stepped into the ladies' dressing room and he killed Eva. In a very quick and decisive move, he snapped her neck."

Constance gasped and lowered herself, shakily, down to the leather couch. Guy, who had stood upon her entering the room, remained standing, not certain if he was allowed to comfort his wife, or if she would want him to.

Elmer said, "Shortly before this occurred, Nina, who had overheard words between Leon and Eva whereby Eva found out that her expected child could not have been Leon's, told this information to Stephen

Grove. Eva apparently decided Grove might be the father. I believe that she decided to put her sights on Stephen Grove, whether or not he actually was the father, because of Mr. Grove's impending career on Broadway. Eva seems to be the type of woman who attached herself to what she regarded as successful or influential men."

Constance said in a slow, shocked mutter, "Yes...she was."

Elmer continued, "When he killed her, since you had just had words with her and the physical altercation, he decided to plant the murder on you. Then your husband came in and Stephen told him that you had killed Eva, which put your husband in a panic and wanting to protect you. He took the body, with Stephen's help and hid it behind the flats in the storage area down the hall from the dressing rooms."

Elmer looked at Guy, who stood with stooped shoulders, as one helplessly doomed.

Elmer said, "The two men decided, at Stephen Grove's urging, that they could protect you by getting rid of the body in the salt marsh. Stephen Grove apparently went under the assumption that it would look like Eva walked out and just never returned. He would not mention the fight you had with Eva to anyone unless he had to. Guy went to take his place at rehearsal, and Grove, who had pocketed your rosary, hid it under Eva's clothing to pin the murder on you, should the body be found. Later on, when the rehearsal broke for lunch and Leon's car was parked in front of the playhouse because he was unloading the playbills, Guy offered to help as a way to get Eva's body out of the playhouse and he put the body in the trunk of the car. Later on that evening, Guy, you took the car to the salt marsh and left the body there, didn't you?"

Guy nodded morosely. "I didn't know about the rosary beads."

Elmer said, "You had your own plan. You wanted the murder to be pinned on Leon, for taking Eva away from you."

Guy let out a sob.

Elmer continued, "So rather than leave the body in the salt marsh where it could not be found, you left it just on the edge of the water halfway on the bank. Earlier today when you went missing due to drinking, you were not really getting drunk. You used the time to walk in Leon's shoes walk out to the marsh and back and put them in the trash."

Constance said to her husband, "Why did you do that?"

"It wasn't just wanting revenge on Leon for…for—I wanted to protect you. I guess I should've realized you wouldn't kill her. That's not something you could do. I don't know why I believed Stephen, but I felt guilty for seeing Eva those times. And I hated Leon."

Constance said flatly, "You hated Leon because he stole your mistress."

Guy began to cry.

"By the way," Elmer said drily, "it was you who clocked me on the back of my head when I discovered Eva's body in the marsh, wasn't it?"

He nodded. "I wanted to make sure you didn't think she got lost and drowned. I hoped you would think it was Leon who did it."

Constance said matter-of-factly, "If Eva had approached you and asked you to provide for her because she was carrying your child, if she had approached you instead of Stephen Grove—you would have run away with her."

Elmer left them alone, went into the outer office, and called the police.

***

Juliet called Robert over to talk with him privately again.

Ed Stiles muttered, shaking his head, "He comes to me saying he wants to work as a stagehand, then he can act like Olivier, now he's a gumshoe. I've got to get into another line of work."

The others shifted in their seats, eyeing Stephen Grove with even more surprise.

Juliet whispered to Robert, "Stephen is very smart, being careful not to incriminate himself, but he was obviously very surprised that Guy was trying to frame Leon. I think he's too dangerous to be either here or brought to Leon's office. I'm afraid of what he'll do if he's cornered."

Robert replied, "I don't want to put anybody in danger, and I sure don't want him to go after me."

She answered, "Let's just give him the chance to run. It would confirm his guilt, and it wouldn't put anyone else in danger. I'm going to ask all the actors to sit closer together in the audience for protection, and I'm going to ask Stephen Grove to go up on stage alone. Would you stay in case there's trouble?"

"Sure thing."

Juliet asked everyone to sit together in one section of the audience, directing those who were scattered among different rows and sections of the theater to come together down front. She motioned for Joan Margolis to come down and sit with them. Joan looked hesitant, but she did so, particularly when Beatrice Longworth beckoned her to sit with her. Leon, who had been standing like a statue, emotionless, at first assumed that her direction would not apply to him but she looked at him sternly. Robert took a few steps toward him and waved him over. Ed Stiles stood like a first mate in mutiny against his captain and motioned Leon to join them. Leon solemnly took a seat in the audience, seeming to understand that his authority was gone for good.

Hardest of all for Juliet was encouraging Betty Ann, far up in the middle of the house sitting by herself, having already watched her marriage and her world dissolve, to come and sit in the section where the actors and her husband were sitting. With steely resolve, Betty Ann came down the aisle and took a seat in the row directly in back of her husband, as if they had been complete strangers.

Juliet said in a loud voice, "Not you, Mr. Grove. Would you please come up here on stage?"

Stephen Grove smirked, "What is this?"

"You get to be the star tonight, Mr. Grove. You've got center stage. Maybe you'd like to explain and give us a soliloquy about how you murdered Eva Breck, tried to frame Constance Burch, and enlisted the aid of Guy Norman to hide the body. What you didn't know was that Guy was trying to frame Leon. He didn't know you had planted his wife's rosary beads on the body and he didn't know you told Constance that Eva was still alive. You convinced him that his wife was a murderer so he would help your plan by wanting to cover up for Constance. It would have been easier if he had wanted to get rid of the body. You didn't count on that." She added, "The police have been called and I suggest that you remain where you are and cooperate with them."

Grove answered angrily, "I don't know what story Leon and Constance are spreading over there with your partner, but this is nonsense. You're not going pin this on me."

"The police are going to pin it on you. We just did a little preliminary work for them."

At the back of the house, through the opened screen double doors, the reddish sunset streaked its glow down the aisles and onto the stage, as if hitting Stephen Grove in a natural spotlight. The stage, and its Gothic setting of an ancient convent in England, canvas painted to look like stone, was awash in an orange glow. They were quiet a moment, feeling the first cooling salt breeze of the evening sift through the screens, giving little more than only a hopeful promise of relief to the heat of the day. They could hear the sound of crunching gravel in the parking lot under the tires of two automobiles.

The police had arrived, and the brilliant sunset spilling into the theater was dotted with the flash of the bubble lights on their cruisers.

Stephen Grove bolted, stage left.

***

Kent Murchison talked to the box office personnel corralled there. He explained there would be no program tonight and, stoically, that the leading lady who had disappeared had apparently been found murdered. It was his moment in the spotlight, and he had their rapt attention.

He told them the police might want to question them and then afterward when they were allowed to leave, the playhouse would be in touch with them. They were shocked, and some of them with that starstruck hero-worship of the theatre world, were dumbfounded that there were at least some occasions in which the show did not go on.

Two uniformed officers and two plainclothes detectives arrived and Kent Murchison directed them to the offices. Elmer briefed them on what had happened. Then Juliet came from the playhouse and approached them.

Elmer said, "This is Miss Van Allen, my partner. Is Stephen Grove still there? How did he react?"

Juliet said, "He ran out the western side of the playhouse. I think his intention is to lose himself among all the people on the beach."

The uniformed police went back to their squad cars to radio for more help, the state police were brought in, and the detectives began getting everyone's back story.

Elmer said to Juliet quietly, "When I called the cops and told them the missing person case Leon reported was now a murder case, they had no idea what I was talking about. That jerk never called it in. He lied."

"Why?"

"That's something we're going to have to take up with him later on."

When more police arrived, Elmer led two of them out to the peninsula in the salt marsh where he had found the body, and he turned over the rosary beads to them on the slim chance they might be able to retrieve fingerprints.

Most of the playhouse personnel who had little knowledge or were not involved were slowly, by ones and twos, interrogated and allowed to leave; the technical crew, and eventually the actors. Guy Norman and Constance Burch, as well as Nina and Gary Pirelli were held the longest. Guy Norman was taken into custody for his role in covering up the murder. Constance kissed him and held him before they took him away and promised that she would get him a good lawyer. Juliet watched them, and said to Constance as the cruiser pulled away,

"I hope it goes well for you both."

Constance muttered, "To forgive, divine."

The search for Stephen Grove was tricky; not only had he lost himself in a throng of people on the beach, but twilight was falling and it would be very difficult to catch him in an area where, as Elmer had observed when he first surmised about Eva's leaving, it was very easy to catch a train or bus or taxi and head for parts unknown. With the proximity to salt marshes, it was also easy to hide.

Chapter Eleven

The sunset was fading, burning off somewhere over the hills of western Connecticut. Only the last leavings of twilight were left on the shore, and in another half-hour it would be dark. On the distant horizon, a shining, bright, round moon was peeking up above Long Island. There were far fewer people on the beach now, slowly moving toward the pavilion and the changing rooms before the park was to close.

Juliet headed for the beach.

"You're not going after him?" Robert asked, grasping Juliet's arm.

"I don't intend to catch him, believe me. I'm just going to scout out the pavilion to see if I can spot him. I won't get too close. Please tell Elmer. He's still with the police."

He hesitated but let her go.

She went down to the beach, but went to the front side of the pavilion instead of the beach side, thinking Stephen Grove might head for the nearby campgrounds to hide, or steal a car, or just use the public phones at the pavilion to call a cab. He could have gone into the men's changing room, and she hoped it wasn't for a hostage, but just to steal someone's clothing.

Those stragglers on the beach, too few in number for him to hide among them now, were people who had waited all day to be alone, couples still lying on the beach together, and a few newly arrived people who had spent the day in their sweaty offices and factories, that come out for a bit of peace and a cool swim and a little bit of heaven before the park closed.

Juliet pasted herself against the building, with nowhere to hide, when Stephen Grove emerged from the bathhouse, wearing a pair of shorts and a white T-shirt, carrying a men's gym bag.

She hoped he would not turn around and see her. His street clothes were likely in the bag, for his feet were now stuffed into worn sneakers too small for him.

The one public phone was being used, while he walked quickly away from the pavilion. He scuffed along, his heels hanging out of the backs of the sneakers, and continued westward along the edge of the beach toward another marshland, as Juliet followed, regretting she hadn't time to call the police or the playhouse, but she didn't want to lose sight of him.

The twilight fell fast now and it was getting dark. Juliet thought that unless Stephen Grove was familiar with the area and knew where he was going, he might be frantically searching for a way out. He finally turned up towards the campgrounds, an open grassy field where a few Streamline metal campers were parked and people sat out on chairs, enjoying campfires. There would be less opportunity for Juliet to hide from him here or escape the notice of the campers who would naturally turn their attention to newcomers to their little community. He continued in his resolute march, waving hello to a few campers who greeted him in a friendly way. Grove, actor that he was, now played the part of a man who lived in the area who was now just coming home from the beach. Except that he was not sunburned. Juliet mused that nobody noticed.

They came at last to area of the grounds where there were no campers, an open, flat field before the highway, with long tufts of waist-high grass. She decided to keep a farther distance away from him, so as not to create a sound in the grass, and to be able to use it to duck under if he should turn around.

Strangely, she thought, he never turned around. He kept pushing forward with resolute focus to reach the Boston Post Road, and then, once on the secure footing of the paved road, he headed eastward. The traffic on the two-lane road picked up as people left the state beach and the restaurants.

He walked into town, into the historical district and the town green, where there stood the historical society and the post office and the railroad station, the postcard scenes of a New England seaside town. He walked up Academy Street to the railroad depot, and Juliet realized he must have arrived in Madison on the train, as most people did from out of town, so he was familiar with its location. He went into the depot and into the men's restroom.

She knew he would be changing back into at least some of his clothes, his long pants and his own shoes, certainly, to ride the train. Juliet found a phone booth and realized she didn't have her purse with her.

Rather than dial O for the operator, she felt it would require less explanation if she called the playhouse for help. She asked a man to borrow a nickel and he flirted with her and presented it to her as if he were giving her a dozen red roses. She smiled and thanked him and closed the door in his face, hoping she had not just picked up an escort for the evening.

The operator connected her with the playhouse and after several agonizing rings, Kent Murchison picked up the phone.

"Hammonasset Playhouse. Sorry to report there will be no play this evening –"

"I know. It's Juliet Van Allen. I'm at the train station. Tell the police and Mr. Vartanian that Stephen Grove is here at the train station where I followed him. I think he's going to take the earliest train anywhere, but he hasn't brought a ticket yet so I don't know where he's going. Please have them send a squad car to the station immediately before the next train comes or we're going to lose him."

"Good lord," he said, "don't get yourself killed."

***

Elmer came up from the dressing rooms below the playhouse where he had been showing the police detectives the spot where the body had been hidden. Police photographers and forensics arrived to investigate the blood spots on the carpeting.

Elmer was about to leave the theater, when he noticed Betty Ann still sitting in the audience, alone.

"Leon's being questioned by the cops right now in his office. I don't know how much longer they'll be. Would you like me to take you home, Betty Ann?"

"No," she said quietly, "I'll wait."

He came down off the stage and walked up to her row. He sat down beside her. After a moment, he put his arm around her shoulders.

"Whatever you and Leon decide to do, Juliet and I will always be in your corner."

She looked straight ahead, but tears glistened in her eyes. "Oddly enough, I was sitting here thinking more about what you and Juliet are going to decide to do."

"I don't get you."

"She was quite the picture up there, like Sherlock Holmes, describing the scene of the crime and interrogating Stephen Grove. I've never seen anything like it, certainly not from a woman, and certainly not from anyone in our sphere." Betty Ann unclenched her hands, which had unconsciously been wringing her white gloves. She tucked them into her purse, and drew out a handkerchief and dabbed at her eyes.

Seeing the crumpled gloves reminded Elmer of when he first met Juliet, alone in her office at the Wadsworth Atheneum when she was in the throes of similar crisis—having discovered her husband had been unfaithful to her. That was a few murders ago, one of them her husband's.

Betty Ann said, "Are you and she going to continue being the Double V Investigators? I do occasionally read the newspapers."

Elmer smiled, "I suppose trouble keeps finding us. We might as well meet it head-on."

"More to the point, are you ever going to romance my friend, or just keep her on retainer as your Girl Friday?"

Elmer's smile faded and his pulse quickened.

She said, "So, you don't have an answer for that one."

He said at last, "It's complicated."

"Don't give me that lame excuse about being from different worlds. My husband and I are from the same world, and here we are, worlds apart."

He said, "Did Juliet tell you that on the way down here we passed by a new suburban subdivision going up?"

"Only one? I'm surprised there's a potato field left in Connecticut."

"I kind of liked it. It was all new and everybody would be new neighbors together. It looked like a good place to start out in life—or start over. You know what I mean."

"Yes."

"But Juliet ridiculed it. I could see it wasn't for her. No mansions, no green lawns or mighty oaks, no educated, cultured friends there in her social set."

"No Negroes, no Asians, no Jews—"

Elmer looked at her. "What?"

"Didn't you know? Lots of those all-American subdivisions have covenants written into them that no non-whites or non-Christians can buy a home there, even if the bank would lend them the money."

Elmer looked away.

"Your friend Robert wouldn't be able to buy the house next door." She looked at him. "I'm sorry, Elmer. I've given you a bigger shock, I think, than I've had tonight. Not all suburban developments are probably the same; you might be able to find one that's welcoming to everybody. But maybe it would be easier, instead of looking for the perfect world for both you and Juliet, to make one for yourselves."

Robert entered the theater from the front of the house, and ran down the aisle.

"I've been looking all over for you. Juliet's gone over to the beach to see if she can spot Stephen Grove and follow him."

Elmer pulled his arm from Betty Ann and scrambled to his feet, "That'd be just like her."

They ran to the screen door at the exit by the stage, where Kent Murchison was coming in.

He said, "Miss Van Allen just phoned. She's at the railroad depot. She found Grove."

***

The eight o'clock train for Boston was about to leave, and Juliet spotted Stephen Grove boarding. Since she couldn't stop him, and the police had not yet arrived, she thought about boarding the train, risking being removed at a later stop on the line when she couldn't buy a ticket. But she decided there was no point in that, as her job with Elmer was to solve the mystery, not to apprehend the perpetrator. She also didn't want her neck to be broken, since Grove seemed to be good at that.

She decided instead to walk down the length of the train, and look into the windows to see if she could see Stephen Grove where he sat.

She found him. She decided to let herself be seen, and she waved to him.

He looked over at her, his expression dropping when he recognized her. He stared with an expression that looked daggers through her, and Juliet felt that if she had accosted him, he would have killed her.

Grateful that he was on the train and she was on the platform, she continued to keep his gaze until the train began to pull away, until the conductor sang out,

"Old SAY-brook...Ni-AN-tic...New LON-don...WES-terly...KING-ston...PROV-idence...BOS-ton. All Abuoohad!"

The train pulled away, the Hartford, New Haven and New York Railroad with its distinctive orange emblem on the sides of the cars. A few moments later, four uniformed policemen arrived. Juliet explained that Stephen Grove had gone.

They went into the station office to have the train stopped at Clinton, the next town over, and to alert the police in that town.

One of squad cars took her back to the playhouse. The box office was empty, the staff had gone home. The actors had been released after giving their statements. As Juliet arrived, Joan Margolis walked out with Beatrice Longworth.

Beatrice said to her, "Well, this wasn't an experience you were counting on, was it?"

Joan answered, "No. I know my husband probably won't be very happy with seeing my name in the papers being involved in a murder investigation. But you know something? I'm glad I came. I was so very glad to see you again, and I think I needed to reconcile myself with that strange childhood I had in Hollywood. I think I can put a lot of ghosts to bed now."

"Good luck to you, Joanie Kelly. Let me hear from you." Beatrice said, kissing her cheek.

Joan got into her car and drove away.

Ed Stiles wiped his face with his handkerchief, rolled his eyes and shook his head, catching Juliet's eye, and muttered, "Jeff Collins said he was off to the nearest bar, and I think I'm going to catch up with him."

Beatrice Longworth went over to Robert, who was sitting on the steps of the playhouse. Juliet approached them and Beatrice, almost chuckling, said "Did you catch him?"

Juliet answered, "I didn't tackle him, if that's what you mean. But I followed him as he boarded a train to Boston and the police are after him now. I expect they'll catch up in the next town."

Beatrice said, "I must say, I'm very impressed. What you lack in stage presence you certainly make up for as a detective. And you," she said to Robert, "you are actually quite a fine actor. What are your plans from here? Or are you secretly a detective also?"

Robert answered, "I'm not much of anything right now, ma'am, but like I told you earlier, I would like to be an actor, or work backstage, or continue to be in the theatre somehow. I don't know how much of that is possible. I guess there aren't too many roles for Negroes unless it's as a servant and I'm not sure I want to go through life playing servants. Especially if I have to talk that embarrassing way they do in the movies."

Beatrice said, "Don't give up hope, Robert. Remember what I said about my connections in Hartford. Are you leaving Madison tonight? Will you be here another day or two? Because I'd like to write you a letter of recommendation. I'm at the Madison Beach Hotel."

Juliet said, "We'll be here until at least tomorrow afternoon. I'm staying at the same hotel. We can certainly pick up a letter from you. It's a very generous and gracious offer."

"Not at all. All right then. When I go back to my digs tonight, I'll write you proper letter of introduction."

Robert answered, "Thank you so much, Miss Longworth. I don't know how to thank you."

"In this business, young man, we all help each other. Nobody succeeds alone." Ruth Maguire and Bessie Baggs piled into Beatrice's rental car and they went to their digs at the Madison Beach Hotel.

Elmer suddenly appeared over the stretch of sand dunes that separated the beach from the playhouse property. He was silhouetted in the dark night by the bright moon. He stood for a moment watching them, then as he approached, kicking sand down the dune, and became visible in the glow over the parking lot cast by the string of lights on the veranda, they gave a weary cheer for him.

Robert said, "Now where have you been?"

Elmer approached Juliet, and hugged her in relief. "I was going to ask the same about you."

It was past midnight by the time the police had finished their investigation.

Leon and Betty Ann Welch left in a cab, without speaking to anyone. His car was held for investigation.

Kent Murchison locked the doors of the playhouse and began his solitary moonlit walk down the long access road out to the Route 1, the Boston Post Road, where he lived in a small bungalow with his sister Billie, who had taken their car. Elmer offered him a ride and he accepted. "I really need the exercise, but I'm dog tired."

Elmer asked, "What's next for the playhouse?"

Kent said, "I'm going to meet with the board of directors tomorrow. Most of them are Leon's family—his father, his two brothers. A few other business associates of the Welches. They'll be the ones to decide."

"What would you like to see happen?"

"I'd like to see Leon bounced on his ass from here to New Haven. But I don't guess that will happen. The rich folks protect their own. Ideally, I'd like to see him removed from his position as co-managing director and have him replaced by someone who actually has a moral compass and a sense of fiscal responsibility. I'd like to see the playhouse reopened for the rest of the season. I'd like to build up the repertory company, our own people, that we can rely on from week to week and only use a few guest actors instead of using mostly guest actors and only a few locals. I've talked about that with Jeff. He'd be interested in staying on and working with two or three other directors to share the work. It will depend on the board. I guess I'll find out tomorrow morning if I've still got a job."

They dropped him off at his little cottage that was sandwiched in between a gas station and a beauty parlor. He had a very narrow frontage but his property extended to beginning of the marshland. A small light pierced the darkness by the back door. In the moonlight, from here, one could see the hard line of the ocean on the horizon. Kent Murchison said goodbye and went into his house.

After dropping off Juliet at her hotel, they drove back to Elmer's tourist cabin. Robert threw his small bag on one of the twin beds and looked around the room, and Elmer watched him, knowing how strange it felt to be released from prison and to find everything so new and unaccustomed, a weird combination of frightening and enthralling. Robert's eyes lit on the television set.

"Oh, wow, that's a TV. I've heard about those. You got a room with a TV? How does it work?"

"Right now, it doesn't. I mean, it does, but there's nothing on it right now. You just get what they call snow. They don't have programs on all night long. The station signs off in the wee hours, they play the national anthem and then it's just snow. It'll start up again tomorrow. We'll put it on early and you can watch the test pattern."

Robert yawned, taking off his shirt, "Elmer, that Miss Longworth, she said I should keep acting and she gave me the name of a fellow in Hartford to hook me up with a job. She's giving me a letter of introduction. What do you think of that?"

Elmer grinned, heading for the shower, "I think life's pretty amazing sometimes. You're on your way, Robert. I couldn't be happier for you."

Robert smiled, embarrassed. "I guess I went off the rails a little bit when I got out a few days ago. A few days? Seems like a lifetime. This has been one weird ride. But it's done more for me than you'll ever know."

"I think I may know a little. You found your way quicker than I did. Hey, Juliet and I want to go to the beach one last time. Okay if we head back to Hartford in the afternoon?"

"That's fine with me. I really feel like a new man now. Hey, I'm actually going to have something to chat about with my poor old parole officer."

"I hope he's a theatre buff."

"Ah, he loves me. I slay him."

***

The next morning, they drove to the Madison Beach Hotel. Robert went to the lobby to pick up the letter of introduction from Beatrice Longworth.

When Elmer knocked on her door, Juliet was just finishing packing and she went back into her bathroom to make sure she had not left anything. She came out with a hairbrush and stood in front of the mirror by the dresser and sculpted the tight curls of her "bubble" cut a little more. Elmer sat in a chair and watched her.

She said, "I'm wearing my bathing suit under my clothes. How about you?"

"No, I'll change at the bathhouse."

"Is Robert going to come swimming, too?"

"He says he wants to walk over to the playhouse for a little while and talk to Ed Stiles. He'll join us on the beach after. Maybe we can grab some fried clams for lunch. I can't get enough of them."

She finished packing and Elmer carried her suitcase out to her car. Robert, Beatrice Longworth, Ruth Maguire, and Bessie Baggs were in the lobby and they decided that breakfast together was in order.

They took a table at a restaurant on the Post Road, a large round table in the corner with the windows facing the long stretch of salt marsh to Long Island Sound beyond.

Beatrice Longworth said, "Having been entertained by the challenge a lobster dinner presented to you, Mr. Vartanian, I suppose watching you eat scrambled eggs will be anticlimactic. Or will it?" She smiled, with a twinkle in her eye.

"I'm going to try very hard to disappoint you, Miss Longworth. But I'm not making any promises."

They placed their orders, and Elmer, who had spent much of the last week observing Robert with concern, noted with pride and poignancy how he looked around the room, seeming to soak in the atmosphere: Patrons, many of them staying at the local motels, straggling in, soft clatter of silverware, and the everyday items so comforting in their not-so-insignificant normality—water glasses, menus covered in plastic, paper placemats with graphics of coastal life; Robert looked down at his own placemat at the clipper ship and the illustration of seagulls perched on the wharf, and, of course, a lighthouse. Then the waitress covered the scene with a large plate of fried eggs, bacon, fried potatoes and toast. Robert was about to dig in, when he saw Elmer take his napkin deliberately and fold it across his lap. Robert did the same.

Ruth Maguire asked, "I'm not at all afraid of appearing nosy. What on earth happened after we were dismissed? Was Stephen Grove caught?"

Juliet replied, "We called Mr. Murchison this morning. Stephen Grove was picked up by the police in Clinton. There will be a bit more follow-up investigation by the authorities and he'll eventually stand trial."

Elmer said, "He met Eva in California before the troupe organized. He was doing some minor film work in Hollywood. Eva was apparently trying to attract the patronage of certain directors, producers, anyone she felt was powerful enough to aid her in her career—although that's the funny thing. I don't believe Eva ever really wanted an acting career. She just wanted an easy path to an easy life, and she tried to parlay her beauty into easy money from well-established men. She found no one wanted to either marry her or support her long-term in Hollywood."

Juliet added, sipping her morning tea, "She apparently saw Stephen Grove as her ticket out of the town that had grown tired of her. But Stephen wasn't interested in a long-term arrangement and told her so. She appears to have taken it philosophically and decided to stay with the company to see what other connections she could make."

Bessie Baggs looked unusually clear eyed. Relieved that the tension was over, she dug into pancakes and coffee. Bessie said, "I don't think Eva would have been with us long, anyway. She didn't seem really interested in acting. It's not an easy way to make a living. I kind of wish I could stay in one spot. I think I'm a little jealous of that Billie Murchison, being able to perform at her brother's playhouse all the time, just getting small roles she can handle. It seems like a nice life here." Bessie paused her coffee cup in mid-air, and she looked around contentedly, as Robert had done, at their fellow diners and at the morning sunlight streaming through the blinds. The windows were open, a soft breeze filtered in and one could smell the salt air and hear the distant cry of gulls.

"Speaking of Hollywood," Beatrice said, "Our play is being made into a picture that's coming out this fall. Claudette Colbert plays my role. Ah, well."

Ruth Maguire nodded, sipping her coffee, "Ann Blyth's playing the Sarat Carn role."

Juliet watched Elmer's ears perk up. She patted his hand, "I'll take you to see it."

Elmer winked at her, and said, swallowing his toast, "The future of the playhouse is up in the air at the moment, but if there's any way Kent Murchison can keep it going, he'd like to. Just as you say, he and his sister are very happy here and don't really want much else. But it's going to depend on the board, which is almost entirely controlled by Leon Welch's family. They're going to have a meeting this morning and decide the future of the playhouse. "

Beatrice Longworth said, "I must say, I was floored when you turned out to be not an actress but a detective."

Elmer grinned, and Juliet, to whom blushing came easily, flushed with pride.

She answered, "It's true that in this line of work Elmer and I have had to wear a mask more than once."

Beatrice said, "I think it's fascinating. I've never known any female private detectives, you certainly don't see them in the movies. We've all read about Agatha Christie's Miss Marple, of course. I think we need more female sleuths. I say hurrah to that."

"Neither Elmer nor I started out to be detectives. I'd like to be frank if I may, Miss Longworth, and touch upon a subject that is sensitive to both of us. You see, for many years I worked in museum administration at a job I enjoyed very much. But in today's political climate—well, you see, when I was in college back in the late thirties, I joined a group of girls for one semester who were trying to raise support for the Lincoln Brigade in the Spanish Civil War, as I alluded to earlier. I'm afraid that rather innocent and noble pursuit, as ineffectual and naïve as it was, nevertheless has landed me in trouble today. I've been blacklisted in my field for suspicion of communist ties."

Bessie and Ruth looked sympathetic, but Beatrice Longworth just looked at her evenly, critically, and took a long time lighting her cigarette. She glanced out the window at the near cry of a gull and blew a stream of smoke into the billowing curtain. "It feels like being a stranger in your own country, doesn't it? But in times such as these, you learn who your friends really are and that's what matters most." She glanced at Ruth and Bessie and Ruth patted her hand.

"How do you keep your courage, Miss Longworth? I've been pretty devastated by this whole affair. And I've begun to wonder what's the point? When you live in the freest society in the entire history of the world, and suddenly you're an enemy of the state because you protested a war when you were eighteen years old?"

Beatrice answered, "Nazis weren't only in Europe. They were here, too. The Bund. They go underground, but they pop up, they resurface from time to time in the form of Klansmen, in the form of America Firsters, in the form of people who decide the world is all about us and them. Their leaders are sick and clever, the followers are sick and stupid. They don't look for friends; they seem to be happier having a variety of enemies. To some measure we can pity them. But the rest of the time, we have to keep watch and be ready to point them out in a crowd for what they are. The only thing that will eradicate their power is our courage."

Juliet asked, "How do you even begin to have hope for the future?"

Beatrice looked at her, as if appraising her, and said, "Think of all those who were oppressed in this country from the slaves, to the Indians, to the immigrants in sweatshops, the Japanese who were put in internment camps during the war. We seem to take great steps back and only little steps forward, but we do move forward. In the meantime, we all have to be our own heroes. And help each other out. I have to hope this will pass, but I can't honestly say whether it will be in two years or twenty. We have two things going for us, one is that Americans don't seem to have a very long attention span. We move on to the next fad pretty quickly. The second is, I do believe we've always had a deep love of freedom and I think that's going to help us overcome this disgrace."

***

Elmer, Juliet, and Robert said goodbye to the three ladies of the theatre and drove down the access road to the Hammonasset State Beach. Elmer changed into his swim trunks while Juliet and Robert walked over to the playhouse, Robert to have a word with Ed Stiles. Stiles and a few apprentices were dismantling the lighting scheme and the set. He saw Robert at the edge of the stage and came down from his ladder.

Robert said, "I hate to see it come down. Kind of a shock. Shame you never got to do the play."

Ed Stiles remarked, "Takes weeks to put up one of these things and only a few hours to take it down. By lunchtime it'll be as if it was never here. I don't know if we're going to get to put up the next one yet. I guess I'll find out this afternoon when the big bosses make the decision."

"I sure would like to come back here someday."

"To act, or work backstage?" Ed Stiles smiled at him.

"I'd even pass out programs."

"You've got the theatre bug, all right. Well, for what it's worth, if they let us continue, you're welcome back to work with me, as far as I'm concerned. You're a good man, Robert."

Robert shook his hand and nearly teared up, but laughed to cover it.

***

Juliet found Betty Ann sitting on a bench on the front veranda of the playhouse. She sat down next to her wordlessly as they put their arms around each other and kissed each other's cheeks. Finally, Betty Ann said, "I can't get the question out of my head as to whether Leon had a vasectomy without telling me because he didn't want any more children, or because he wanted to be able to continue to have his affairs and not worry about getting any of his mistresses pregnant."

"Has he made any explanations to you, any apology?"

"No. And I haven't demanded any."

"Betty Ann, why?"

"Because I'm six months pregnant and this is not a good time to be going through divorce court. Juliet, I'm not like you. I don't have a career, despite my Wellesley degree, I really don't even have an occupation to pursue. All I've ever been trained for, all I've ever pursued was career marriage to someone whose family was as wealthy as mine. It sounds sordid, but it's put a very nice roof over my head and until now, not too many worries."

"Then you and Leon will simply go on as you are?"

"I sense what we are is going to change, whether either of us wants that or not, when the baby comes. And maybe even sooner, depending on what the board of directors decides today. There's a couple of silent partners but for the most part it's Leon's family. I suspect they gave him the running of the playhouse because they didn't want him in the family business." She tried to laugh, "Leon's business skills and his desire to work, I'm afraid, are similar to mine. Unfortunately, we're perfectly matched."

"You're not perfectly matched. You have integrity. What keeps you from pursuing a career is a fear of consequences. I'm sorry you had to find all this out through Elmer and I."

183

"Yes, but look where your ambition has got you—blacklisted."

"Yes. I've just about stopped looking. The blacklist is a pretty deep trench and there's no climbing out of it."

"I'm sorry. At least you have a trust fund to live on, don't you? I mean, has your father reinstated that?"

"My father and I have patched things up, yes, but I still want to work. Elmer thinks I should go back to painting." Now Juliet tried to laugh, unsuccessfully.

Betty Ann remarked, "I like Elmer. I mean, I know he's an ex-con, not part of our crowd and all that. You know what I like most about him?"

"No, what?"

"The way he looks at you. I wish somebody looked at me that way."

***

Juliet returned to the beach. More people were arriving in the late morning and it looked like it would be another crowded, hot day. She finally saw Elmer sitting under a rented umbrella. He was wet from having just come out of the ocean and his hair was slicked back like Johnny Weissmuller playing Tarzan. Rivulets of water dripped down the patch of dark matted hair on his chest. His upper body was muscled, his stomach was flat and hard. His legs were muscular and the dark hair on his shins was pasted wet to his skin. She dropped herself on a towel next to him.

Juliet suddenly felt a little shy about stripping down to her own bathing suit, but realized ruefully that it would be ironic to fear intimacy when one was just a speck on the long beach with five hundred other people. She laughed off her nervousness and slipped out of her skirt and her short-sleeve top to reveal her coral-colored one-piece suit. Elmer clearly noticed, without ogling her, that it flattered her figure. He took a sip from a bottle of Coca-Cola and offered her a sip. She took the bottle from him and put her lips to it.

"Umbrella and everything," she said, "You know how to show a girl a swell time."

"I thought the sun would be too much for your fair skin. How was Betty Ann?"

"Sad, depressed, but strangely resolute. I get the sense she doesn't love Leon as much as she's hitched her wagon to him. It's a sad thing. Women of the wealthier classes, ironically, seem to have no value of their own except being part of a wealthy man's life, and poor women have very little opportunities for education and so marriage is a matter of survival for both of them. I pin my hopes on the new middle class for strong, independent women. I love Betty Ann dearly. I wish I could help her. But I really can't."

"But what about your own prospects for independence?"

"Meaning?"

He drew his knees up to his chest and flexed his strong arms over them, clasping his hands together and looking thoughtfully out over the waves and at two small children digging in the sand with a plastic shovel.

He said, "Leon hired me. He doesn't even like me, and he knows I don't like him, but he hired me anyway. He could have gotten a professional detective, certainly one that didn't have a prison record. Is that because was he just being lazy, grasping at straws, grasping at the first name he knew, or did he think there would be some particular advantage in having an amateur look into his problem? I'll never know, because even if I ask Leon straight out, he'll never give me a straight answer. He's the kind of guy who just doesn't."

She asked, "Are you unhappy with the way the investigation turned out? Or do you think there's more to it? Do you think we found the real killer?"

A child's beach ball blew in their direction and Elmer, smiling, tossed it back to the boy and his sister who ran down the beach. "Oh yes, Grove did it. No, it's not the outcome that bothers me; what I mean is, I can't help but be suspicious about Leon contacting me. I guess you know me well enough by now, Juliet, to know that my past hangs pretty heavy on me. I don't think I'm ever going to shake off having been in prison."

"Look at it as a reset on your life. It brought Robert into your life. That's a great thing."

Elmer grinned. "Yeah. Robert was the only good thing about it. Sure took to this theatre stuff like a duck to water, hey?"

"You knew he would, didn't you? You brought him here hoping it would revive his acting interest and maybe give a fresh start and something that he liked to do."

"No, I was grasping at straws. Fortunately, Robert didn't need much of a push. Maybe he can shake prison off better than I did."

"I'm glad you brought him. I like Robert."

Elmer said, "So Robert's got a new path to follow thanks to Beatrice Longworth. But where do we go from here? This is the first job anybody hired me as a detective."

"You were hired for the Litchfield murder case at the horse show last summer."

"Yeah, but that was a setup. The guy knew I'd been an ex-con and amateur and he wanted to get away with making me a patsy. It was dumb luck we tripped him up."

"It wasn't dumb luck. We got the goods on him."

He laughed. "You sound like a gangster."

She smiled archly. "I'm learning the lingo. My father also paid you when you investigated the murder mystery at the New Year's Eve party last year."

"I'm not sure he was paying me for my services or just paying me to get rid of me. But I took the money, yes."

"What is this getting at, Elmer?"

"I don't have too many other skills except for being a janitor and driving a truck. And finding murderers. The hotshot reporter from *The Hartford Times*, Rattigan –"

"Lord, Rattigan." She shook her head.

"He labeled us the Double V Investigators, for Vartanian and Van Allen."

"How come you get top billing?"

"So, why don't we do it?" he said.

"Why don't we seriously become detectives?"

The sea breeze rippled through his collapsed pompadour. "Ever since the blacklist, you haven't had any luck finding work. It may last for a few more years, yet in the meantime I know you're not crazy about living off your trust fund. So why don't we try it? We make a good team. But we have to find out if we need any license. I probably couldn't have the business ownership in my name because I'm an ex-con. I doubt the police would give a license to an ex-con. I certainly wouldn't be able to carry a gun."

She answered, "Hold off, I'm not doing this is if it involves guns."

"No, no, I'm not saying we should have guns. I just mean that private eyes always have guns in the movies and the police probably are going to be wondering about that."

She said, "Before we start having business cards printed, we're going to have to talk a lot about how we want to run this, how we want to market ourselves or if we want to market ourselves at all. Forgive me for being so mundane, but my background is in marketing, after all."

He said, "And we're going to have to decide what kind of cases we'll take. Tell you flat out, I don't want to do any spying on cheating husbands or wives. That kind of stuff seems even more dirty than murder, if you know what I mean."

She laughed, "More dirty than murder!"

He chuckled, "I don't want to be hiding in the bushes with a camera shooting photos of a couple having sex just so somebody can blackmail somebody else. I want to help people who need our help. I want to do some good. Find murderers. Missing people, maybe. Who stole my tiara, that kind of thing."

"Tiara?"

"So far the only people we've worked for are rich people. But I'm open to cut rates if we find a worthy cause among the people on my side of the tracks."

"Double V Investigators."

"Maybe your father's lawyer, Mr. Endicott, can guide us through filing papers with the state or whatever it is we have to do."

"I have to admit, Mr. Endicott is better at filing papers than he is at actually offering a defense. He's a paper shuffler from way back."

"So you want to do it, Partner?" He offered his hand. She looked at his hand, large, tanned and strong, and she slipped her small, white hand into it and felt his warm grasp.

"Okay, Partner. It's a deal."

They walked to the edge of the water on the hot sand, weaving in and out of blankets and beach chairs and umbrellas that formed little islands on the beach, all representing individual domains. The beach was where people could disrobe to the barest of garments and yet not be concerned with modesty, could observe and listen to those around them and yet never interact, maintaining the appearance of minding one's own business with complete decorum. It was democracy pared down to blankets and sun tan lotion.

They stepped into the cool water and waded out into chest-high depth. Ahead of them lay the hazy, long strip of the Long Island, which, being a barrier island, left this part of Long Island Sound almost placid. There were none of the crashing ocean waves here or the threat of undertow.

Juliet launched herself, floating on her back, her arms extended, looking above at the immeasurable deep blue sky. He swam a distance away and then swim back again.

She righted herself. "We're going to need business cards."

He smiled. "Yeah."

"We're going to be seeing a lot more of each other. Do you mind?"

"I think I'm ready for that, if you are."

She said, "Robert told me you have a good singing voice. I'd like to hear you sometime."

He answered, "From right here, the playhouse standing on the rocky point, that would be a nice picture. You should paint it."

"You're a nag."

They said nothing for a while, just floating and paddling in place, circling around each other. Then Elmer began to sing in a powerful, resonant voice, "Softly, As in a Morning Sunrise" from the Sigmund Romberg operetta *New Moon.* Juliet stood still, no longer floating or paddling but just listening to him.

"My lord, Elmer. You have a marvelous voice! You sound just like Gordon MacRae."

He chuckled and dove under the water.

***

When they climbed out of the water and stepped back onto the sand, their bodies refreshed but laden again with the heaviness of gravity, he took her hand as they walked back to the blanket. They saw Robert coming across to them from the playhouse and motioned him to their umbrella.

Robert said, "Glad you came out of that water just now, I'd never have found you."

Elmer said "You ought to go in, the water is great."

Juliet answered, "Yes, you could get cooled off for the ride home."

Robert looked back up at the Pavilion, "They rent suits up there?"

188

"Yep."

"Okay. Sounds good. I'm getting hungry, though. Anybody ready to eat?"

Elmer said, "Yeah, I want fried clams. How did it go at the playhouse? Did you see Ed Stiles?"

Robert said, "He's a nice guy. Little gruff and hard, but a nice guy. Mr. Murchison came by and we talked a little and he said that the playhouse is going to be shut down for a few weeks but it's going to resume for its last couple of shows in late August and early September. He said if I don't have anything else cooking, I can come back and work, and maybe there'll be a spot for me next year if I want. And guess what?" He pulled an envelope from his shirt pocket, "A genuine pay envelope with $25 for working at the playhouse. I got a week's salary for two days. I gotta tell you guys, I'm flying high right now."

***

In the late afternoon they were dressed and back into Juliet's 1949 Lincoln Cosmopolitan. Elmer drove, Robert was in the passenger seat and Juliet sat in the middle just as they had on the drive down. Elmer snapped on the radio to Vaughn Monroe singing, "There I Go," and headed down the Boston Post Road, past the cottages and clam shacks and farms. They drove past the train depot where Juliet had followed Stephen Grove and she thought of him as they drove by it. Then they turned on to Route 9 and headed north back to Hartford. Juliet felt a curious sensation of having been on vacation for a long time but instead of wishing she did not have to return home, she felt glad they were going back and glad that she and Elmer were going to start formally on a new partnership.

She saw in her mind's eye the image of the playhouse on the rocky point from the vantage that Elmer had suggested she paint. She thought perhaps if she could do a small painting of that, it would make a nice birthday present for him.

When they reached Hartford, they dropped Elmer off first and then Robert because they lived in buildings not too far from each other in the same neighborhood in the north end of town. Then Juliet drove her car back to her father's mansion on Farmington Avenue.

***

Elmer found a letter in his mailbox and took it up to his apartment. The room was stale from having the windows closed in the heat of the past couple days, and it suddenly looked small and claustrophobic to him, and too hot on this summer day. He envied Leon's celebrated playhouse air conditioning.

The letter was from a boyhood friend from his old neighborhood in Waterbury, Connecticut, who now lived in Boston.

"Dear Elmer,

I hear you became a detective. I need your help…"

The end

***

Connecticut summer theatergoers really did enjoy July 1951 with Lillian Gish at the Clinton Playhouse in Clinton in a play called *Miss Mabel*, and George Bernard Shaw's *Candide* starred Olivia de Havilland. Melvyn Douglas starred in *Guilty* with Signe Hasso, and the Ivoryton Playhouse in Ivoryton featured *The Chocolate Soldier*, and *A Streetcar Named Desire* with Claire Luce, and *Rain* with baritone Lawrence Tibbett, as well as Joan Bennett in *Susan and God*. The Somers Playhouse in Somers produced *Light up the Sky*, and *I Remember Mama*. *The Show Shop Theater* in Canton produced on *Out of the Frying Pan*.

However, though the Hammonasset State Beach in Madison, Connecticut, is a real place, the Hammonasset Playhouse never was.

***

Receive updates on my books with my newsletter and get your free eBook copy of the first book in this series, *Cadmium Yellow, Blood Red* at www.jacquelinetlynch.com.

A museum heist, a missing child, a murder, a recent ex-con and an even more recent widow. How many times do we have to pay for our mistakes before life sends us a reprieve?

Juliet Van Allen, museum administrator, discovers that her artist husband is having an affair with another woman. Elmer Vartanian, recently released from prison for a museum robbery, is coerced into helping scout her museum for a heist by a gang that has kidnapped his daughter. Juliet's husband is murdered. Did she kill him? She needs an alibi – so does the ex-con.

Cadmium Yellow, Blood Red is the first book in the Double V Mysteries series set in New England in the late 1940s and early 1950s.

If you like the romance and charm of a classic film, this "cozy noir" will remind you of an era when dramatic stories were elegant, subtle, and even a grim dark alley might lead to the glamour of evening dress and a champagne cocktail.

Enter a world where Modern Art meets old-fashioned murder and take a back seat in Juliet's sleek 1949 Lincoln Cosmopolitan for a fast ride to outrun danger – *now*.

"As a heroine, Juliet successfully blends "damsel in distress" with "independent businesswoman," sidestepping the wealthy heiress trope that could easily have flattened her into a caricature of a character. Even more enjoyable, however, is the way in which Elmer Vartanian is fleshed out. He is neither brash knight nor tortured hero; rather, he comes across as a decent man trying to piece together a good life for his family. His attempts to find his daughter and circumvent the fate laid before him were what kept me turning pages (or flipping Kindle screens, as it were)." Alice of "Hide and Read" book review blog.

See the further adventures of Juliet Van Allen and Elmer Vartanian in these volumes of the Double V Mysteries series:

Cadmium Yellow, Blood Red (No.1)
Speak Out Before You Die (No. 2)
 Dismount and Murder (No. 3)
Whitewash in the Berkshires (No. 4)
Murder at the Summer Theater (No. 5)

Other fiction:

Meet Me in Nuthatch
The Current Rate of Exchange
Beside the Still Waters
Myths of the Modern Man
Collected Shorts

Non-fiction books:

Ann Blyth: Actress. Singer. Star.
Comedy and Tragedy on the Mountain: 70 Years of Summer Theatre on Mt. Tom, Holyoke, Massachusetts
States of Mind: New England
The Ames Manufacturing Company of Chicopee, Massachusetts
Movies in Our Time: Hollywood Mirrors and Mimics the Twentieth Century
Classic Films and the American Conscience
Calamity Jane in the Movies

ABOUT THE AUTHOR:

Jacqueline T. Lynch's novels, short stories, and non-fiction books on New England history and film criticism are available from many online shops as eBooks, audiobook, and paperback. She is also a playwright whose plays have been produced around the United States and in Europe, and has published articles and short fiction in regional and national publications. She writes *Another Old Movie Blog* on classic films, and the syndicated newspaper column *Silver Screen, Golden Memories*. For updates and special offers, please see: www.JacquelineTLynch.com.

Made in United States
North Haven, CT
21 May 2023

36812382R00108